ADVANCE PRAISE FOR

THIS IS HOW YOU FALL

"*This Is How You Fall* had me hooked from the opening lines—exceptional writing, utterly engaging characters, and a story that shifts between thrilling, heartbreaking, and hilarious before its final poignant ending. This literary piece of noir is for keeps."

—OLEN STEINHAUER
New York Times best-selling author of *The Tourist*

"Characters so real they follow you home—and park threateningly across the street."

—BEN LOORY
Author of *Stories for Nighttime and Some for the Day*

THIS

IS HOW

YOU

FALL

ALSO BY KEITH DIXON

FICTION

The Art of Losing

Ghostfires

NONFICTION

Cooking for Gracie

PRAISE FOR *THE ART OF LOSING*

"A moral fable with deep-tolling resonance . . . *The Art of Losing* [has] more heft than a lot of novels twice its size."

—FRANK WILSON, *PHILADELPHIA INQUIRER*

[Starred review] "A descent into darkness that can only end in calamity, but the reader, swept up in the narrative momentum, can no more look away than [the characters] can avoid damnation, if not death. Dixon has written a cautionary tale that is not easy to enjoy but even harder to forget."

—*BOOKLIST*

[Starred review] "Dixon is too good a writer . . . so well and darkly done."

—*KIRKUS REVIEWS*

PRAISE FOR *GHOSTFIRES*

"Brilliant . . . a brave, chilly look into the human soul."

—DANIEL WOODRELL,
NEW YORK TIMES BOOK REVIEW

THIS

IS HOW

YOU

FALL

KEITH

DIXON

f THOMAS & MERCER

Printed in the United States of America.

Published by Thomas & Mercer

PO Box 400818
Las Vegas, NV 89140

ISBN-13: 9781611099867
ISBN-10: 1611099862

For Margot, with love and affection

Special thanks, once again, to Ellen Levine

PART ONE

✚

PENNY-WISE

ONE

SALLY GODSTREET, TWENTY-FIVE YEARS OLD, good with knives, looking sharp in her tailored chef's whites, told me she'd sell me the pool table in her basement for a song, get her sister, Kimber, to stop throwing parties around it. Kimber wasting her afternoons in bed with the blinds drawn, nights in the basement, shooting pool with old high-school friends and some rougher trade, too, smoking joints and listening to country music at top volume until the neighbors phoned the police.

I remembered Kimber as a teenager who kept to herself, mostly, read Beverly Cleary books and sang Pat Benatar songs into a hairbrush in front of her bedroom mirror; but then I hadn't seen her since their father's funeral.

"Just get rid of her," I said, sipping coffee in the Chime Creek Country Club kitchen while Sally's doing prep with her morning crew. Sally can manage a line cook who speaks almost no English with a hopscotch of jailhouse ink running up his arms, have him turn eighty covers a night, but she hasn't the nerve to tell her own sister to turn the music down. You lose both parents, I guess it's going to have an effect like that. "Tell her the parties don't stop, she's out."

"I'm all she has," Sally said.

"You'd be doing her a favor, kicking her out."

Thinking, *How come if Sally's paying the mortgage she doesn't just tell Kimber to pack her bags?* . . . Maybe Sally's feeling that with both parents gone she owes it to her sister to help her work this one out. You know: Be there for her.

Sally extended her bottom lip and blew a wisp of hair out of her face, then swiped a smudge of flour from her temple, with one wrist. Two gestures that would loop in my mind's eye later, in bed, after I had switched off the light. What she did, daily, leaving me with little moments I'd revisit staring at the ceiling and wishing I could have a smoke.

"How could I do that?" she said. "It's her house, too."

"You're paying the mortgage, aren't you?"

"Just take the table, will you?" she asked.

"See if it fits in Rolly's basement. If the table goes away, maybe the parties will."

And said Kimber had promised to be there to let me in so I could measure it.

The history Sally and I shared with that table couldn't have been far from her mind when she offered to sell it to me. I'm wondering if the moment has the significance for her it has for me, or if she no longer allows herself the luxury of regret. I've known romantics cured of their dreamy tendencies by life's disappointments. This needn't be an entirely bad thing—my father might have avoided prison by curing himself of that lousy romantic streak of his—but to see Sally so unemotional about an object that hummed like a struck tuning fork in my imagination was altogether heartbreaking.

Which explained my funny mood as I was driving across town a few minutes later: dejected, exquisitely unrelaxed—in a sort of permanent nonsmoking panic attack. I detoured by the bottle shop to pick up a gift of a fifth of bourbon for Kimber, and even paused in the parking lot to noose a pink bow about its neck, thinking that I'm doing Sally's dirty work, here, telling Kimber that I'm here to see if the table's going to fit down my uncle Rolly's basement stairs and maybe take it away.

I parked in the driveway and rapped on the front door for at least five minutes. The only answer was the buzzing of the crickets in the hedges and, down the block, someone pulling a stubborn mower starter again and again Kimber thinking she can stand me up, maybe I'll just go away? I wiped sweat from my face and squinted up the brick face at the gabled roof in the hard sunlight. It was an exquisitely sad house, tidy and practical, sure, but also haunted in the way that only a once-happy home can be, and with the lights off, Sally's car gone, and the front door firmly locked, it had me thinking it's looking a lot like a dwelling abandoned ahead of a coming disaster. I tried the doorbell, waited fuming for another five minutes, and then walked around back, trailing my hand along the thistly hedge, to let myself in, the mower roaring to life the same instant I located the key in its usual place, the hollowed-out rock beneath the old juniper. A rockabilly tune had been playing on the car radio, and I began whistling the melody as I hopped up the deck stairs—"Matchbox" I think it was, or maybe "Gone Gone Gone," one of my father's durable favorites, the notes rising, along with my blood, to the idea of moving freely alone through Sally's house—though the song died on my lips when I reached the top step to the pool deck and found Kimber, wearing only a bikini, fully reclined on a lounge at poolside.

It's no small thing to run up on a woman in any state of undress and discover that she's ignorant of your presence—in moments like that it's just you alone with your conscience, and this can be cold company indeed. The temptation was sharpened when I realized that this was Sally's green bikini from high school, taut halos of fabric the color of American money that provoked something deep in my reptile mind. A few simple truths presented themselves for inspection, among them the realization that Kimber, following her sister's example, had come to possess the sort of body that could electrify a stretch of beach from one hundred yards, husbands looking up dreamily from their sandcastles, wives reaching absently for their cover-ups. Her mouth full and bow-shaped, blushed coral against tanned skin, and you sensed within the perfect white teeth one would expect of a dentist's daughter. Envy the words that roll from such a mouth: Those lucky consonants, caressed with a tongue-tap, kissed and sent on their way. She wore sunglasses dark and depthless as pools of motor oil, the color plagiarized by the glossy hair spilling around her neck and shoulders, her toes hooked into the style of tiger-print heels the women in the underwear magazines wore when they hiked up and down the runway. I'm remembering Kimber at age ten, cultivating a habit of adorning her fingers and toes with butterfly stickers. Now a tattoo of a serpent coiled around her bare ankle, heading upward from her instep. I imagined that she was dozing away her hangover, insensible to my hammering on the front door, and had allowed myself maybe fifteen or twenty seconds of appreciating the shining length of her tanned body against the green bikini, the steel key warming to my tight grip, when her lips moved, asking, "Enjoying the view?"

She sat up cross-legged and lit a cigarette, stirring awake my mad itch for a smoke, and made no move to cover herself. My aunt sometimes accused women who dressed this way in public of *leaving little to the imagination*, but I was inclined, in that moment, to think the problem there was not so much with the clothing as with my aunt's imagination.

"Jake Asprey," she said.

"Kimber. Long time. I'm here to measure the table."

"Worried it's too small, Jake?"

She raised her head, revealing a withering smile listing to starboard, and showed me my reflection in her sunglasses as she exhaled smoke through her nose. My mouth hanging open in that reflection so I closed it.

"Too big," I said, compounding my embarrassment.

"I find that's hardly ever a problem."

I said, "I'll just let myself in."

"Why don't I join you?"

"No need," I said.

6

But she was already rising and leading the way inside under the vined trellis, three feet in front of me and lit by her own personal cinematographer in the alternating shade and hard midday light, my eyes fixed to the spot between the tanned wings of her shoulder blades, where the bikini clasp grasped itself. That coloration—Lebanese blood gracing their history on the mother's side, Sally and Kimber lightly browned even in midwinter, and altogether Persian-skinned through summer. Two supremely handsome parents had created supremely handsome daughters, a triumph of braided biology. It was hard to see past those attractive features, so you could say I followed Kimber indoors willingly enough, propelled by the blunt force of her beauty. But I wasn't altogether confident about what would happen once we were inside.

The kitchen was tunnel-dark, shades down with bright slices of sunlight around the edges, and the air conditioning was surging at full blast. Kimber, poised, turned and shivered and crossed her arms under her breasts, and for a brief moment the room seemed to turn like a gyroscope. She'd pushed her sunglasses up to pin back the surging waves of her hair, and was frankly assessing me with unusually clear, green eyes. Was it a trick of the light, maybe her features sharp where Sally's were soft?—as if the DNA, aware that it was doomed to a shortened life span, was intent on making its mark more quickly.

I held up the bottle of bourbon by the neck.

"For you," I said. Kimber's arms remained crossed and, unsure of what to do, I blinked and set the bottle aside on the counter, thinking that the bow I'd tied there—well, all it did was make me look like a fool. "I guess I feel badly about taking the table."

"Sally's trying to get me to go. Thinks by getting rid of the table she'll get rid of *me*."

"She doesn't want you to *go*. She just worries things are getting a little out of hand."

"You know how good she had it when my parents were still around? They would let her get away with anything. She'd go out seven nights a week, would sneak back in at sunrise. But now that she's paying the

7

bills," she said, and let her hands drop, "she expects me to live like a *nun*."

I'd been ready for a confrontation, but not one packaged in an oblique come-on—the bathing suit, the setup. Kimber drew a thoughtful drag from her cigarette and took one cunning step closer.

"Listen," she said, her voice lower, her gaze level, "why don't we work something out, you and me? Make nice, be friends. It doesn't have to be this way. You could just leave the table here, talk Sally out of getting rid of it, maybe come over now and then and play it when you like. You make out. I make out. Okay?"

She reached out and, incredibly, lay one wrist lightly on my collarbone.

Her bedroom was fourteen steps away.

For Christ's sake, I thought. Have the sense to know the difference between what you want and what you don't.

"Kimber," I said, "work it out with Sally. I'm not getting in the middle."

That did it. She raised her right arm and, without taking her eyes off me, sent her cigarette ember spinning into the sink from ten feet.

"Yeah, well, you *are* in the middle," she said. "Fucking up my good time."

She snatched the bottle off the counter and swiveled slow—showing me everything I wasn't going to get, not today or ever—and padded lightly back out to the deck, closing the door and leaving my vision dripping with the mapped silhouette of her body against hot white light. I remained there in the kitchen for a moment, feeling as if a tornado had just savaged the room, then showed myself downstairs. The tape measure told me that the table wasn't going to be a problem—I could hire four movers for an hour, have them quietly carry it in through my uncle's garage, along the back hall, and down the basement stairs. Then Aunt Zooey and I could lead him down the stairs with a blindfold, take it off, and in the silence that followed, while he was working his way through his astonishment, I'd say something like,

There you go, Minnesota Fats, something stupid like that, the sort of simple joke he enjoyed so much.   Sally's basement still contained old fly rods and photographs and sewing machine parts, artifacts from her parents' canceled lives. Her father had been my dentist all my life—I still vividly recalled those moments when he'd lean in to have a look at my open maw, breathe a sigh of mint and, beneath it, the tobacco that had killed him. When I was a boy he always took great care to prevent pain, to the point that even the sting of the numbing needle was cloaked by a quick application of topical anesthetic, a second shot available if you asked, the process somehow gentled along by endless, soothing patter about the joys of tying your own trout flies. He's coring your tooth like an apple and you're sitting there numb and somehow caught up in his latest effort with a caddisfly. When the cruelly symmetrical news came—the same pancreatic cancer had taken his wife three years earlier—I believe a collective prayer went up from his patients: We wished him a painless end, though the effect of the last few months on Sally made it clear that maybe the prayer had gone unanswered. Kimber went back to Florida after he was buried, though I believe Sally was the only person who was surprised when Kimber was sent home six months ago with a grade point average approaching zero.

And right there, I think, you have the crucial problem with the family enterprise: You go on being family even after they let you down. You can't ever ask them to leave, not really, and you sure can't walk away yourself, so what you've got to do is this: You've got to find a way to make them *want* to leave, which can entail giving up things you enjoy plenty yourself, things like the very pool table I was here to measure, the item upon which Sally Godstreet had lost her virginity nine years earlier, after a pool party, back when she was just another child in a well-off family, two loving parents upstairs and her whole future ahead of her. On the afternoon of her father's funeral I found her downstairs gazing at that table with a strange look on her face, as if she'd gone and lost her keys on it or something. At the time she was halfway through getting her degree at the Culinary Institute of America, and until her father had suddenly fallen ill and the X-rays had announced that his future had been radically telescoped, she'd been getting ready for a summer job cooking for free for a two-star Michelin in Provence. Now that had all been wiped away, Sally home indefinitely to care for Kimber and pay the mortgage. To watch Sally chalk a cue while staring at the green felt expanse that morning was to witness someone experiencing *three* deaths—the enchained loss of mother, father, and ideals. Lingering there on the stairs, the faint music of cutlery on plates upstairs, I didn't trust myself not to say something stupid, and instead retreated back to the kitchen to hide behind my beer.

With the measurements finished I was tempted to use the front door out as a flagrant *Fuck you, too, Kimber*, to seal the nature of the relationship, but I guess I just like people, and chose instead to trail her image up the basement stairs and out onto the hot pool deck. The lounge was empty, the bottle of bourbon open beside it, two fingers down already, and then Kimber surged dripping up out of the pool, hoisted her tan, lean length up onto the deck, the green bikini gone a shade darker and clinging to every curve of her body, her hair sleek down her back. She flipped her hair forward over her shoulder and stood there twisting it gently to squeeze out the water, watching me.

"You were wrong," I said. "It's just right. The fit."

"Is it?"

"Maybe tomorrow, the next day?"

When she said nothing in reply, twisting her hair with the water coursing down the length of her body, I turned and walked down the deck steps to return the key to its home. And because I can't ever let people go, I glanced over my shoulder as I went around the side of the house. She was facing away from me now—dragging one toe in the water with her hands resting lightly on her hips—but staring at me over her left shoulder, her expression enciphered by those piercing green eyes. I felt the strangest urge to wave, and gave in to it, but her hands remained where they were. Her expression, too, remained inscrutable, and for a moment I entertained an incredible thought: that Kimber

Godstreet wanted to sleep with me. That mad thought entrained by a crucial qualifier: that her older sister had not only lost her virginity on the pool table downstairs, she'd also done so while dressed in the same green bikini Kimber now wore. Both of these facts known to me because I was the person with Sally when it happened.

Later, at the dinner table, I asked my uncle, "What's the deal with Kimber Godstreet?"

Rolly's mouth was full of roast chicken, so he held up the thumb and forefinger of his right hand and rubbed them together in the universal sign for wealth. Rolly, who'd spent his entire adult life selling a car he could never afford at retail, understood money. And he knows that the subject of money never fails to provoke my curiosity—finding yourself burdened with twenty-seven thousand dollars of unpaid bills will do that to you. But it was with more than my usual amount of interest that I leaned into his response.

"What," I said, "you think she's got money stashed somewhere?"

He swallowed.

"No," he said, "that's what I'd like to do to her thigh."

My aunt swatted him with her napkin.

At the sink, after about ten minutes of plunging the dirty dishes elbow-deep in sudsy water, I found myself thinking about the snapshot of Kimber that my mind's eye had taken as I'd walked around the corner of the house. Something about Kimber's refusal to wave back made me want to revisit everything that had passed between us, every word and glance. I thought, *You must get yourself back to college, and quick. You've only been here a few months, and look at the trouble you're already courting.* It was madness to engage Kimber, to surrender to the cruel implement of her beauty—but her resemblance to her unassailable sister, her green eyes, and her refusal to wave had triangulated me and, transfixed, I was helpless to resist.

Whatever I happened to be thinking, I was jolted out of my daydream when my aunt, returning to the television from a quick trip to the refrigerator, dropped an ice cube down the back of my shirt.

TWO

THE NEXT EVENING I'M AT the Skeller to meet Rolly after work, the door propped open to the street and people hurrying by, with rain forecast only nothing falling yet. I'm sipping a glass of milk knowing Rolly's going to arrive in a bit, we'll share a drink and he picks up the tab. I ought to be picking up the tab, Rolly pulling strings to get me this job after the previous lifeguard let someone drown on his watch, but right now the money just isn't there.

The bartender, Doyle, said, "Rolly selling any cars?"

"Eight Caddies this month already."

"That's a lot. He make much off them?"

"Enough they're thinking of a cruise."

"Yeah, only I don't see Zooey being good on a boat."

"The Dramamine makes her sleepy," I said. "I get the impression it's not a problem, her being in bed the whole time, if you get me."

"They do okay for an old couple," Doyle said.

A minute later Rolly walked in, tie already loosened, umbrella still in his bag.

"Say, Doyle," Rolly said. "What's the kid drinking?"

"Milk," Doyle said.

"How about two Sazeracs, good Peychaud?"

He sat beside me as Doyle walked up the bar to lift out a bottle of brandy and the good bitters.

"Every time I come in here," Rolly said, "I think I'm going to catch you having a smoke."

"I haven't cheated once. The morning's harder."

"I got depressed back when I quit. Man, did I go down. I could hardly get out of bed some days. All that tobacco coming out of my system, Zooey sleeping in the guest bedroom a couple of days saying I smelled like an ashtray. Truth is I guess I might have been a little irritable, chased her out for a few nights."

Doyle set a frosted glass in front of Rolly on the dark wood bar, another in front of me, rubbed the rim of each with a lemon peel then tipped out the chilled brandy drink and I leaned forward to have a sip. Jesus, that was good, goes all the way to the tips of your fingers, sets your mind buzzing, has you feeling things are going to work out okay. Have to leave the car and Rolly drives me home if I have another. In that little moment of uplift thinking I was never irritable after quitting smoking, just felt that mad itch, an itch that seemed to live—well, you could say it lived in the place where the match used to strike, drinking a glass of milk the only thing would scratch it, milk seeming like the wrong choice at the wrong time, even in summer you'd want something stronger, but it always worked.

He said, "I worried you'd get depressed like that after you left school. Lay in bed all day, can't think of a reason to get up."

"Rolly, you know I didn't leave. They kicked me out. Don't make me talk about this again."

"I just don't get it is all. You had all A's."

"A's and one B. Why're you making me talk about it?"

"I just think it's wrong, a good student and they send you home."

"You owe that much money—" I said, "—they'll kick you out whatever your grades are."

Rolly upset for a moment as he's sipping his Sazerac, I can see he's thinking about this money and where he stands on the subject. All of it from the last account we thought was clean, the IRS looking back finds a problem with it and every cent of the twenty-seven thousand dollars of tuition I'd already paid out of it, suddenly the Dean's inviting me in and waving letters she's getting that are postmarked Kansas City saying *This is your notice of our intent to levy.* They want to recover tuition I already *paid?* Okay: I call the agent assigned, say, *I'm out there making myself a better citizen with a dad in prison, you want to take my tuition?* He says, *We don't consider education an essential living expense.* I say, *It's looking pretty essential to me.* He says, *Your father owes a debt to society.* I say, *It's beginning to look a lot like my debt,* and he hung up. What Rolly's thinking: He's caught between wishing he could help me, the nephew he all but adopted at age fourteen, and wishing his con man brother for once would pay his own debts, my father, who at his sentencing lectured the judge but never once said *Thank you* or *Sorry.*

I quit smoking that very same night the Dean told me I wasn't coming back next semester, not until we squared this bill bigger than a down payment on a house, quit smoking to show myself I could be strong where my father was weak, show him I could drop the same pack-a-day habit he never got out from under, even in prison. Feeling like I was acting tough, not smoking or giving in, using a glass of milk now and then as I had to, and how silly is that? Who drinks *milk* to get by?

How many kids you know think they're rebelling against the old man by *quitting* smoking?

Rolly said, "You ever get mad at him? Your dad."

"Every day. Only it's the opposite of the smoking thing, worse at night, laying there thinking about him and listening to you and Zooey talking in bed."

Rolly hesitated.

"You hear us?" he asked.

"Just talking."

"What do you hear?"

"Zooey asking, *How come he said yes to the lifeguard job . . . ?*"

"And I should tell her what?"

I sipped my Sazerac, feeling good.

"It didn't hurt," I said, "that Sally already worked there."

"She's the chef upstairs, you're down on the pool deck."

"I have coffee with her now and then."

"You ever talk to her about school, your dad?"

"No, see, Rolly, I want to get away from him when I'm with her. I just think about him at night, how mad I am about everything."

"But you still love him."

"I do."

Rolly sighed and sipped his drink.

"Yeah, me too," he said. "That little punk. I want to wring his neck, tell him to wise up, all that time I spent looking out for him. Since he was six years old all he wanted was to make a dollar out of fifteen cent, you know he'd make a lemonade stand only he'd cut the mix with water and sugar to stretch it? Mom and Dad thinking I'm so much older than he is, they tell me, *Roland, you need to set an example for your little brother,* I want to answer, *Isn't that your job?* Now I'm Mister Honest selling Caddies, make my bones on the fact I'm the only straight shooter in the valley, he's still the same. How does he do this?"

"Do what?"

"Get us fixing his problems."

I want to ask Rolly which problems he's talking about. To hear the state of Pennsylvania say it—the high-priced attorneys and county prosecutors and seen-it-all judges—my old man's problems largely had to do with fraud, money laundering, obstruction of justice, conspiracy, witness tampering, and a host of other garden-variety state- and federal-crime raps. To hear U.S. Marshall Raymond Tibbens, the man who'd brought my father in for sentencing, say it, his problem was that he didn't want to grow up, accept a few simple truths the rest of us knew pretty much from birth. To hear the bulls from the State Correctional Facility at Slippery Rock say it, he's no problem at all, the nicest con they ever did mind. My mother, being dead, has no opinion on the matter. To hear my old man say it, though, the real problem with Jacob Cameron Asprey Sr. is just that he's a romantic at heart. Except his opinion is the one that counts least in matters like these. And his name is my name—and Rolly's, too, sort of, which I guess points to what Rolly was talking about, what I think about late at night. Walk the straight and narrow all you want, be the only honest Caddy dealer in the valley, the most popular, the most trustworthy, you're still brother to the con man doing time in Slippery Rock just across town. Why it seemed appropriate that in my effort to get a prize education, set myself apart from my name, it was my name that came and knocked me right back down to where I'd started.

Rolly saying, "It was hard being his big brother. Mom and Dad always telling me to set him straight, he's got all the personality and I'm telling him about putting yourself out there with integrity. Meanwhile he's cutting his lemonade with water and sugar and telling me I'm playing a sucker's game. He was *six*. When he gets older, you know, he has better I guess you'd say *luck* with women than I had. As a teenager fooling around, I mean. Okay. We both get lucky as grown men. I get Zooey, build a happy life with a woman like that. His good fortune he met your mom, God rest her, the best thing ever happened to him; difference is Zooey's around to keep me in line and your mom, God rest her, isn't."

But Rolly doesn't believe in God, not really, and I sipped my drink almost gone now and looked out the door at the silver light. Rolly knowing I rely on him for advice; so far what he's offering up makes sense, even when I tell him, in high school, that I want to go to Bucknell. He'd asked, *Why an expensive place like that? Why there?* Back then we still believed the money in that last account was safe, unwashed, legally obtained, mint. Enough to get me through with the help of a job in the kitchen after class and the scholarship. *Why there?* he asked and I wanted to say, *Rolly, you may as well ask,* Why not prison? *Because they don't have people like my father there. So that's where I'm going.* Then, after they kick me out, I learn that you can't transfer credits from a school you owe money, and no bank in the world will loan you money when the IRS has a levy against money you already spent. I go to Bucknell to get away from my father once and for all, only my father brings me right back.

"Things okay with Sally?" he asked. "Seeing her a lot after being away."

"We had a couple of years to cool off."

"You mad at her?"

"Not *mad*, no. Stung, like hurt, maybe. Okay? But friends."

"How do you go back to that, being friends? Like Zooey and me saying we go back to being friends. Married this long, interested, we don't want to be friends. Why would you want to be friends?"

"It's not up to me."

"You sure it wasn't you?"

"No," I said, "it was all Sally. The split."

He's trying to get me to look back in time when what I'm after is to break from the old man who's three-quarters of the way through his 148 months in Slippery Rock, shed that old self like a snakeskin doesn't fit, and find myself born-again as Rolly's boy. Rolly the only honest man in the valley. And now I'm somehow eligible for a second look by a woman who'd given me a summer at sixteen and then cut me loose. Hungry, too, for the possibility I spy there on the pool deck at Chime Creek. Sometimes wondering, *Well, what if I were to get mixed up with one of those rich women? Would that fix things?* An imprecise response, sure, it's just that sometimes I imagine that I can even *hear* it, money: Have the impression that I can actually *hear* money calling me, my reaction similar to what happens when someone blows one of those silent dog whistles. Watch my dog, Coop, on his bed, see him snap awake and lift his head, ears pricked up to the sound of something no one else can hear: That's me, when money calls. The feeling there when I told Werner Schmidt, the general manager of Chime Creek Country Club, that I'd be his lifeguard, make sure nobody drowned, and stay away from the wives, though I didn't necessarily mean that.

A feeling that I was saying yes to a new idea of myself, some possibilities for change there.

"Sally's mistake, then," Rolly said.

"You drive me," I said, "I could have another."

Two hours later, done brushing my teeth, maybe a little too buzzed but I'll be okay with enough water, I walked back into my bedroom in time to hear Rolly say goodnight to Zooey and click out his light, then realized I'd forgot to feed Coop.

Five years ago I'd discovered him rooting through our garbage, a Labrador limping on an infected foot and his ribs showing. I identified. Asked my uncle could we keep him and I don't think Rolly had it in him to tell me no. We took the pup in and named him Cooper and fed him until he was nice and happy and fat and loving, a real face-licker and tail-thumper; but soon enough we learned the queerest thing about him. Weeks after we'd got him, after it had become plain enough to him and everyone else that he was going to be loved and fed and cared for and never, ever go hungry again, I made the mistake of sidling up to him while he had his nose in his food dish. I reached out to scratch his ears, let him know I was happy to have him there, and next thing you know I'm riding to the emergency room with my hand wrapped in a white dish towel saturated with blood, the wound doubly painful because it was received on a mission of delight.

I fed him now and stood at a safe distance yawning and blinking and marveling at how *needfully* he approached his food bowl. We'd been having problems with a bear again, the summer drought bringing one down from the mountain, famished enough to hunt through garbage, maybe even come after some livestock, and I had the impression that Coop sensed the bear was out there and any minute might come after *his* food. That was Coop for you—worried about his food when he ought to be worried about himself. The dog ate not just with his jaws but with his entire body, as if his entire body were hungry. Hunger doing its hunger thing.

I'm remembering my first night at Bucknell, a similar feeling of hunger, only mine had nothing to do with food. I was green and twenty-two years old, already doubly removed from my surroundings—by my advanced age, and by the understanding that while the other first-year students were fresh from private school graduations, I'd spent the last couple of years working as a mechanic in the same dealership where my uncle sold Caddies while I scraped together enough money to attend college. I was walking home at ten o'clock that first night, stinking of garlic from my shift cooking at the cafeteria, thinking of Sally Godstreet and smoking my last cigarette of the day, when my roommate, whom I'd talked to for all of ten minutes, passed me going the opposite way in his new black Saab convertible with four other guys from my hall, all of them talking on cell phones over thumping music, the car heading downtown—you could say on a mission of delight. I stepped out of reach of the streetlight and watched them go by, my heart pounding. It was all pimped and primed, that Swedish automobile, and as it hummed by I imagined that this was *money*, this car—money passing me by without so much as a sidelong glance as it headed away in the opposite direction, kissing its fingertips and bidding adieu forever.

THREE

LATE THE NEXT MORNING, POOL deck baking under my feet, the crowd of
tanned wives having slipped away one by one to their private tennis
lessons, I lifted the skimmer out of the guardhouse in order to circle
the deck, straining out forsythia leaves and the other unidentified crap
that always found its way into the water; would foul the drains you
didn't watch out. I was still dipping and straining when Hippolyte, the
alcoholic head greenkeeper, walked the deliveryman across the green to
oversee the filling of the fertilizer tank, the painted white pipe off beyond
the West Gate kept distant from the buildings hidden by a low hedge
and locked down like Fort Knox. Hippolyte granted the truck driver
entry, supervised the coupling of truck to tank, and then, incredibly,
stood at a short distance smoking a cigarette while the poison flowed.
The deliveryman considered the cigarette, seemed to sense doom at a
glance, and walked a distance away to talk on his cell phone until the
tank was full.

I was halfway around the pool when my cell phone began to hum on
the lifeguard stand, Rolly calling to ask me to pick up a pint of vanilla,
and of course I was too far away to do anything as it vibrated its way
across the perch, just waited there with my hands on my hips, looking

at the deck and shaking my head as it reached the edge and tipped over, dunking with a real pitiful *plunk* into the deep end, and sank.

Water-resistant, the manual said.

But not water*proof.*

I stood there with my head down, eyes closed, and hands on hips, until I heard a rhythmic tapping high above and looked up.

Sally stood at the wide café window, her burnt-blood hair tied back by a white scarf, tapping a coin against the glass to get my attention. Her beauty, as always, seemed like a category error: These were looks that could have been used to sell things, to market elixirs and oils and white-sand beaches, and the hoarding of her beauty for its own sake seemed curiously old-fashioned. Why have the weapon and not use it? For one terrible moment I felt myself trapped, drunk on the milk of two sisters, each entirely out of reach.

"Eat?" Sally mouthed.

I nodded.

She gestured with her chin: *Come on up, then, sport.*

I posted the NO SWIMMING sign, snatched my red lifeguard sweatshirt from the guard-shed hook, and walked upstairs to find Sally in the kitchen in her whites. You could say I was proud of her—this woman who could have walked runways in Paris and Milan instead managing a kitchen crew full of scarred knuckles and tattoos and pierced eyebrows, had a nickname for each of them, and who was not afraid to call out lazy work where she saw it. Proud of her because I'd known her well back in those days Kimber had been talking about, when she was just another girl looking for her identity in a little fun and, failing to find it, doing her best to pretend she knew who she was. In a lifetime you have maybe one, two relationships like the one we'd had: a single summer at sixteen together, lives linked in total secrecy—because, I liked to think, we were too selfish to share the news about something that seemed so fragile. We were children then, and now, whenever I saw her running a kitchen, I experienced a hot flash of what felt like mourning: She'd become a grown-up. You could see it in her face, not just in the resignation and the urgent, ever-present exhaustion, but in the light that seemed to have gone out around her. Sally would always be beautiful, perhaps even unfairly so. But at twenty-five she looked thirty, and considering her from across the room you might find yourself wondering what thirty would bring to yourself someday. I followed her around the kitchen as she dipped her fingertip to taste the stocks and sauces on the stovetop, and then, incredibly, dove deltoid-deep into the trash can to see what saleable food had been wasted, lifting out a big handful of scallion tops and cursing the kitchen in general, saying they were going to be put out of business if they kept it up, not watching their food cost base, even though the idea that they'd go broke was an outright lie. Sally did fifty or sixty covers every day for lunch, twice that many for brunch, plus they had a full house every night of members willing to pay thirty-six dollars for a hanger steak would cost you eighteen at a bistro downtown.

"You meet the wives yet?" she asked, digging in the trash again, and then, satisfied, scrubbing her hands clean at the sink.

The "wives" being the women who swarmed my deck all day, never so much as dipping their toes in the pool. The wives being the spouses of the husbands who bought Cadillacs from my Uncle Rolly, husbands Rolly had given square deals for twenty years running, and cashed in to get me this job.

Werner having given me two pieces of advice as he led me to the door after hiring me.

One: *Just make sure nobody drowns.*

Two: *and stay away from the wives.*

"Every one of them, I think," I said.

"Lovely, aren't they?"

"I suppose."

She lay a couple of lamb chops on the counter, dusted them with salt and pepper and ground fennel seed with her fingertips raised to eye level, then gently laid them on the grill. Smoke curling up and I realized I was hungry.

"I think a few of them are divorced," I volunteered.

"Right."

"Still kind of young."

Sally looked away at the chops, poking at them absently with her finger even though they'd only been on the grate for thirty seconds, then back at me.

"What?" I asked.

"Come on, Jake," she said.

"What?" I asked.

"Don't do that."

"Don't do what?"

"You know what I mean."

"You think they're out of my league?"

"Listen," Sally said, "I like you, Jake. You know what I mean? I *like* you. So just take my advice on this one, and don't worry about this league, that league, whatever league. That's not what this is about."

"I was just asking," I said.

"You've got to stop falling for the wrong people. That's how you fall every *time*."

"Since when do I do that?"

She really gave me the eye on that one, and went back to pressing the chops. Sally had met my last girlfriend, when I brought Bethenny home for a weekend, hoping for the best—okay, maybe hoping to piss Sally off, sure, thinking of how she'd cut me loose after our one summer together—and things hadn't gone well. Place yourself in the scene: the favorite home pub, the tense second beer, the interloper girlfriend asking the old friend what it was like, growing up in such a bourgeois fantasy. Later, when, with shaking hands, I managed to paper-cut my index finger on the check, Bethenny silenced the table by drawing my finger to her and taking the blood-beaded tip into her mouth, her bright-barred eyes over my finger fierce on Sally and seeming to say *Yummy*.

Sally chose not to answer, sluicing a grassy stream of olive oil into a smoking pan and laying sliced fennel over it—the burner so hot the oil flashed up in a quick lick of fire—flipping the crackling pile over and over by tossing the pan, lifting a bottle of white wine up by the neck and drawing the cork out with her teeth, dumping the wine into the pan with a careless splash—rosemary fumes rising now—swirling and swirling the boiling pan all around like a hypnotist's tool, laying a knob of butter in the middle of it—still no utensils—just using her hands and the motion of the pan, swirling and swirling. And then she expertly poured the sauce out on a hot plate, giving the cooked fennel some real height in the center and gently topping the pile with the smoking lamb chops and a pinch of salad made of what looked like celery leaves. Instead of sliding it toward the pass-through, she casually sent the plate spinning toward me across the counter, and the dime dropped: It was for me, this plate that ran thirty-eight bucks in the next room.

"No time to let the chops rest," she said. "Criminal as that is. Eat. Before Werner sticks his head in."

I went at it like Coop. The chops were charred on the outside, cherry-red inside, and when I took the first bite a muscle began to twitch in my left eyelid, it tasted so good, that electric salty good goodness that goes right to your spine, and I lay my head back breathing steam to cool off my mouth. I could taste the money that had gone into them, and I was thinking I ought to save one chop to bring home to Rolly, man, he loved lamb with a little mint jelly, but I couldn't stop myself and in just a few moments the whole plateful was gone except for two gnawed bones.

"You know what Werner told me the day he hired me?" Sally asked.

I slid the plate back her way.

"Stay away from the husbands?" I asked.

"No, see he didn't. You know why? Because he didn't *have* to say that. And doesn't ever, not to anyone else with half a brain. But I warned him about you. I said, *Werner, he's got this thing, he falls for girls that he knows are trouble.* That harpy you brought home? *Werner,* I said, *remind him to watch out, maybe he'll actually listen if he hears it from someone other than me.*"

I moved the plate a little to the left, a little to the right.

"She wasn't a *harpy*," I said.

"She was a harpy. That act with your finger?"

"Why'd you tell him that, anyway?"

"You see that lunch you just ate? You see that pool out there, those underwear models lying around it handing you money? You see the landscaping, the view, the mood? This is the kind of world you move through when you work here. Every *day* you get this stuff. It's a good job, Jake. And I don't want you to fuck it up because you went all dreamy on me."

"I don't get *dreamy*."

"Yes you do. Sit tight, keep your head straight, maybe in a couple years they'll give you a staff job here, an *executive* job, and then you've got it made." She picked up my plate and turned away toward the dishwashing station. "I'm getting one myself."

"*Are* you?"

Her back was turned as she lay my dish in the rack, though even facing away from me she couldn't hide the blush burnishing her ears, the blood-bright neck and cheeks.

This was the only time Sally ever blushed: When she wanted my approval on something.

She said, "An opening's coming up in the business office. The genuine article. You know: the suit, the company car. Enough bonus money in three years to open my *own* place, do it the way I want to. Werner and I already talked about it."

I'm thinking: and this is how *you* fall, Sally.

"He's going to want an MBA type, don't you think?" I invited.

"I asked about that. He tapped my shoulder with his finger and said, I don't want MBAs. I want *problem solvers*."

"Sally," I said, "in my experience these things can go either way."

"It's a wrap, trust me," she said. "How about the pool table?"

"Some table," I said.

"I bet she tried to cut some sort of deal with you."

"Sort of."

She snorted in disgust and shook her head.

"That kid," she said. "You don't want to know what it's like having a sister like that. Listen to me on this one: Jake, you think the wives are a risk? My sister is twenty times worse. Do yourself a favor and don't get mixed up with her. I *have* to stick by her, because I'm all she's got. I figure, so long as I'm in her life, if she needs money she'll come to me instead of cooking up some scheme. But she sees a guy like you, she thinks, *Here's a guy I can work an angle with.* Promise me you're not going to let her get under your skin."

And that sort of pissed me off, too, Sally telling me not to let someone get under my skin when *she* was the one who had left her mark on me. Through all the time we'd known each other there had only been that one summer between us, about as consequential a time as any moment can be—but still, just that one hit of sweetness, and the cryptic remark that had followed its exquisite start on the basement pool table: *I trust you,* she'd said, and in the end I guess what she had been saying was, *I trust you to remain my friend, if this doesn't work out*—because we went right back to that two months later, when she told me it had to end. And now, when she was telling me to stay away from her sister—I guess I might have easily said, *You were the one who got under my skin. But you turned me away. And that excuses me—that officially ends my tour of duty. I put myself out there for you. And you didn't answer.*

"Kimber's making so much trouble for you," I said, "I guess I can see why you want to get rid of it."

"When do you want to pick it up?"

"I'll try to put it together tomorrow."

"You do that," she said, "I'll owe you."

She reached up and gave my bicep a single tight squeeze, leaving a damp imprint of her hand on my sweatshirt, and I felt a moment of psychic pain: With hurt, with love, with fear and admiration, I realized that this was the same gesture she'd used nine years ago when, after the pool party ended, she gripped my arm and asked me to follow her downstairs, saying, *I want to give you something.* We left her parents swimming in the pool, both of them slightly buzzed on afternoon beers and the bright heat, clearly fully occupied by each other. The interior was so chilled by the air conditioner that our teeth began to chatter, Sally stepping to the basement doorway and momentarily placing a hand on the frame, as if to steady herself. Neither of us spoke a word—not even when Sally, at the bottom of the stairs, shivering in that green bikini, stepped to the pool table, swiveled in the dark, and leaned back against the rail with both hands, her chin lowered in what might have been shame or doubt, but her eyes wide and level and nakedly unguarded as she draped both arms over my neck and, with the skin of her burning belly pressed tight against me, delivered a lemonade kiss whose sweetness I can still taste.

Eight weeks later she would visit me after dinner with her hair still wet from the shower, and walking beneath dripping elms she would tell me that it was over. *But, please don't make me tell you why*, she said. *Please, Jake. If you love me, don't make me tell you.* I gave her that much—I left her standing there and walked back home in the rain. At the time I was just naïve enough to believe that I'd get over her, and my education—my passage into adulthood—the slow realization that some wounds carve themselves so deeply they change the shape of you forever.

It wasn't until I was in bed that night reading that I remembered the cell phone at the bottom of the pool. And I'd promised Zooey ever since Rolly started in with the blood thinners that no matter *what* I'd always, always have my phone on me. I would have just left it, got it in the morning, but I go now I know if I need to buy a new one on the way to work tomorrow. So I dressed and went down the back stairs to avoid passing Rolly and Zooey's bedroom as I went out. They'd want to know what I was doing, plus Rolly'd be asking me to pick up a pint of ice cream on my way, Zooey reminding him he wasn't allowed to have that anymore. His car was blocking me in so I lifted his key off the hook, grabbed a clean towel, and climbed in behind the tiller of his Cadillac, feeling a little silly but also a little pleased, which I guessed was probably how Rolly felt every time he drove it, too.

The Beach Boys playing on the oldies radio Rolly likes; nice to be driving in the cool night air, my mind going back again and again to that moment when Sally, turning in her bikini, had given me that strange look, somehow ashamed yet proud at the same time, and leaving it to me to ask myself if I was able to meet her gaze. I was already in love with her then, and twice as bad off after that. I did fall for the wrong women, and she was one of them. *I trust you*, she'd said, after, and I thought, *Well, no one's arguing with that, Sally. But we're going to find out if I can trust you.*

The slate walk leading up to the gate was a cindery gray in the moonlight, the heat of day still radiating upward from the warm stone against the descending chill of night. I unlocked the gate, hearing each footfall as I strode to the mirrored rectangle of the pool and crouched before the water to look over the edge. My cell phone rested there at the bottom, the pale fluorescent light of its glowing face illuminating the blackest recess of the deep end of the pool, where it had ended its tumbling fall—and somehow the water, which always seemed shockingly cold during the heat of day, felt warm now as I shucked off my sweatshirt, kicked my flip-flops to the side, and dove in to go after it.

I sat in the car afterward with the heater blowing, listening to the radio, waiting for my teeth to cease chattering. The Beach Boys were asking "Wouldn't It Be Nice"?—and I sort of sang along, not really knowing the words but somehow understanding the music just the same as I put the car in gear and decided to take the town road around the course home. It was the same drive Rolly had taken me on earlier in the summer when I'd asked him to spell me for the last year, I'd pay him back. He asked me to join him for a drive, and it was as we were passing around the golf course that he'd dropped the news that they weren't going to get the loan he'd checked on, the goddamn parasite bankers, Jake, and all the real savings tied up in their retirement funds, no way they could touch a penny. The only other money the house, and they hadn't planned to sell it for another five, maybe ten years, Jake, no way to come at it but to come out and say it, but I just wasn't going back in the fall.

But he had something for me: He'd taken Werner—you know from the club?—taken him to lunch. And had got a job for me.

There . . . , he said, and pointed through the rain-blurred glass at the lights of Chime Creek, the curved drive inviting even in this weather.

We both observed this change of fortunes in silence for a moment.

Look, he said, *you're not from the sort to ever give up.*

It might've helped Dad to know when to quit.

It might have. But he couldn't, because that's what you came from. People who keep pushing even when they know they're beat. Good can come of that.

He pulled over to the side of the road, the rain going against the roof of the car, and told me a story about Grandpa, the day the hired strike-breakers had come to the house in a line of pickup trucks, muscle from Philadelphia dressed in longshoreman hats and coats and bearing pick handles, a dog chained into the back of one of the pickups. Rolly and Jake, still young boys, shushed inside with Mother, standing at the window watching the dog strain and strain on its hook to get at Grandpa, who stood on the porch cradling his hunting rifle. The strike-breakers had walked around Grandpa's car, whacking the headlights and taillights in turn with their pick handles until the dun-colored grass and brighter patches of coltsfoot were twinkling with busted glass. Grandpa had watched them do what they had to do, his arms crossed over his rifle and not saying a word nor even giving them much attention, the strikebreakers saying they'd be back tomorrow if Grandpa didn't tell his boys at the plant to call it off, that they'd be bringing five dogs to set on the men on the picket line tomorrow morning at first light. Rolly and Jake still inside at the window watching the strikebreakers walk back to their trucks with their pick handles dragging in the mud when Grandpa casually raised up and shot the dog in the head. The dog went down like its legs had been kicked out from under it, just a pink spray hanging in the winter air, the strikebreakers frozen in their tracks, and in the silence that followed, Grandpa lowered the smoking barrel of his rifle as casually as he'd raised it and both boys had clearly heard him say, *Now you've only got four of them to bring, you tick-bred sons of bitches.*

I didn't have the heart to tell Rolly that this was the second time I'd heard that story.

The first time, it was Dad telling it, I'm age fourteen, the two of us sitting in the back of a police cruiser outside of Palmyra, New York, the cruiser with its lights going, no siren, Dad's handcuffed wrists getting in the way of the little hand gestures he always used to support his stories while the state cop searched his car, and I listened with the helpless love of a kid who knew that his childhood was about to die, that we were both in mourning for one age even as we were beginning to understand that another, far more troubled age was upon us.

It was the same story, both times. Yet it carried vastly different meaning when spoken by Rolly, with his defeated eyes, the soaked golf course visible through the rain-kaleidoscoped glass, than it did when recited by the man who'd planned to run for Canada from a prison sentence, his fourteen-year-old son in tow, but hadn't made it four hours out of town before the taillight he'd been too cheap to repair had caught the interest of a bored cop.

FOUR

A CLATTERING RAIN POUNDED THE backyard just after sunrise, fat flooding torrents pouring from the gutter just outside my window. I blinked and stretched and considered the gushing sluice of the drainpipe—the first rain we'd seen in weeks—then pulled the covers over my head with all the delight of someone who has been let off the hook, if even for a single day. Thirty minutes later my aunt knocked on my door and entered with an anxious expression, bearing the phone. Werner. Had I mistakenly viewed the weather as a sign to sleep in? Yes. Yes I had. Unfortunately the intricacies of insurance and liability, coupled with certain recent unpleasant events that were better left undiscussed, regrettably required that the club have a guard on duty even on rainy days for the remainder of the summer, and would I please get myself to work as soon as possible?

The rain clearly wasn't going to let up anytime soon, so I wrapped myself in my uncle's red jacket and, after a bleary-eyed drive through the rinse-cycle streets, a paper cup of tepid coffee in my fist, I climbed the cold, slippery steel ladder to my post, with a music player in my pocket piping music in through headphones. Hood up, hands in my pockets, the music like a lullaby, chin on chest, warm rain tickling my bare feet, and the faint odor of Rolly's aftershave going up my nose, I began to feel a bit like a kid who'd safely escaped a freak rainstorm for a warm tent and, not entirely uncomfortable, subsided into a nap. I suppose I would have happily slept clean on until lunch, but when a cold hand gripped my bare foot my lower mandible, hanging slack in sleep, snapped up so forcibly my lower and upper incisors clicked together, and I surged forward and damn near stumbled right off the platform into the deep end. I pushed my hood back and blinked in the rain, found Werner standing there beneath a golf umbrella in his good suit and shined shoes and immaculate haircut, waiting for me to compose myself.

"I figured it was all right to sleep," I explained, and swiped my dripping hair out of my face.

"And right you were. I'd like to apologize for the unpleasant work environment. In retrospect, it seems a bit cruel, having someone keep watch over the pool during a monsoon. I could ask our attorney to have a word with the insurance company. Have a coffee with me in my office? Five minutes?"

I imagined Sally glaring down at me from a window overhead, reminding me: *Don't fuck it up.* Werner and I had never spoken easily or at length, but here was what appeared to be an invitation of significance. Delighted, Werner. Just have to put out the NO SWIMMING sign and lock the gate before I leave. One can't be too careful.

Werner's secretary, Wendy, was waiting for me, rising as I approached, swiping my damp hair back, Werner inside the office at his desk with two cups of coffee on a silver platter along with a sugar bowl and a silver pitcher of cold milk. The picture window to our left revealing rain-blurred grounds, workers still at work pulling tarps over the sand traps. Hippolyte was simultaneously directing the men and attempting to light a cigarette in the driving rain, and having what looked like no luck with either. I licked my lips and angled the silver pitcher to tip out a cup of coffee and douse it with a double shot of milk. Werner hadn't bothered to rise from his chair, one of those perfect leather chairs that tilt and swivel, the thing Rolly said he loved most about his own office, that good chair that announced to the world you had money and were ready to play.

"Sorry about the misunderstanding" I said "I hope that's not what this is about."

What did this moment remind me of? Oh yeah: an afternoon when I was a kid, ran into him in the coat closet. Retrieving my blazer after brunch, picking up Dad's coat, his date's spring jacket, too—Eloise Parker, it would have been, because she loved the club and would beg my father to bring us for Sunday breakfast—the jazz band murdering "My Sweet Embraceable You" behind me in the dining room. I must have been only ten or eleven years old, judging by how anxious I was when I found Werner there in the coat room polishing the brass hat stand with a white handkerchief. Before I could back out he looked over his shoulder at me, still polishing intently.

You're Jacob's boy, aren't you? he asked. *Also Jake?*

Yes, sir. Also Jake.

Heard you're quite a swimmer. Quite a swimmer.

I didn't answer.

Silver medal in states last summer, was it? he invited.

Gold.

Some precious metals on that wall of yours.

I didn't answer.

I gather you like it? Swimming.

I said, *I like the way it leaves me hungry all the time.*

Ever consider swimming for the club team, son?

Yes, sir. It's just that it's too far to come all the way across town after school.

Werner pocketed his white cloth and stepped to the coat rack, quick as three viper strikes, snatching out the correct pair of blazers and Eloise's linen coat, frowning slightly as he paused to brush away a speck of dust from her collar. He helped me put my own blazer on and lay my father's over my left arm, then held out Eloise's coat, which I grasped eagerly, ready to make my escape.

Except when I took hold of it he didn't let go of it.

A favor, if you'd be so kind, he said. *Let your father know the club has somehow gone and lost his dues check again. It must have been our mistake, I'm sure, as he wouldn't let it happen a* fourth *time, would he?* Still holding that coat tightly, and smiling faintly.

Ask him to forward another, and quickly, will you? And extend my apologies for the club having made this dreadful mistake.

And then he let go of the coat. As I backed out of the room, Werner grinning benevolently at me, I realized that he'd planned the moment, that he'd been waiting in ambush, polishing an already gleaming brass stand. That was how I felt now, there in his office more than a decade later—as if what was about to happen wasn't about me, not really, that I was just going to be a part of a scene that had already been framed.

"No need to apologize," he said. "Perfectly normal for a lifeguard to guess that a rainy morning is his chance to sleep in, have the day off. Did I ever tell you I was a lifeguard here, Jake?"

I said *No,* he hadn't told me that.

"That very chair you sit in. There for two summers."

I said He must have enjoyed the job if he came back for a second summer.

"Indeed. And worked my way up from there. A promotion, then another. And now here we are. I respect people who come in at the ground floor, Jake. Business school has its merits, of course, but our best decisions aren't made by the actuarial tables, are they?"

I said I supposed not.

"A good way to start, in that guard chair. You get the lay of the land, literally and figuratively. You know—take in the mood, the customs, the social geography. Everyone comes through that pool, the wealthy and not-so-wealthy, young and old, women and men. You see the interplay of friends and enemies. Even the husbands can occasionally be goaded into a lap or two. And there you are, above it all, so to speak. Seeing."

"It's—I seem to have mostly the wives."

"So many of them with free time," he invited. "So few ways to fill it."
I'd been warned about this. Before my interview, Sally cautioning me
that Werner routinely held business meetings in which no business was
conducted and conference calls that were devoted entirely to the unsea-
sonable weather and power lunches in which the only subject of conversation was his daughter's recent poetry award. Sally's own interview
for the position of executive chef a fourteen-minute discussion on the
subject of women, and of Werner's dawning understanding that, while
one couldn't live with them, one also couldn't, paradoxically, live without them. Werner's aim in these events, as best as Sally or anyone else
could tell, to deny you any useful preparation, draw a bead on just
how much eleventh-hour reserve of knowledge, social capital, and con-
fidence you possessed. I feared that I was undergoing one such test now
and had thus far failed to draw the passing grade of his interest.

I drank my milk with coffee and said, "Sally seems to think they're
going to trip me up."

"The wives?"

"She tells me I fall in love too easily."

"Do you?"

"Only when I can't help it."

"I have a theory," Werner said, "that romantics are destined for
unhappiness. Something about their unwillingness to see the world as
it is. Always wishing it so, wishing it so, when of course it never is.
Why aren't they more sensible?"

"It's not up to them, though. How you get to be a romantic, doing
things don't make any sense."

That was my father speaking, but Werner lay back his head and
looked at the ceiling and laughed, a genuine laugh, and I felt an electric
thrill as he crossed his hands over his trim stomach and smiled at me.
Thinking I wanted Werner to like me and sensing that for the moment,
at least, he did, for the first time in his presence I felt comfortable
allowing a moment to pass in which the only sound was the rain tapping against the window.

"Your father and I were friends, you know," he said. "Before all that unpleasant business with the IRS."

"A long time ago."

"The friendship?"

"The unpleasant business."

"Don't remember much of it?"

"It's others who do the remembering."

"The subject makes you uncomfortable."

Condescending now, and I suffered a hot flash of rage.

"Werner," I said, "why did you invite me here?"

He drummed his fingertips on the desk for a moment, then leaned back in his chair and watched me expressionlessly.

"I was the one who introduced him to de Soto," he said. "Your father approached me at a Christmas party. Here at the club, actually. He said the business was beginning to stick and he needed a good man."

I remembered that year, when the real estate plan began to come together and my father sold his first building. All at once I'm seeing money where for a long time there had been none. For Christmas I got what I'd asked for and then some, the first time in memory. In May we had our first visit from Janvión de Soto, a.k.a. "Tico," a.k.a. the Magician. *The Magician is coming,* my father told me, *watch for him,* and that was how he seemed to arrive, the way a true magician would—I was alone in the kitchen on a spring evening, listening to the heavy weather outside, and turned to pour myself a glass of pink lemonade. When I turned around again he was just *there*, having arrived silently, as if he'd materialized out of thin air from the freak rainstorm outside, smelling of ozone, water rolling and dripping from the brim of his black hat and long black coat all over the kitchen floor. Looking down at me with fierce blue eyes. I stood there with my mouth open until he grinned at me and said, *Well, get your father, boy.*

"It would seem," Werner said now, "that the good man I recommended wasn't so good."

"My father is to blame. He knew what he was doing."

"Still," Werner said, "I can't help but think that none of that would have happened if I hadn't introduced them. It was born in the instant I placed them together."

I said, "It took me a while to get over that."

Werner sighed, rose from his chair to come around the desk and sit on the edge in front of me with his arms crossed, through the window the clouds moving right to left in a slow retreat from the advancing pressure.

"I knew something was wrong when Rolly calls me in June, invites me to lunch," he said. "I knew they'd just let two mechanics go, things slow down in the summer, maybe he wants to put together a business thing, a discount for club members buying new cars? But he wouldn't let on, and it was uncomfortable, that lunch, like any moment when you know a decent man is stretching himself for something he cares deeply about. Laying down his pride along with the check. He brought me to the Semaphore, a four-course lunch, wines with every course plus a Sazerac before, and it wasn't until the last course that he dropped it on me. He was a little looped, said, Werner, Jake isn't going back. They went after the last bit of money he thought was safe and they *got it*. It's all gone. And not one bank's willing to help him out, not with *his* history. Rolly's a good man, of course, so he had the decency not to come out and say it, what was there between us, that I owed you. But the truth was still there, both of us knowing that de Soto was my responsibility. Instead he said, *Jake is* your man, *Werner, he's someone you can trust, and he needs to land on his feet.* Tears welling up in Rolly's eyes by now. I was embarrassed for him, so I let him go on. *There's not a job to be had out there anywhere,* he said, *even if you do have a college degree. If Jake can't get a job, what will happen to him? We all know where these things can lead. The apple doesn't fall that far from the tree. But you give him that same job you started with, who knows?* And he picked up his drink and said, *Maybe even end up with a job in the main office.* And then he took a big drink but kept his eyes level on me while he did it."

We sat there in silence for a moment, in appreciation of Rolly's courage. He was always in things for the long haul, didn't mind swallowing pride or blood when it was the right thing to do, though I considered the likelihood that that little stunt had cost him his entire July bonus, that four-course fucking lunch, when Rolly didn't even *like* fussy food—he just knew that Werner did.

"I don't want to sound ungrateful," I said. "But since we're being honest, I have to tell you that a summer job doesn't really balance things out. What happened."

He nodded and looked at the ground, and I could see he was already ahead of me, three and four moves, that he'd already worked that out.

"You may have heard," he said, rising to stand over me, his arms crossed over his chest, "as I'm sure Rolly had, through one of his beloved customers, that we have an executive position opening up. Entry-level, not-great pay but a good year-end bonus. Management level nevertheless."

"Sally mentioned it. What you said about problem solvers."

"An apt description of you, yes? That minefield of high school, everyday, with your history, must have been like rolling a rock up a hill. The other kids knowing what your father did, where he was just across town. Some of them even living in his condos, I'd think. How did you get through it?"

"I swam," I said.

"Doing what you had to do. A problem solver."

I sat there thinking, *I thought we just agreed I was a romantic.*

"What if we were to give you a shot at it?" he asked.

"The job?"

"Yes, of course."

"Sally seems to think that you promised it to her."

"You'd be good at it." He tipped his head to gesture to the pool. "See the way you navigate those wives out there? More difficult than much of what we do here in the office, Jake. Like I said, important decisions aren't made by the actuarial tables. They're made with your *character*."

"Sally's my oldest friend in the world."

Werner opened his hands in mock surrender.

"I suppose that's why they call it business," he said. "This could be good for you. The kind of move that sets a life in motion."

"If this is really what you want to do, why does it have to be this one? Why right now? We could wait until another spot opens up."

"That could be years, Jake. No one else even close to leaving. Why don't you think about taking this offer? Sally can wait. To be quite honest, she's so good where she is I'd be reluctant to move her. Maybe you and I could work something out—you stay, things look good? Maybe in a few years we talk about covering tuition. Transfer your credits, take a few classes at night at Penn State. A year later you're done, degree in your pocket and a career ahead of you here," he said, and here his voice went low and soothing, and he leaned down close and damn near whispered in my ear, "Get the *old* life back, Jake. Like none of that business ever happened."

"What happens," I said, "if I say no?"

He seemed surprised by the question.

"I could keep you on as a waiter in the off-season," he said. "But we both know that you'd take off the moment something better came along."

Suddenly the room felt just a notch too warm, even though my hair was wet and the air conditioning was doing its temperature thing with ruthless efficiency. I set down my milk and coffee and realized, with the bitter sting of recognition, that I wasn't going to be allowed to finish it. The meeting was over.

"Werner," I said, "are you saying you're going to let me go if I don't accept?"

He walked around the desk and regained his seat, then replaced his reading glasses and opened the manila folder on the blotter before him. The glass discs of his lenses reflected the rain-blurred window-light, and for a moment he was entirely poker-faced, like he wasn't there at all, just a suit and a voice with money behind it.

"The position opens up in thirty days," he said. "Let me know by the end of the month."

To hear my old man say it, the problem with Jacob Asprey Sr. is that he's a romantic. He was always falling for things that were overpriced, for things that cost too dear against the bottom line, because Werner was right—that's what a romantic is: someone always wishing it so, wishing it so. In my father's particular case, the wish pursued was an ideal of himself as a wealthy individual who had shaken his factory roots once and for all. When the math didn't quite add up, he didn't shrug and accept that it hadn't worked out—no, what he did was this: He changed the math. And then kept on changing it. If you were to type his name into an Internet search engine you would soon find yourself reading phrases like *obstruction of justice* and *conspiracy to commit* and *fraud* and *forgery* and *witness tampering*—the usual nonviolent felonies that set the con man apart from the general criminal population. At least, that's the way he sees it. And here, again, we run into that old, old problem: That the way my father sees things really isn't relevant. When people hunt for your name and instead encounter the word *felony*, they generally make up their mind about you very quickly. And it is my great misfortune that we share this name, because searches for my history invariably turn up that word, too. Imagine, if you will, my fumbling explanations in banks, in innumerable departments of motor vehicles—to cops, to clerks, even meter maids. *It's not me. It's just my name.*

It has always seemed appropriate to me that your undoing and the thing that prevents you from avoiding your undoing should be one in the same. My father, when first convicted of being a fraud, could have paid his way through—the entrained fine and service, with the record wiped clean after. Being a good and true fraud, however, he instead did this: He attempted to defraud his way through the fine, the service, compounding his mistakes and deepening the punishments exponentially. That's how it is with any criminal soul. The gambler cannot rise above the gambling life because when he is finally given the opportunity to do so, he will find a way to gamble with that opportunity. The alcoholic cannot rise above the drinking life because when he is finally given the opportunity to do so, the pressure of the opportunity will provide him the excuse to have a drink. This is because when you have it bad, the way my old man did, the disease is not some component of your personality to hold in check. No, when you have it bad, the disease is *you, you* are the problem, your name and your blood, and how are you to get around those? You never break free of the laws of your own nature—your own gravity, which wants to bring you low, and keep you there.

Revisit that cold winter night the Dean showed me the letter postmarked Kansas City, the one saying *This is your notice of our intent to levy*, and told me I wasn't coming back in the fall. That night it felt as if it were my own native gravity dragging me down, my own physics squaring the math. Sidewalks icy that evening, spring trying to escape the snowy confines and, for the time being, failing, the thwarted effort somehow appropriate to the defeated mood. In my bedroom I briefly considered the silver closet crossbar, wondered if it had the strength to hold my weight. When you reach a good and true bottom, anything is allowed. But it was life I was after, not oblivion—so I pieced myself back together, sat at my desk, and put a trembling pencil-point to paper. I wrote for two hours without a break or pause or flinch, hunched over the table with my tongue out of the side of my mouth as the words flowed forth. I felt about four years old. I don't think I blinked once. I knew of an eminent writer who spoke of *getting it all in* with his fiction, that being the true test of story, if you'd *got it all in*, and that was what I did now—I put it all in, where I began, what was behind me, the events that I'd finessed or passed over or just plain denied, the vanity and greed beneath it all, and why I needed to return here in the fall to escape the misfortune that had attached itself to me since the day the Magician, dripping rainwater from his hat brim and coat, had materialized in our kitchen and made my childhood disappear.

I closed the letter this way:

I write this, finally, to acknowledge the most damning fact—the one that visits me every night, brings me awake into the terrible rinsing clarity of 3:00 a.m. But you must listen closely, because even on paper, even with the written word, I find that I can't bring myself to say the words louder than a whisper. Dean: I knew all along.

I knew what was going on: That my father was rooking the government. But I did nothing to stop it, and this is how I pay my debt to society: not in the locked cell (as my father does), but in the simple act of being truthful with you—the person who has the power to send me back to myself forever. There is dishonesty in my past. But I believe that being a good person is something you work at everyday. And I am trying today.

Will you help me?

When I heard the tick of Bethenny's boots on the stairs, like the rapid *chocky* click of a timely clock, I realized that a moment I had been avoiding all my adult life was finally here: I was about to tell someone the whole truth about my past. That time last winter I brought Bethenny home with me for a weekend—to meet Rolly, to meet Zooey, and therefore experience their silent but palpable disapproval—she had asked about my father but I gave her the same old half-truth I gave everyone else: *He's gone.* Most people, including Bethenny, reading that to mean that my father was dead along with my mother, and I never felt the need to correct the misunderstanding.

The document on the table before me a first step toward setting that right. The secrets I kept—vanishing every Wednesday afternoon for an unidentified weekly obligation, fielding phone calls behind locked

doors—had electrified the air between us, prodding us toward argu-
ments that woke the neighbors once a week and, for better or worse,
extreme habits in the bedroom. She seemed determined to break me,
Bethenny, to force me to confess to my sins—though her primacy, at
least in regard to the bedroom, was forever being qualified by her particular weakness: Surprisingly, Bethenny de Maurier had the pornography thing. I say *surprisingly* because much of it seemed to capture
everything that she categorically opposed in the arena of gender and
fairness. And I think she *did* object to pornography—academically,
ethically—yet her blood demanded it and, sometimes visibly cross-
purposed, she answered the call. She couldn't get off without watching
it, which meant I was consigned to watching it, too, and soon came to
know its arcs and disappointments and jeweled sweet spots. I also came
to know the three or four plot structures the films follow—you know
them, too: For example, the television repairman arriving in his sleeveless shirt, the helpless housewife in her faerie outfit, and then the
unforgivable music and sudden shedding of clothes and the terrible
grimacing, as if the actors were in pain. To protect her dignity, Bethenny
insisted on buying the top-dollar kind: the priciest, slickest pornography money could buy. Which isn't saying much, because even this was
a letdown. Here it was, the best quality she could find, and what was it?
The repairman, the helpless housewife . . . the only difference was that
they used a quality camera, and had bothered to set up some lighting.
Occasionally you could see the microphone wandering down into the
shot. It was the best pornography money could buy, and it was still a
very sad affair all around. The set seemed to be in need of about ten
hours of cleaning before you'd even want to sit on the couch. There
was a poignant quality to Bethenny's fidelity to these films; she had
resigned herself to hunting through the thickets of her own cast-off ideals for a fulfillment she seemed to know she would never experience.
That was sex with Bethenny: the collusion of two souls whose best
efforts merely served to deepen the feeling that something was missing.
I began to wonder what I saw in it, sex with Bethenny—maybe that it

43

was so familiar, in that it reminded me of another activity I couldn't get free of: going broke.

I was all nerves when she entered the room in her black tights and sweater, her boots and chains, the expansive and expensive hair loosely gathered by a scarf at her nape. Book bag lowered to the floor, she considered the scene for its relative immediate value. Finding none, she sat in the chair opposite me, crossed her long legs, and lit a cigarette in search of entertainment. A beautiful woman, in every way the sort of lovely snare Sally had accused me of falling for—we both already knew she would go on to a modeling career in New York and a heroin habit after college. She was damaged, emotionally: Someone in her past had hurt her deeply, and she was tallying strokes of revenge with her subsequent relationships. I was damaged, too. For some relationships, that's all you need.

She wasn't cheating on me.

Not yet.

"Writing again?" she asked. "More entries for the little book?"

The notebook I kept: another secret that nettled her. A rare case where the power structure of the relationship was clear. I never let her read it. That would soon change, when I showed her what I'd just written.

"Something different this time," I said. "This one's actually true."

"Who's the hero?"

I thought about it.

"I don't think," I said, "that there is one."

"Isn't that the truth," she said, and walked into the back to take a shower. I sat watching the empty chair, the outlines of her body still carved into the air and occupying the space like a rumor or a threat, and I thought, *She comes at things with pain. She leads with it. Don't expect the process to begin anywhere but there.* So I left the pages where they were, knowing she'd be more likely to read them if she imagined I'd accidentally left them out, and went into the kitchen to put together some dinner for us. The shower cut off and I soon heard her hunting down her lighter in the living room. First came the snap that announced the lighting of her next cigarette; then a wide silence, and in terror I realized that she was reading it, the letter, that it was happening, and that now, finally, someone would understand. I imagined complications falling away, that moment when pain meets pain and calls it good. A clear channel. I would tell her I wasn't coming back to school and explain why—the deception, the avalanche of felonies, the debt to be paid. We would sit facing each other, gripping hands.

Except it didn't work out that way.

Something went wrong, in fact, just a few pages in, because instead of empathic silence, the breathless absorption of all I had laid out, I heard a plosive gasp, a sharp exhale, and ten deliberate steps leading toward the bedroom. The door cracked shut, followed by the chunky *chock* sound of the latch. Even then, before I had any clear signs that a real disaster was brewing, that the heavy Bethenny weather was on its way—even then, I think I knew what would and must happen. Because there is only one outcome when *you are the disease.*

"Bethenny?" I said through the door.

"*I surround myself with people who reflect my weakness.*"

"Keep reading. You'll see where it leads."

"Then you talk about being ditched by *her*, that one from *high school*—what was her name?"

"Sally," I said.

"And equate me with the others? How? *Why?*"

She was too fixated on the big unanswerable questions, Bethenny— the hows and whys. Because there is such a thing—there is such a thing as looking too deeply, lingering too lengthily on the unknowns, giving them more than their fair share. This was, after all, a woman who had sincerely lobbied for compulsory philosophy majors for all students, with only selective minors. She had named her cat Kierkegaard; above the convex of her breasts, a tiny text of tattoo asked, *Supposing truth is a woman—what then?*—a question I was forced to contemplate at length whenever we made love. That was her doom, the compulsion to closely examine questions that are bound to send you to pieces—which I suppose made it my doom, too, because you're irretrievably linked to those you invite into your bed and your life, linked by the force fields the emotions exert.

"Bethenny," I said, in my sincerest calm-Jake voice, the voice that was required nearly every time she'd taken an extra Ritalin and I'd find her plucking her leg hairs out one by one with tweezers. On those days she'd throw glass ashtrays at me and shout at me for being *too nice*. "Bethenny, I was talking about my family. If you keep reading you'll see what happened. It's worse than you think. I've been lying to you. He's not dead."

"Ah, but you weren't just talking about him. You were talking about *the people I surround myself with*. And I refuse to be diminished this way. I refuse to be reduced to a set of principles. I have a theory, Jake—would you like to hear it? Very well. I have a theory that a person becomes a chef because she's secretly hungry all the time, that a person becomes a teacher because he secretly wants to learn, that a person becomes a doctor because he secretly wants to heal his own pain. In other words, people minister to an idea of themselves. They provide the relief that the world has failed to provide for them. So what does that say about aspiring writers? However talentless they may be? Are they attempting to rewrite history, and present themselves as the hero?"

I lay my head forward against the cool wood.

"It was just an experiment," I said. "A folly of the pen, of the mind. That's how you move forward. You put it down, and then shape it from there."

"You're talking like a true writer now, Jake-O. Proud of you, old boy. But you know what any real writer needs, if he's to succeed?"

Metal scraped against wood.

"He needs *adversity*," she said. "Because really, Jake, what is an artist without a quest? Without that, he's just a man alone with his indulgences, eh?"

The sound I'd just heard—I realized it was the wastebasket being pulled out from under the desk. A sulfurous scrape and pop followed, and it didn't take her very long to burn my journal and my letter. It took only a few minutes, in fact, to reduce that bound notebook and those fourteen loose pages to ash with one of the kitchen matches she kept handy for a cigarette after sex—though it did provide me with enough time to reflect on just how fragile words are, how in need of our protection, how vulnerable to the human elements, to opinion and commerce and need and, worst of all, interpretation. The journal went first, and I imagined I felt a rush of heat radiating through the door—as if the story of my life could generate so much energy. Then she burned the letter one page at a time, announcing each fresh page for the fire, telling me her theories as she advanced through the confession. And I realized that this was correct, this ending—no, it was better than correct, it was *symmetrical*. At first I was laughing, sort of, though I suppose I was also weeping. At first I saw it as some sort of special joke that only I understood—but then I realized that the joke was on me, and when smoke began to drift under the door I told her I was going to kill her. I think I actually meant it. I think I believed I was going to do it when I got through. This sensation of predetermined defeat had been with me since I was fourteen years old, this winnowing away of alternative endings, and I found myself wishing I could go back in time and tell my younger self: *Don't worry. There's no need to struggle. Because it's not up to you. First you lose the television. Then you lose the car. Then the bank account. Then the father.*

But don't stop there—keep going. Lose your home, then your street, then your city. An entire coast, a continent, a sea, a sky. A world.

Lose further; lose faster. Lose your *family.*

Lose your entire life.

"*Stop*," I pleaded.

But she only laughed, cruel laughter that communicated no pleasure.

When I did get through—bashing my way with my shoulder until I knocked the hinges out of the wall—I found her sitting calmly beside her smoldering bonfire, legs crossed, still wrapped in her bath towel, a second towel wrapped tightly around her hair, and in the moment just before the first heavy drift of smoke curled out into the hall and the fire alarm began its Klaxon-sound, she looked at me levelly and said, "And now you've got your quest, Jake-O."

That being the moment I chose to quit smoking.

FIVE

THE NEXT DAY, SON OF a bitch, it's a heat wave, one hundred and ten down in the suffocating space of the basement because Kimber pulled one of her jokes or whatever and switched the air conditioning off, and dripping sweat like it's a Roman orgy wouldn't you know we strain and curse and wrangle the thing to the top of the stairs and then find that we can't make the turn to get it through the hallway and out the back door? I'd squared the math for getting it down Rolly's steps, hadn't bothered to check that we could get it out of Sally's basement, figuring, *They got it in, didn't they?* Standing there with four weight-pile gorillas in muscle shirts, each clocking twenty bucks an hour apiece, eighty already and eighty more just to bring it back down and every one of us looking at the table, shaking his head, and wiping sweat off his face and flicking it away.

At this point we'd all pretty much given up.

"Too tight," gorilla one said.

"Too wide," gorilla two said.

"Too *high*," gorilla three said.

Gorilla four, silenced, turned his head to the side and, incredibly, spat on the tile floor as casually as he would in the dirt. Kimber chose this moment to make her entrance. Dressed in that same green bikini and heels, sunglasses pushing her hair up and back in two surging obsidian whorls, one hundred gleaming teeth on display, she opened the door in an onrush of hot white light and clicked across the kitchen tiles to the refrigerator. At the counter, her back turned to us, she mixed up a pink lemonade and stirred in a shot of vodka from the plastic bottle in the cabinet, and if she was aware of those five sets of eyes on her taut rump as she stirred and stirred, she didn't let on. Finally she swiveled, gracefully, one heel fixed in place, a bullfighter turning a perfect veronica, and raised the glass to her lips, her eyes unblinking on us as she drank deep. Then she pointed at the table with her drink.

"That side of the table comes off," she said.

"It comes *off?*" I asked.

"How do you think they got it *in* there, Einstein?"

And then she turned again—another perfect veronica—and clicked out the door with her drink. After the latch *chocked* shut, gorilla one gave a low whistle.

"Slick," he said, "you got to go *after* that."

I'm thinking, *I don't get back to college, this is going to be me in ten years: the laborer groaning and smooching and rubbing his fingertips together in the air everytime the Mrs. leaves the room. But getting nothing at all. A guy always moving but never going anywhere.*

I raised the hem of my shirt and wiped my face.

"I would," I said, "but I'm afraid she'd bite me on the neck after it was over."

"Man, it'd be *worth* it. You got to go *after* that."

As it turned out, I did go after her, found her on the lounge poking at a cell phone with a ruby nail she'd chewed just bit, the imperfection somehow making her seem more real, less a caricature as she sipped her first drink of the day. I was still pissed off and irritated and because of that I was no longer intimidated by her looks.

"*How* do you get the side off?" I asked.

She never even bothered to look up.

"Figure it out," she said. "Sally tells me you're smart enough. That's all she'll tell me about you. But I happen to know, Jake, that there is something there between you—"

"Hey, this is *going to happen*, you know. The table's leaving. Your little world here's changing."

And I actually felt it go, that unwise remark, tried to whistle it back, snatch it out of the air and put it back in my mouth unspoken, but of course you can't. She looked up at me with her big eyes already beginning to swim a little bit and, oh, fuck *me*, then it happened: Her lower jaw trembled, just a little bit—this being the house where she lived with her parents and then watched them both die just a few years apart, each time Kimber holding one hand and Sally holding the other as they expired, and no matter how much you think you understand that, you really don't. You just don't. Her world had been turned inside out in a way even I couldn't understand. Even the extreme I'd seen didn't come close—losing a mother, a father in prison. I still had him around to resent, at least. I knew he was still out there receiving the signal.

"Ah, Kimber," I said, backing up a step, "ah, Kimber—I'm sorry. I'm so sorry."

She lowered her sunglasses over her eyes and gave me what looked like a smile but was not, an expression that hewed closer to pain, and I stood there tripping over my shame until gorilla two stuck his head out the door and said, "We *got* it," and rather than compound my stupidity I sloped back inside to get the fucking thing *out* of there.

With the table secured by canvas straps inside the trailer, gorillas two, three, and four climbed into the back for the ride, and I hopped into the cab with gorilla one. As he started up the truck the front door opened. Kimber stepped into the doorway holding her second drink of the day, her body framed by interior darkness.

"Hey, *Jake*," she said.

I stuck my head out the truck window. She raised her glass and took a long drink, then smacked her lips and smiled.

"You owe me one," she said, and shut the door.

You owe me one. That remark the first thing that crossed my mind when, just a few hours later, after the celebratory dinner of a rare steak and a bottle of French wine to seal the gift, Rolly already itching to get downstairs and play, the phone rang and Zooey, with that extra note of excitement in her voice, said it was for me. And that it was a girl.

I did *owe her one,* after all—or rather, the universe did, owed her one, and I guess it had picked me to be the one who paid. And I was accustomed to paying the debts of others. I'd been doing it all my life.

"Why don't you come meet me?" she asked.

People rarely surprise me anymore.

"Sally told me to stay away from you," I said.

"Why would she say something like that?"

"She tells me you're trouble."

"Really, Jake," she said, "there is trouble, and then there is trouble. Maybe you stick around, you decide that my kind of trouble is sort of fun. You get in it. Then you get out. And life goes on."

Faint country music played in the background, the genre, organic to its environment, reminding me that I was engaging not the city but a wilder, less tame terrain to which I was poorly suited.

"You never even cared about that table," I said. "Say it."

She laughed.

"Not really, no," she said. "You were the one I was interested in."

"What was that business with the bathing suit? You, laid out like a crime scene."

She laughed again, confident now.

"That was for your benefit," she said. "Because I'm quite aware that something passed between you and Sally. A woman knows, Jake. Oh yes: A woman knows. What happened between you that was so important she won't even talk about it?"

"I'm hanging up."

"Come meet me. We'll have a chat. Make up. And we'll stop talking about the past. Instead we'll talk about the other thing."

"I'm hanging up."

"The pool hall in Zion. I'll be here all night."

And that stopped me cold, hearing mention of that place.

The pool hall being the last place I went with my father before he went to jail.

She said my name once in the interrogative as I gently placed the receiver back in the cradle. I turned and discovered Zooey hovering ten feet away in the fluorescent kitchen light, pretending to rearrange glasses in the cabinet.

"Who was that?" she asked.

"That," I said, "was Sally's younger sister."

"I think about their parents all the time. Just terrible."

"Pretty bad, I guess. Sally's handling it better than she is."

"I saw her at the gas station the other day, filling up," Zooey said. "Jake, wearing nothing but a *bikini*. Walked inside to pay with the money tucked into her *top*."

"I believe it."

"A figure like that—don't you think she'd show a little more modesty?"

"I guess she got my attention well enough," I said.

Zooey stepped close to me and did the Zooey-move: held my chin between her index finger and thumb while looking into my eyes.

"Jake," she said, "I can see that this is going to be a *character building* summer."

Still holding my chin and gaze, she nodded once, and then snatched her knitting off the table and walked into the TV room.

Rolly downstairs practicing trick shots and sipping a glass of brandy, looking pleased, humming an old Dave Brubeck tune as he chalked up and leaned over the green, and in that moment if I'd been given the option to choose a future, I believe I would have chosen Rolly's. This simple life he lived that seemed to make him so happy.

"Kid," he said, "I can't tell you what a surprise this table is."

"I was happy to do it. You deserve it."

"I was thinking I have the boys over once a week after dinner? Like a club."

"That would be great. You could see them more that way."

"Anyway, kid, I love it. Zooey won't mind, do you think?"

"No, she was in on it all along."

I sat watching him play for a while, listening to him hum "Pick Up Sticks." I'd spent less on the table than he had on that stunt with Werner, done less for him than he'd done for me, but you wouldn't know it to see him feeling so satisfied.

"Kimber called me up," I said.

"Uh-huh."

His back to me. He leaned down over the shot, concentrating. Rolly always the sensible one, sticking with the slow burn of the dealership job with its steady trickle of pay, bowing and scraping and selling, selling, selling, hustling while his younger brother, who had always outshined him as a boy, once again outshined him by opening his own business building and selling condos, a business that, according to my father, began to take off the year it opened. At an extended-family Christmas dinner that year Rolly had sat with damp eyes, his napkin foolishly tucked in his collar and knife in one hand and fork in the other, gravy dripping off the knife, as his little brother said, *If the dealership ever folds and you need a job, Rolly, come asking. I'll find something for you in the office.* Rolly knowing that this flashy kid, nearly ten years his junior, was playing the books, but unwilling to call him on it in front of the whole family. Even after that, when the indictments came down, Rolly big enough to visit long after dark, hat in hand, and tell his brother, *We are here for you, for the boy. Family.* I guess I wasn't surprised to hear him say that—sitting in the dark at the top of the stairs in my pajamas, listening to the whole conversation, I realized that I'd always known Rolly would be there, because it wouldn't occur to him that family had any other choice. That was what you did.

"What'd she want?" he asked.

"I guess she's still figuring that out."

"People who don't know what they want, Jake—people like that are no good to anyone. They look to you to *tell* them what they want, and when they find out you don't know what that is they hate you for it."

I thought about it for a moment.

"I think the problem," I said, "is that I seem to know what *I* want."

"And you feel she might help get you there. Where you want to be."

Thinking *that's an irritating remark*—a challenge by plain sense I did not possess and never would—and for an instant I understood Dad, the path he had chosen. You had to use whatever you had at hand, and for Dad that thing was charm. Dad had outshined Rolly all his life. But that didn't mean he'd enjoyed it. For Dad, outshining Rolly was just the counterweight to the heavy gravity of living up to the older brother's steady ways.

"Play?" I asked.

He let me break and I got all of me behind the cue ball for once, didn't shovel it off to the side or crack it off center, but fired it right into the rack with all my might. How often does that happen—that you get all of yourself into something and watch it explode? I strode around the table scarcely waiting for the cue ball to stop rolling before firing the first ball in straight, rolling another along the rail, then a double bounce, a few chip-ins, two lucky breaks, then another, and even gravity seemed to like me, even gravity acting like it's on my side on this one, the miscues and mistakes all going my way. Rolly silent now. I was, too, but of course you don't stop to feel doubt or second-guess yourself when you're on a streak, you just go forward with it. Neither of us had ever cleared a table on a single turn before, even back in high school when, my situation a little funny with Dad in prison, Rolly would bring me to the pool hall for a couple hours every Saturday afternoon. When the last ball dropped in I gave a small but decisive nod to record the moment, considered the emptied green, and swiveled with a helpless grin that said, *Can you believe it?*

Rolly sat motionless on the folding chair, arms crossed and legs out straight, brow creased with dismay, staring at the felted rectangle before him, cue laid up against the wall like he'd known all along he wasn't going to get his chance.

After a beat, he said, "Quite a run, kid."

We considered the half-empty expanse of the table.

"That's never happened before," I said.

"Better luck next time, I guess."

He stood up and picked up his glass and looked into it for a moment, a searching expression on his face, as if he'd lost something in there.

Finally he said, "Get the lights when you're done, will you?"

He hiked upstairs and I stood chalking up again and watching him go, feeling like something had got into the air between us, something not quite right, though it wasn't until the door clicked shut that I realized what it was. I'd attached a little footnote to the sweetness of the gift. *The guy gets you a job and what do you do? You pay him back by showing him up on his own table. The very night he got it.*

Which was exactly the sort of thing my dad would have done.

The difference between us being that Dad would have enjoyed it.

SIX

I PLANNED NOT TO GO. I figured, *put Kimber aside, Jake, take Sally's advice,* and hid out downstairs shooting pool until I was sure Rolly had gone up to bed, humiliated for the both of us and unwilling to face him. If he saw me upstairs he'd softball one of those Rolly-jokes my way, *Time for bed, Fast Eddie*—forgetting that things didn't turn out so well for Eddie, or his girl, in the end—and then he'd deliver his best smile, only the smile wouldn't quite close the sale. The smile wouldn't quite get where it was trying to go. So I waited for the sound of the freezer door opening and closing—Rolly moving in to get a bite of vanilla while Zooey was brushing her teeth—and when I was sure he'd gone to bed I walked upstairs and found most of the lights out, Coop on the couch lifting his head and thumping his tail to see if I was going to walk him, and in a single instant the unbearable thought of heading off to bed alone turned my own best intentions against me.

Kimber drinking a pineapple juice with vodka, a single cherry atop the melting ice, the little tin can of pineapple sitting in front of her so she could sweeten more as she went. That always gets me about women—the sweetness thing, always sugar in their tea, the ruby-colored cocktails, the treats and cadged candies hoarded and dined upon, as if life had failed to do its job of giving them their fair share, leaving it up to them to settle the account on their own. Women have a unique talent for this, the ability to square the math and make sure everyone gets his due in the end, and as I considered the functional posture Kimber employed on her stool perch, the language of her body all in italics, I found myself wondering what she had in store for me. She would get her way, eventually, unless her sister intervened. You could say it was madness to come and see her but I had promised myself that anything was allowed and, anyway, some acts of discretion are beyond even the most prudent men, and I am certainly not one of those—but even so, I hesitated at the front door and, contemplating the checked male aggression charging the air, I sensed that I was about to learn something about myself.

The singer on the juke telling us about "Friends in Low Place" now, Kimber, there at the corner of the bar, reflecting the country mood, with a short denim skirt framing the center of her gravity, against the frayed hem the shining length of the tanned thighs, a white button-down tied at her navel, and brown suede boots that reached up to her calves hooked into her stool's footrest. All six pool tables were occupied, the stools overlooking the tables mostly full tonight, stage and dance floor empty behind that, nothing usually going for music until Friday and Saturday nights. Everyone here looked to be getting pissed on the dollar beers that were the pool hall's claim to fame, most of the men dressed head-to-toe in denim with hunting licenses clipped to their jackets, the rest in sleeveless black T-shirts, shouting the name of a metal band in seventy-point Canterbury. The few women all cleavage and curve and black eye shadow gathered together in bundled promises of wised-up sexuality—yet the tattoos on display were sweetly childish—unicorns and rainbows and hearts—as if their four-year-old daughters had been the artists, leaning in with buzzing needles in their little gloved hands. I had dressed in my old college sweatshirt and jeans and flip-flops, feeling now a bit like a walking version of that pink bow I'd tied to the bottle I gave Kimber.

"Hey, Jake," Kimber said, rotating toward me with her whole body and lifting her gaze over the hot wattage of her smile. "Hey, man. Surprise. I'm happy you came. Why don't you take a seat here, let me buy you a drink?"

For a moment all conversation in the bar ceased, the *click-thump* sounds from the tables paused—even the juke seemed to do a double take between songs, and I felt the room prepare itself for a transfer of power. You could read the mood-shift in the air: Because every one of these guys had been sitting here all night wondering how he was going to get the marbles up to step over to Kimber and ask if she wanted a drink. Now she's buying a drink for the queer in the college sweatshirt any one of them could have stomped in the parking lot without breaking a sweat.

I had visited this bar twice before as a kid with my dad. That first visit would have been in the afternoon—I knew that because the steel mill whistle hadn't yet creased the air, firing its rocking blast all across the valley, the warning bugle of an advancing army telling the town that men were about to flood out looking to drink, fight, and fuck away the disgust and heat and risk of an eight-hour factory shift. I didn't know what the business was about that day, figuring it was just more of what my dad always called *men stuff*. I followed him inside and he sat me down at the PAC-MAN machine, a whole stack of quarters at my elbow, then strode into the back with Sally's uncle, Colonel Tom, who owned the bar, to talk through what he'd come for. The woman behind the bar sat watching me while she smoked a slim, helping me pick her favorite country songs from the juke and, when my dad was delayed past the stack of quarters, even bringing me one of those little cans of pineapple juice like the one sitting in front of Kimber now, plus a dish of cherries from the plastic container on the bar top. A couple of smoldering drunks watched me soddenly from the bar, though not one of them dared to speak one word about my presence, knowing the Colonel would cut them off. Soon the little dish of cherries was gone, the can of pineapple juice emptied, and when the woman turned her back to draw a beer from the tap I went looking for them—past the stage, down the hall—the open door to the Men's Room revealing one swaying drunk lashing the piss trough as he sang "Tutti Frutti" in a hoarse voice, then approaching the dogleg with the office on the right, I heard my father saying, *Please, Tom. Please, please. I have to have all thirty. Fifteen isn't enough.* Judging by Tom's answer, fifteen was going to have to be enough for a little while. I had never heard my father beg before, and the sound of his voice speaking those words turned my bowels to water. I was still rooted in that spot when my father stepped out of the office carrying a paper bag beneath his arm and whistling to himself, only the whistle dried up on his lips when he spotted me.

That was my first visit to Colonel Tom's bar.

The second being later that night, long after midnight, on our way out of town to run for Canada.

And this was the third.

Kimber knocked on the bar and said, "Hey, Colonel Tom, look who's here," and Tom, whom everyone referred to as the Colonel though he'd never gone anywhere past buck private and had spent all of Vietnam in Leavenworth for breaking a staff Sergeant's wrist, limped our way from out behind the bar, same old tarantula-black T-shirt, worn denim jacket over it, his long graying hair hanging down, good teeth because he grew up in a good home only didn't make much of it, and saying my name in that smoke-singed voice of his.

I'm thinking, *How did you travel from Sally's dad to* this?

And already I'm getting twenty-twenty vision on where this night is going. Because just about everyone I know has a Colonel Tom in his life. Charismatic, less dependable than the weather itself, and always on the make; mine happened to be my dad, but for most it's that distant relative you see only so often, maybe once every couple years, your parents finally having run out of excuses, relenting and certainly going a little more snappish and tense than usual with each other before the visit, though for all of Colonel Tom's charm, you, the kid, can't see why, as he's just loaded down with the kind of stories your dad never tells you. The time he got stranded in Mexico for a week, for example, and had to ride across the border under a train with a couple of Guatemalan gangsters heading north to pull a hit. Or the time he fell in love with a Las Vegas blackjack dealer and damn near got talked into a card-counting scam. Or the time his Alaskan fishing boat was hijacked by the Moscow mafia and he was kept tied to a chair for over two days, until ransom was established in the form of one hundred cases of Scandinavian vodka. And during all of this the Colonel is giving you little sips of his Old Fashioned, maybe letting you eat the cherry and even take little pulls on his cigar whenever the adults leave the room, getting perhaps a little too tipsy to be driving, though nobody makes any attempt to stop him or take his keys, even when his stories darken a good sight into the subject of his training as an army sharpshooter and the kills he'd heard mentioned on the range. And then, noticing that the adults have retreated into the kitchen and are actively washing dishes and even openly discussing how late it is, he'd look at his watch and gasp and light a last cigarette, give hugs all around, and sway off into the night, everyone relieved to see him go and wondering aloud as soon as he's gone how many more times they're going to have to go through this—even though you're already asking when you'll see him again, and can you go on that fishing trip he invited you to? The answer always being *No*. Colonel Tom was Sally and Kimber's uncle. And Sally had been that kid on the receiving end of the stories and the sips and the slugs of cigar smoke, somehow feeling a rough equivalent of a crush, wishing she could be just like the Colonel when she got older.

Unfortunately, Sally's admiration for this charming, funny, crafty, mischievous uncle had cooled significantly when she learned that the Colonel had tried to have himself written into the will just days before Sally's father had expired. A riot of visitors downstairs, all of them here to help but accomplishing nothing, making the experience more exquisitely painful, food and dishes stacked up everywhere, trays of inedible lasagna no one would ever eat, and Sally, seeking escape, went upstairs to give her dad his Oxycontin, because as the physician said, *There is no such thing as addiction at this stage*, and opened the door to find the Colonel leaning over his befuddled brother's bed with a fountain pen and a notarized document, the Colonel backing up with both hands raised defensively, saying, *Sally, this isn't what it looks like. He wants to do this.* Sally had hauled him out of the house by the collar even though the Colonel was half a foot taller than her, actually threw him down the steps and forbid him to set foot in the house again.

All this playing in my mind with the Colonel limping my way polishing a glass.

"Hey," Colonel Tom said with real pleasure, "hey, Jake. Been some time."

"Since I ran into you in Atlantic City."

He rubbed his stubbled chin and did his best impression of a man momentarily drawing a blank, nodding softly.

"Oh yeah," he said. "Sure. I still owe you that twenty bucks, don't I?"

"It was thirty, Colonel."

"Right, right. Wasn't my night, was it?"

"It didn't seem so. Seeing as how you had to tap me for bus fare home."

"Drinks on me tonight, then. Square up."

"I'm having just one."

"Playing it cool for the new job, huh?" He gave a low whistle and shook his head. "Chime Creek. A smart piece of property. Quite a bit of tail there, too, I guess."

"I wouldn't know."

He thumped a beer in front of me, the beer just a little too excited about being poured into the cold glass and spilling over onto the countertop.

"Young buck in the prime of life like you?" he asked. Probing now. "That dog don't hunt. Jake, have I ever told you about my Kowa scope? That thing—with that thing I can see you a half mile away as clear as if you were sitting right here in front of me. Sometimes if I'm driving by the airport, I'll pull over on that big high turn, lift that Kowa out of the lockbox, and have me a long look at the Chime Creek pool deck. Just dream myself clear into a metropolis of wealthy tail, watching those women laid out on their lounges. Though I'm guessing what they're hungry for is likely what they're seeing up in that lifeguard chair, make them feel young again. And you all too willing to play along. Unless you have something going with the beauty Miss Kimber here neither of you are letting on about."

"He's just a friend, Colonel," Kimber said. "Right, Jake? Here because he owes me one. He's the one took the table."

Colonel Tom put a foot up on the ice chest and began to chew a toothpick. His denim jacket gapped open and, incredibly, I got a quick glimpse of holstered steel.

"You going hunting after work, Colonel?" I asked.

Kimber put her hand on my leg.

"No," he said, giving me a grin, "no, just hedging my bets against some of the meth dealers who've taken a shine to this here place. A little SD9 with one in the barrel, eight in the pipe. I keep it for insurance purposes. Do you know any meth dealers, Jacob?"

I said I really didn't think so.

"And lucky you are," he said. "They're an impatient sort, as you might imagine. Because most are on the product themselves, which means they want what they want, and they want it yesterday. It's not quite the country club life, is it, kid?"

"I guess not," I said.

"But, then, the country club isn't quite what they'd have you believe, either, is it? I mean to say, you're *staff* there, Jake, am I right?"

"The lifeguard."

The Colonel nodding now, polishing a fresh glass. Warming up.

"Uh-huh," he said. "And when you're staff—well, it's not like you're part of the family, is it? Not really. No, it's more like—it's more like you're a sort of *pet*."

Kimber's hand gripping my leg now, gripping it *hard* and holding tight.

"No," I said, "it's more—"

"And like most pets," he said, "like most eager little puppies, your job is to hunt and fetch and dig, right? Just root around for that little treasure they've sent you after. And then give a little thump of the tail and roll over to have your belly scratched. Only they don't do that, give you a scratch, do they?" He leaned in close and gave me a level gaze with his amphetamine-bright eyes. "No, Jake, what they do instead is this: They give you a good *kick*."

Sally and me, you could say we're smart but not wise. We can do our own taxes, sure, and finish the Friday crossword no problem, and maybe dash off a term paper without *too* much trouble—but we can't see more than a day ahead and know what's going on. Whereas guys like the Colonel, in my experience, are the other way around, everything a mess, nothing adding up, always a beat behind with the law and the bank and the traffic cop—I *swear* I was going to pay that fine, mac, don't impound the car, I'm *begging* you—but the Colonel Toms of the world, they look at you and it's like they can see you tomorrow. Where you'll be, what you'll be doing, and what you want. That was what he was doing now: looking into me tomorrow, and what was he seeing?

Werner. Werner saying, *Get the old life back, Jake.*

"It's a job, Colonel," I said. "A little trick for the summer. It's not so bad."

"Sure," he said, "but it's not so *good* either, is it? Oh, they *talk* about how you're a team, you're part of the Chime Creek *family*, right? And yet I have it on good advisement that on this very night there is a delightful party of the dressed-up-dance-plus-punchbowl genre with likewise bullshit going on for *all members* in the fair Comanche Room. Some of the lyingest, thievingest cocksuckers in our fair city are to be found there tonight, invited because they *are members*. You may be a decent boy, Jake. You may even be a delightful boy. And you have been told that you're part of the family. But you are not invited. Because you were born *you*."

"Why're you hacking on Jake, Colonel?" Kimber asked. "He came here to make nice, didn't you, Jake?"

"I ought to be going," I said.

The Colonel snatched up my half-empty beer, filled it up again, and I could see by his aggressive hospitality that I wasn't going to be allowed to leave, not until I'd heard them out. The little flash of steel inside his jacket said so.

"I'm hacking on him," the Colonel said, "because, well, I'd like to see what sort of *man* he is. I mean to say, is he the hot-headed sort, the kind to get worked up about nothing at all and do something *stupid*? Or is he a cool customer, Mr. Cucumber in an icebox?"

He plucked a cigarette from his breast pocket, the Winston filters Bethenny used to smoke. She liked the hillbilly cachet, her friends going in for Dunhill or Gauloise Brunes, hoping the little colored sticks would help them affect a country club pose, Bethenny going the same direction she went with the pornography—going downmarket and somehow liking it. The tobacco reminding me of the wet earth smell of her after sex, when I'd kiss her neck, her shoulders, her collarbone, spent but somehow finding myself excited all over again by her beauty, moving down her body, Bethenny reclining speechless with the lit cigarette between her fingers having forgotten about it, the smoke trailing away, her eyes closed into the moment. Now, with Colonel Tom placing that cigarette between his lips, I was thinking of Bethenny, the little deaths she had provided me. Supposing truth *is* a woman? What then? Is a glass of milk supposed to help with that, too? I think in that moment I missed her. It's entirely possible in that moment that I even loved her.

"It's just a friendly beer," Kimber said.

But the look the Colonel was giving me as he applied the lighter flame to the tip of his cigarette didn't say *friendly*. What that look said was *business*.

"Let's say," he said, exhaling smoke, "let's just suppose, Jake, that a couple of boys do some business together. Do business and a little money trades hands, everyone goes home happy. *Except*—and most people don't understand this about the kind of business I do, the kind of business I'd like to do with you—the most difficult thing about this kind of business is making sure everyone stays happy *after*. And you do that by remaining a cool customer, Mr. Jake. Cool as the deep freeze, if you catch my drift."

"I'm not here on any business at all," I said.

Feeling like I was a little slow in the jaw. Like my mind was doing its mind thing, trying to get its story straight before saying a word, while my body was all raw nerves telling me to run.

"Jake," he said, "haven't you realized that it's *all* business?"

"We'll just be heading out, Colonel," Kimber said, glancing at me. "Come back another night."

"No, no," Tom said, his eyes never leaving me as he reached out and tapped his ashes in the sink, "because right now, like I said, we're finding out what kind of man Jake here is. I ask, Jake, because, see, I knew your daddy. Knew him well, played cards with him. Had a drink with him. Hell, I even *worked* with him. And the debt to society— well, it pays out *both* ways, high and low. Right now he's paying his debt to high society. But Jake, your daddy's still got to pay his debts to the *low* end, too. And maybe this is how it plays out." He set down the glass and leaned back against the bar, his flat reptile eyes betraying all the simplicity of his tabloid soul. "Because, son, see— I *knew* what sort of man *he* was. And I'm thinking there's a bit of him in you."

"Thanks for the beer," I said, and stood up.

"Oh no, Jake," he said, sorrowfully. "You think you can just leave in the middle of it, when we're talking business? You think I'm just going to let you walk out of here?"

"I'll be seeing you, Colonel," I said.

"Sure," Tom called after me, "I expect you will be."

Kimber called after me, too, a question of some kind, though I didn't hear what she'd asked. I was sent on my way by a sharp-edged taunt offered up by one of the men at the tables, the guy mimicking me in an effeminate voice, a couple of snickers chasing me out into the cooling night.

SEVEN

I WAS UNLOCKING THE CAR door when Kimber called my name again, walking my way with her hands tucked into her back pockets, her gaze a little sheepish.

"The fuck was all that about?" I asked.

"I'm sorry, all right? I didn't know it was going to be like that. He asked me to bring you on up tonight so you could talk. But he's harmless, Jake. He just wants to find out if he can trust you, so he leans on you a little bit. Okay?"

"He didn't seem harmless, with that fucking piece of artillery tucked into his armpit. What are you doing hanging around him, anyway? Sally told me all about the stunt he pulled with your dad."

"Give me a ride home, okay? I'll explain everything."

Before I could object she climbed in the passenger seat, looking out at me through the glass, biting her lip. I hesitated for a moment, wondering what Sally would have to say about this, and thought, *Take her home. Take her home, send her back like a rejected application, and you're done with all of it. You leave her here at the bar? Then you owe her all over again, that's how she gets her hooks in you.*

The cooling night air inverting the heat equation, the drive spooky and fog-bound. Before I'd gone even a mile I was using the wipers to clear the condensation off the glass, driving no more than twenty miles an hour, even that pushing it a little on the curves. Visibility like that, you feel like you could pile right up against the worst wreck and not have a chance to even flinch, though Kimber didn't seem worried, casually lit a cigarette with the dash lighter and sat back, rotated against the door to watch me. Zooey would give me a look when she smelled the smoke on my clothes, though in that moment I didn't care.

"Give me one, will you?" I asked, suddenly dizzy with anticipation of giving in.

"He really got to you, huh?"

"Yes," I said, "he was ringing my bells."

Kimber plucked the cigarette from between her lips, reversed it, and handed it to me, then gave herself a fresh one. I hesitated, then drew the smoke in and felt the overmastering pleasure of resigning yourself to a long-suppressed urge, even one you know is bad for you, the good clean nicotine buzz cruising my bloodstream as I did the best I could to see the road ahead.

"What's he want with me?" I asked.

"He won't say. Honest."

Honest. Christ, like she was trying to convince *herself* that she was telling the truth. I let the silence hang, and another quarter mile down the mountain, she said, "Look, if you want to know, he's after something that you have."

"What is it?"

"I don't know."

"*Honest*," I said.

"Really, I don't know. I only know he needs something you've got, just wants to *borrow* it, he said, and that what he really wants is for you to stay quiet about it, after. That's what he was talking about. The not talking thing. *Can he do silence?* he asked me."

"I can't believe it. That you think I'd get mixed up with someone like him."

"It's a lot of money, Jake. You can't believe how much money."

"I can guess how much. And I'll have to earn every penny."

"He said he'll give you thirty thousand, Jake."

She'd known that number would shake me, now her turn to do the silence thing.

Another quarter mile and I asked, "What about you?"

"Five for me, if I get you to go along. All you've got to do is hand something over. And stay quiet after."

"Who gets hurt?" I asked.

Because that was what mattered: I wanted to know who was going to pay.

"Pull over," she said.

"Forget it."

I adjusted my grip on the wheel.

"Pull over," she said, "and I'll tell you."

It wasn't the wise thing to do—placing myself in that situation alone with Kimber—so why was it that I felt somehow *unburdened* as I braked and turned the car off the side of the road? Maybe the nicotine cruising my bloodstream for the first time in weeks, maybe the heady invitation to park on a lonely avenue with an unqualifiedly beautiful woman, or some strange cocktail of both lightening my grim outlook— but I felt relieved, even alive to what would come next as I cut the engine. Was it possible that revenge against Sally was there in my heart? The crickets sighed rhythmically through the open windows, offering approval, and I sat breathing in Kimber's perfume, which, in the close space of the car, reminded me of nothing so much as the scent of possibility itself.

"Tell me," I said.

Kimber slid across the seat toward me, and time seemed to go syrupy and slow: I realized I was still ambivalent about what would happen— but then she reached past me, raising her arm and pointing out through my window, her breasts pressing candidly against my arm as she looked past me. I followed her gaze through the thinning mirage of fog toward the far lights of the college. She could only be pointing to one thing— off in the distance, beyond furlongs of moon-frosted grass, the glowing, the incandescent white hilltop, the arcadia of Chime Creek under its warm landscaped lights, and I imagined even from this distance I could hear the faint music of the band playing in the Comanche Room, the debutantes waltzing in white gloves with boys in blue blazers. Irritation boiled up into my throat: Colonel Tom was right, I had been told I was family. But I was most certainly not invited.

She turned her face fractionally toward me, her body warm against mine, so close that her hair slid liquidly over my shoulder as I breathed in pineapple and cherry.

"You want to know who pays?" she asked. "*Those fuckers.*"

The rich. Those who have. *Those fuckers.* Something unwholesome within me seemed to give a nod of agreement, swivel into terrible alignment with her. This wasn't a partnership. No, this was more like what you feel for your enemy's enemy. I raised my hand—intent, I think, on resting my palm flat against her collarbone, hoping to maintain the necessary distance—but when my fingertips touched the glossy weight of her hair all strength seemed to abandon me and then, without realizing how, we were clinched into a grappling kiss, the press of her body, with its curves and lines, its alternating points of softness and hardness, setting my belly burning—though even swamped with lust I was aware of how lethal our impulses are, how powerful and persistent and freighted with risk. I sensed her own desperation, too, the bewilderment and hunger in the urgency of the kiss, and I understood that she was as frightened as I: She had realized that her looks were a weapon even she couldn't control. Helpless as we both were, we might have continued—would have continued—if the interior of the car hadn't suddenly brightened, the light rising into a crescendo of roaring sound that peaked in the clattering bellow of a passing truck. Kimber pulled back as the *blatting* horn passed over us, and for an instant she was profiled, astonished, by hard white light—and then the moment was past and we were plunged in darkness again, the only sound the truck rattling away down the hill, and the crickets sighing in time with the quiet panting of our breaths.

I thought, *Jake, you do this? You lose Sally forever.*

I sat leaning against my own door, unable to meet Kimber's gaze, surprised to find the cigarette still burning between my fingertips.

"I had a crush on you for a year," Kimber said. "When I was twelve. Did you know? But you never had eyes for me. Sally was all you ever wanted."

"We shouldn't talk about it."

"I didn't even know what it meant, the feeling. I was so confused. I only knew that I wanted to be around you."

"Hand what over?"

"Jake," she said, "they won't even know that something's gone missing."

I said, "Hand *what* over?"

She said, "He wants your key."

I pitched my cigarette out into the night, and started the car again. There would be no second kiss. It was almost over—this *fiasco*, this joke scheme, this disaster in the making. I rolled back onto the pavement with both hands on the wheel. The air was clearing. I could see the road ahead now, taking curves faster, confident I'd get through. It was almost over. And when it was, I could go back to being a lifeguard and wondering when and how money was going to enter my life.

"He's going to rob the place," I said. "Of all the stupid—they'd be on him in a heartbeat. They'd be on *me*, on you."

"No," she said, shaking her head. "No, not at all. It's not like that. Something outside that he says they don't even know they have."

"Something *outside*? That doesn't make any sense. All they have is fucking *grass* out there."

"He said they won't even know it's gone. Whatever it is. He swears to me, Jake, all that money just to sit by and stay quiet and no one hurt."

"Five won't get you anywhere when you're in jail."

"Nothing like that, Jake. You know what I could do with that five? I could get some *wheels*. Wheels and a black dress. This Camaro across town, painted black. So glossy you'd think you could go for a swim in that paint."

"And where would you go with it? Back to the pool hall in style?"

"Hollywood, brother, park myself at the bar at Formosa every night with an unlit cigarette and pretend to look for my lighter, find me a movie producer with money and live the good life. Maybe get an acting job. Just like that, a new life. A new me."

"Kimber," I said, "I've tried that and I can tell you it's no good. You can't get away from yourself just by going somewhere else. Why don't you stay here and try and make it work?"

"Because I don't have it in me. I know I'm supposed to want that. But I just don't."

"It's not going to make any difference, going to another coast."

"Jake," she said, "if I'm going to keep on being me, I'd rather do it in a warm climate. Understand?"

"You're doing it without me, then."

We rode another mile in silence, Kimber seething away about how she was going to get me to do it, the lights of her street up ahead when she said, "You can't tell me he doesn't make a little sense now and then."

"Sure, he makes lots of sense. Right up to the point where he says he's going to rip off Chime Creek."

"Thirty thousand dollars just fell in your lap."

"What's he doing to get money like that?"

"He won't tell me," she said. "I just know it's safe. Not one person hurt. That's the best part of it. I told you: He says they won't even know it's gone."

I felt like telling her I didn't believe her on that one, either, but there wouldn't be any point. You do it, you don't do it—the thing to do is make your decision and then push aside the regrets. Assign yourself a future. And the future I was picturing had nothing at all to do with this girl or Colonel Tom or any of them.

The house lights were off, all the windows blank, which meant Sally wasn't home yet. I pictured her alone in the kitchen office now, nothing but the little lamp on as she checked receipts, confirming orders for tomorrow—did she hear the music coming her way from the Comanche Room? Why wasn't she in there with them? Why wasn't I? Why wasn't Kimber? The only thing between us and those who had been invited was who you were born to be, and who had decided that?

"What was that he was saying about your father?" she asked.

I parked out front and left the car running.

"They pulled something together," I said, "a ways back."

"You have any idea what?"

I thought about it for a minute.

"I guess I really don't want to know," I said.

"He seems to think you owe him one."

"I'll be sure to pass the message to my dad," I said.

"You could go back to school with that money."

Which pisses me off, thinking, *Sally, that was between us.*

"Let me guess," I said. "Now Colonel Tom knows."

"I sort of let on, okay? That you needed the money."

"Terrific."

"You do it and it's all behind you for good. You could leave, Jake. Just like me. We do it. And then we're both gone for good."

I didn't answer and she sat there scratching at the seat fabric with one chipped ruby fingernail. Scheming of ways to hold on to me, and I'm thinking, *There's just one way, the hard and direct route, because that's where all things converge, especially when you have looks like hers.* Which happened to resemble Sally's half a lifetime ago. I suppose it troubled me, that resemblance. I didn't like it. But my blood did.

"You want to come in?" she asked. "Have a bourbon? It was your gift after all. You ought to have some."

I did want a drink. I think, in fact, I wanted about four of them, to rinse myself of the entire night. That hot stone still burning in my belly, but for once, just this once, I looked inward, in search of my identity, and found a well of strength in the unlikeliest of places: in weakness. The truth was that I did want Colonel Tom's money, and I did want

Kimber. But another truth was that I was too straight and too simple and—most importantly—too fundamentally yellow to imagine myself into either fix.

"Kimber," I said, "do me a favor and don't call me anymore."

The door gave a surprised squawk as she shoved it open and climbed out with two *chocky* chunks of her boot heels. She cracked the door shut again, then leaned down—so close that her words spread a frost of condensation on the window as she spoke.

"I'm not the one who's going to be calling, Jake," she said.

I watched her let herself in, her words evaporating off the glass into the night, the taste of cherry and pineapple on my lips like a terrible reproach.

Ever had your parents shake you awake in the dark, nothing but the hall light on? Telling you, *Get dressed. Quick.* It happened to me more times than I care to count, though it's a relief to note that all save one were to rouse me for a swim meet hours and hundreds of miles away, my first obligation in the pool falling some time around eight o'clock in the morning, and my father never once complaining about what this required of him. We'd wake so early the starlight would still be out, Dad just a shape over me in the dark holding my ankle in a firm grip until I sat up, he'd always say the same thing: *Get dressed. Quick.* My clothes would be laid out at the end of the bed and most mornings I'd lay back down and fall back asleep and he'd have to come back in and repeat himself. The second time I always obeyed, got dressed and walked downstairs, the duffel bag with my sweatshirt and a few comic books I'd put together the night before on the counter. He's at the kitchen table with the little lamp on, usually drinking coffee and having a piece of toast. I'd get some orange juice and toast myself, and when we were ready he'd carry his coffee mug out to the car, tuning the radio to the old rockabilly station on low volume, the Burnettes and Bill

Haley and Buddy Holly. I'd roll up my sweatshirt and use it as a pillow against the glass and often I'd be asleep before we were ten minutes out of town, blink and sit up and that quick it's full daylight as we're turning into the parking lot of the pool, and he'd turn to me and here, too, always say the same thing: *Time to swim, Jake.*

Except it wasn't like that on our last trip together. That night, after the first visit to the Colonel's bar, the image of the whistle dying on my father's lips troubling my sleep, I woke in the dark with my father holding my ankle, and he said, *Get dressed. Quick,* except there was no swim meet tomorrow, no clothes at the end of my bed, and, confused near to the point of tears, I thrashed around in my drawers, found them nearly empty, located some clothes on the floor and dressed and walked downstairs, where I found two packed bags waiting for me: The first full of clothes, the second filled with my comic books and my photographs of my mother and my schoolbooks. They were too heavy to lift so he carried both for me, and we drove north out of town with a light snow just beginning to fall, taking the mountain road this time though I couldn't understand why until he cut the lights still rolling and turned into the empty parking lot of Colonel Tom's bar. He drove around back and parked, leaving the engine idling, "Rocket 88" playing quietly on the radio, and then turned to me and sounded the one familiar note of the evening. *Time to swim, Jake,* he said, and then plucked a flashlight from the glove compartment and hopped out of the car. I watched him walk off into the woods, could see the beam of his light swiveling around in the dark, moving forward like a man who knew where he was going. Soon the beam was passing out of sight and I waited listening to the radio until, ten minutes later, I saw the beam of his flashlight heading back. He walked out of the woods with a package under his arm, the package just like the one he'd been carrying earlier, only this time the whistle didn't die on his lips when he saw me. This time he kept right on whistling until he dropped himself into the seat next to me with a deep sigh. He'd cut his right palm, had wrapped a clean rag over it to slow the bleeding, the rag already beginning to soak through red, though he didn't seem much concerned about it. I sat looking at the rag for a moment, watching the color spread and darken, my heart pounding in my chest, and then he turned to me and asked, *Ready?* Before I could answer he put the car in gear, and by the time we were on the highway he'd got himself worked up to whistling again, even turning the music up and drumming on the steering wheel with his good hand, looking aside now and then to give me a confident grin. Around sunup I noticed a sign that said we were now entering the state of New York, and it occurred to me that it was the first time I'd ever been here, though I had no way of knowing that I'd only be there a few hours before a busted taillight would put a quick end to the trip in Palmyra, New York.

Rolly was at the freezer as I let myself in the back door, the refrigerator spilling its yellow light into the dim kitchen, my uncle looking at me over his shoulder with a pint of Breyers in his left hand, a spoon in his right, and a guilty look on his face. Plus he had the little television on the counter switched on and tuned to a dance party show, the sort of mindless programming he loved but Zooey quietly disapproved of, said when he had the insomnia it was the only thing that did help him sleep.

"Kid," he said, "promise me you won't tell."

I dropped my keys on the wall-hook.

"You can't be doing this every night, Rolly," I said. "What did the doctor say?"

"Promise me, kid."

"Okay," I said, "it'll be between us."

"You want a little dish?"

I felt a little like Sally in that moment, the way she was with Kimber, figuring, well, if I sit with him he'll just have a little, I say no and go upstairs, he'll have a lot.

"I'll have a glass of milk," I said.

"This *is* milk," he said.

So we sat at the kitchen table, the fluorescent lights under the cabinets giving the room a nice low light brightened occasionally by flickers from the television broadcasting its late-night crap, and we each had a little ice cream, Rolly eating out of the container so Zooey wouldn't see two dishes. We're agreed on this, Rolly and me, on bad television's wonderful side effect: It temporarily halves your IQ. This can be a good thing, sometimes. Especially late at night when you can't sleep, can't switch your mind off. Bethenny might have benefited from watching it now and then. Eating our ice cream and watching this coked-up joke emceeing the roomful of dancing teens, with his hat turned sideways, a gold chain around his neck, a mike up in his face as he tries to talk like a brother, with all the hand gestures and the rest of it, introducing the next song—just two minutes of that and I felt about six years old. I felt as if I'd suddenly have a difficult time writing my own name, or tying my shoes.

"I must be getting old," he said. "I just don't get this stuff."

"How do you know when you're old?"

"I'll tell you," he said, "the first morning you wake up and find that you somehow managed to hurt yourself in your sleep. Did Werner talk to you?"

"About?"

He dragged his spoon across the ice cream.

"One of my customers let on about a job opening up," he said. "Apparently, Werner doesn't want some stiff out of business school. He's had bad experiences with a couple prima donnas who want to talk profit sharing from day one, only they don't want to do any *work*. He wants someone with a good head, maybe someone willing to be shaped a little bit into his mold."

"Yeah, we had a little talk. The other day, when it rained."

"And?"

"And Sally seems to think the job is hers already."

He set his spoon down.

"Who gave her that idea?" he asked.

"I guess you could say Sally gave it to herself. With a little help from Werner."

"So you'd be taking it from her. From her point of view."

"That's the problem."

"Still," he said, "maybe a friend like Sally would understand."

"I doubt it."

"Honestly, kid," he said, "even if she didn't, this is your *life*. Nobody understands the value of loyalty more than me. Than I. It's loyalty pays the mortgage on this house, people coming back to me every four or five years because they trust me, know they can count on me. But kid: There is such a thing as giving loyalty more than its fair share. You and I have both seen what can happen when you stick by someone a little too long."

I let that one lay where it fell. He knocked on the table once, just once, like a judge dropping his gavel to end the proceedings, then gathered up my dish and spoon and put the pint back into the freezer. I switched off the television and followed him upstairs so tired it actually seemed as if I were drunk, but after I'd brushed and washed and rinsed the day off, I lay down, and what happens? I'm awake, exquisitely awake in the face of the two unavoidable things I must do tomorrow, two face-to-face meetings that I do not want to have, and I thought, *No, Rolly,* this *is how you know you're old: When you're always wishing it were the day after tomorrow. And then suddenly you find out that it is.*

I turned on my side and knew it would be a long time before I slept.

There in the dark I heard my aunt ask, "Was that Jake in the kitchen?" and Rolly, who was right, said, "He's hungry like Coop."

PART TWO

✚

THE ESCAPE CURE

EIGHT

"I SAW COLONEL TOM UP at the Zion Tavern," I said.

Sally hardly registering the remark, focused as she was on the pans before her, the duck legs and potatoes she was searing, shaking and swirling the skillets, getting the duck just right over a lot of heat, some extra duck fat in the pan with the potatoes to help them along, make them nice. I'd timed the visit with the lunch rush, busier than usual today because one of her cooks had called in sick and Juan doing the expediting while she handled the sauté station.

I'd come here to tell her that Werner had offered me the job, thinking I'd do it while she was too busy to give the news her full attention.

"Kimber's hanging around him," I added. "Where she's finding those characters she's been bringing home."

"That surprise you?"

"I didn't know she was that close to him."

She added two pinches of parsley and garlic to the potatoes, tossed everything around just by flipping the skillet, then spun around quick as a dancer, ducked low to lift a steel bowl and two handfuls of frisée out of the lowboy, tossed the frisée with a few spoonfuls of vinaigrette and then arranged it on two plates as carefully as you'd lay a house of cards, quick spun back and lifted the duck legs out, laid them over the frisée and scattered some potatoes around, then sent the plate sliding toward the pass-through, saying, "You got two duck sarladaise."

She spun back, checked her tickets, dropped a knob of butter in two pans and waited for it to foam, then gently slid in two sea bass filets.

"Kimber always had a thing with him," she said. "A little too close, if you ask me."

"You used to like him."

"Who wouldn't? He shows up, lets you sneak a couple beers, takes you for a ride on his motorcycle. Kid stuff. Then you grow up. See him for what he is. Only she never quite got there. The understanding never quite made it."

"You think he's dangerous?"

She looked over her shoulder at the pass.

"Goyo: overdressed," she said. "Replate."

"Yes, chef," Goyo said.

"I know he hangs around some fucking sketchy characters," she said. "Kimber bringing this guy around one time—it wasn't like he was casing the joint. It was like he was considering burying us in the yard and moving right in. She goes in the next room to apply the lips, the eyes, he asks me for a beer, looking at me steady like he's figuring out how hard it would be to get me in bed."

"You give him the beer?"

"Jake, I would have given him a fucking steak dinner if that would have got him out of my house. Of course I gave it to him. Big fucker with a funny name, and *long* hair, Jake, like jet black hair gathered in a braid runs all the way down to his waist. Built like a kickboxer, like his favorite manner of fighting is to break your nose with a head butt. I'm uncomfortable even being around him. I casually say, *What sort of work do you do, Mr.—? Mr. Lightpainter,* he says. *What sort of work, Mr. Lightpainter?* Figuring he's going to tell me he bench-presses couches."

"I know him. Rolly used to buy lamb from him, has a shop in Zion."

"Only that's not what he says. What he says is *I'm an associate of your Colonel Tom.*"

"Bodyguard, loan shark—"

"Yeah, I imagine. Plus he's on something that's doing funny things with his pupils, dilating them way past normal."

"Just about hallucinating there in front you."

"Then he says, *What sort of work are you into Mrs.—?* And I said, *Never mind the name, you can get it from Kimber. I'm a cook. Like in a restaurant? Yes, genius,* I say, feeling a little insulted, so I want to send the ball back at him, and I say, *up at Chime Creek. I'm the executive chef.* He grins when I say that. *Chime Creek,* he says. *Well, I'm a butcher.* And then he tries to sell me on some venison he just got in. Says *Maybe I come by next week?* "You got two sea bass, one branzino. Juan, wipe the fucking—clean the—wipe that shit off the plate."

"Yes, chef," Juan said. "You got two lamb fennel, chef."

I pictured Colonel Tom leaning toward me last night, the little bright flash of stainless steel at his armpit.

"You figure Kimber would ever let herself get mixed up in something bad?" I asked, watching her obliquely. "Hanging around people like that?"

"She's just getting her kicks, grow out of it soon."

"Unless she doesn't."

Sally was quiet for a moment, swirling and flipping potatoes in the pan, thinking and thinking, this one already bothering her, already on her mind. Maybe another thing keeping her awake at night over and above the noise from the basement. She hadn't wanted to get rid of the pool table. She'd just wanted to get rid of the type of guys the table was bringing around. Because she wanted her kid sister back.

A couple of tickets spat out of the printer.

"She mixes with those guys enough, anything's possible," I said, thinking, *Just come out and tell her Kimber's in trouble, damn near got you in trouble, too.* "You know how it is."

"I swear," Sally said, and now she's looking at *me* obliquely, like she's testing something out and wants to see by my expression how it plays, "I'm thinking about kicking her out. After a certain point—sometimes the best thing you can do for someone is let them go."

"Chef, you got two branzino," Juan said.

"You ought to separate her from him," I said.

"Yeah, well," she said, "I've already got a full-time job."

And that was the opening I'd been looking for—that was the invitation I needed to let it all spill out about Werner, the job, that I was thinking of betraying her and, why not?, thinking that maybe, just maybe, she deserved it for making love to me and then cutting me loose.

"Chef," Juan said, looking more than a little anxious, "you got two branzino, four duck sarladaise, two lamb fennel all day."

Plates from the fry station and the grill were ready in the pass-through, and the tickets were spitting out as fast as they could print.

"Do me a favor—Juan I *got* it—do me a favor," Sally said, "and drive by the house on the way home. Let me know if his car's there. I swear, Jake, if she's bringing him around I'm going to kick her out."

And I'm thinking, *But you can't, Sally. Because it's her house, too, like you said. If you have that with someone you can try to push them out all you want, but they're not going to go anywhere.*

"Chef, those two branzino on the fly, chef," Juan said, knocking on the pass-through.

"Does Rolly like the table?" she asked.

"*Chef*," Juan pleaded.

"*Fuck*," she said. "Jake: Chop this. No, like this—cubes, cubes."

I began slicing up a couple of peeled potatoes while Sally checked on her duck legs and quickly laid two branzino filets in a pan, but the pan was too hot and the oil roared to life, flames jumping up from the back of the pan. Juan rapped on the pass impatiently.

"The table? He was crazy about it," I said, slicing. "I really messed up, though."

"What happened?"

"I sort of got on a hot streak."

"You beat him. You beat him on his own table."

"Yeah," I said, "I ran him on it. He didn't even get to play."

Sally gave a low whistle.

"I bet he was nice about it, too," she said. "Getting beat by you."

"Yeah, he was sweet."

"I *hate* that," Sally said.

And then the potato slipped and I sliced the knife across my knuckle and thumb, and dropped everything to the floor in a clatter of steel and wood as the blood burst through my gripping fist.

No one really worrying until I mentioned that I was feeling dizzy. Blood wept through my clenched fist, dripping now and then to the floor. Juan, who was a museum of line-cook tricks, went to his locker and selected a stick of deodorant from the top shelf.

"Is this going to hurt?" I asked.

"I am thinking maybe a little," Juan said.

The two Mexican cooks and the dishwasher were standing in the locker room doorway speaking quietly in Spanish to one another, their tone bearing a lilting melody of barely restrained hilarity. Sally sat beside me, looking more than a little concerned. The printers outside were doing their ticker-tape thing, tickets piling up, but nobody seemed to care. I wasn't terribly surprised to feel so dizzy. When it comes to other people's mortality, I'm tough as a trauma surgeon, but when it's my blood leaving me, emptying me out . . . when I told them I had to sit down: I think that was when they decided that the entertainment on hand was worth falling into the weeds a little bit. I didn't allow myself to look as Juan leaned in, the savior doing his savior thing, just lay my head back against a locker and watched the fireflies wheel about behind my closed eyelids as he *salaamed* over my fist, opening up the wound to press the deodorant stick right against it. Hurt? I hammered my free hand against the bench until the pain eased. After a minute he dared to withdraw the remedy, examined the results, and, in a calm voice, declared the cut ready to be butterflied.

He wrapped me up skillfully while the others watched. The three cooks in the doorway were sharing quiet remarks at my expense.

"You speak espanish?" Juan asked.

"No."

"Good," he said.

"What's this then?"

The doorway, previously occupied by the amused faces of the kitchen workers, was now occupied by the sterner, sharper features of Werner.

"We're getting complaints on the wait," he said, and then he noticed me.

"A little ding, boss," Juan said.

Werner considered the garnet trail leading from the pass-through to the locker room.

"How little?" he asked.

"He's okay in like a week maybe. Two tops."

"Sally," Werner said, "if that's an entire finger? Or a third-degree burn? Insurance doesn't cover it. Someone injured who has no business being in the kitchen. Next we're sued. Then I'm out of a job. Which means you are, as well."

"Understood, Werner," Sally said.

"This is your kitchen, is it not?"

"It is."

"Everything that happens here reflects on you, does it not?"

"Understood, Werner."

"It was my fault, Werner," I said, feeling somehow clear-eyed, as if the pain had done me some good, had blown the sawdust out of my head. "I was getting in the way in the middle of the rush."

"I'm so relieved we've cleared that up. Now: these tickets piling up. Are we planning on getting to those today? Or shall I inform the diners that the kitchen's just not up to the job and they'll have to get their meals tomorrow?"

He watched Juan and Sally file out, then turned on me.

"This is your day off," he said.

"Yes."

"And you know that you're *not* to be on the grounds on your day off."

"I do."

"Or even to be on the premises as much as fifteen minutes before or after your shift."

"I do."

"This is not encouraging. In light of our, ah, discussion the other day. Which, no doubt, you've given due consideration."

"I have. I am."

"Have you made your decision?"

"It's—I may need a few days."

"This job, while entirely deserved, was a favor I did your uncle Rolly. And I'm not accustomed to having my favors turned back on me."

The understanding, when it arrived, was almost like a physical symptom—I actually rocked back in my seat with the force of it. Three simultaneous jewels of knowledge, a simple syllogism leading to one conclusion, arrived together: first, that Werner *was an employee, too.* Just like me. Second, that Rolly had realized this, that any employee would have to do the bidding of the members so long as enough powerful members were tapped for their support. And third, that Rolly had known that all he had to do was make it *sound* like it was a favor. Knowing that Werner would understand what was really going on. Thereby allowing Werner to save face. Hence the sad-sack routine at lunch. In other words: What had seemed like a favor had really been a command, summoned forth by Rolly after twenty years of climbing the walls. I imagined him there in his office—in the chair that told the world he was here and was ready to play the game—phoning his best customers one at a time. *We've always had a good relationship. You know you can come to me for a good deal. And now I need to come to you for a favor.* The problem: If I turned the job down, it wouldn't just be Werner I was saying *no* to. I'd be denying Rolly, too.

"I understand," I said. "But I'll need some—I'll need some time to smooth things over."

"Remember: the end of the month. I need an answer."

"I'll have one for you."

With that the tension seemed to dissipate.

"Would you like to have that looked at over at the hospital?" he asked. "I know a good man could sew you up. Like it never happened."

"I'll be all right," I said. "I just bleed a lot."

"Yes," he said, "you would."

And then the short drive across town to the second event I'd been putting off that day—the edifice of stone, the medieval escarpment, with its witchy tower, where as a kid I'd imagined princesses would be hidden away by jailers with iron keys, the sparkling razor wire over the fence and the expanse of dun grass. My wrapped hand ached, despite the three tablets of ibuprofen I'd chewed in the car, thinking that grinding them up would help the anesthetic get where it needed to be more quickly, but it was no matter, I'm finding the comfort I need in the routine: year, make, model, license number of my car, sign-in, the unbelievable wait with the unbelievable visitors in the unbelievable room, the unbelievable coffee that was an affront to the human senses, the surrendered wallet and keys, the metal detector, buzzed through the electric door by the guard who by now knows your face well enough to give you a little nod, and then, as I entered the room, my father turning and rising from his chair in his brown jumpsuit, a smile broadening on his handsome, tanned face as he spoke our name.

NINE

"I'LL TELL YOU, KID," he said, "I didn't know if you'd make it today."

This was our little game—together pretending it was possible I wouldn't show even though I'd never missed a visit, always driving up from Bucknell, sometimes in questionable weather in a car that seemed to want to come apart at highway speed even under the best of circumstances. I had come close to pushing the commitment to its crisis once, after a delay on a cold February morning—first by my breakfast shift in the kitchen, then by my boss, who wanted to talk about how I didn't seem to be *enjoying my work*, and then again by the car that would not start. In winter it required every ounce of the experience I'd gained working summers in the service bay of Rolly's dealership just to keep running. I was actually begging it when the engine received the message from the Almighty and roared to life, but a freak whiteout surprised me at the highway, the plows out before I'd gone five miles, and, pushing with as much speed as I dared, I was passing an eighteen-wheeler in chains on a steep descending right turn just before Lock Haven, the wind gusting a whiteboard from right to left, when suddenly the plowed patch of road ended as neatly as a full stop on a telegram bringing nothing but bad news. I had perhaps four or five seconds to react, though this only allowed enough time for me to realize that the gusting wind would get its way, keep me moving straight when right was what was required. An old tune from the eighties was chiming on the radio, and the lyrics died on my lips as my car passed onto the unplowed turn at what must have been seventy miles an hour, a high limestone wall to my left, the path carved from rock before I was born, and I knew that the wind, trying to shove me off the road the entire trip, would get me at last. Yet my car, which tended to shoulder its way through the wind like a linebacker, now seemed to carve along smoothly, with no resistance, and when I dared a look to my right I realized what had happened: The truck driver passed had spotted the unplowed stretch and recognized what was about to happen. He'd put his accelerator on the floor, the steep grade all too willing to oblige his heavy load, and he'd cruised into the turn just a little ahead of me, sheltering me from the terrible river of wind and bringing me safely through in his softly baffled wake. My knuckles were white on the wheel as I came out of the turn, the plowed stretch mysteriously beginning fresh and clean on the downhill straightaway again, and I leaned over so that I could look up through the passenger window. He was looking down at me from his high window grinning brightly, as if he'd just pulled a lovely trick. He gave me a thumbs up and pulled the cord for his horn, two quick blasts that rocked the valley and made my heart stand in my throat, and then he was gone somewhere up ahead while I pulled to the side to let the shakes subside, Boston singing "Let Me Take You Home Tonight" on the radio.

That day, too, my father had said the same thing, *I was worried you wouldn't make it*, and for once, having earned honesty with a true brush with death, I was inclined to tell him the truth, say I *did* often wish I could skip a visit, just one, because I'd begun to gather the upsetting impression that somehow I was in prison, too, that even though I was allowed to come and go I was still somehow walled in by the four high fences, that even when I left I was still somehow inside. And though I was a free man, entirely rational by any measure, I *still* carried a genuine fear that one of these visits the attending bull would say, *Sorry, kid, we've decided you have to stay this time*, and drop the bracelets over my wrists. Often giving a sidelong glance to the guard as I came through the door, as if to reassure myself that this wasn't what was going to happen the moment I passed through.

"But I always make it, Dad," I said.

"I know, I know—only Rolly wrote me a letter, told me you were lifeguarding. I figured maybe you couldn't get away."

"I told them I wanted Wednesdays off before I agreed."

"That was smart, going into the job knowing what you want." He turned to look at the couple at the next table, the wife unwrapping a gift of a ham sandwich she'd brought for her husband, then looked back at me. "You used to like swimming."

"I did. I guess it was my favorite thing."

"Only now you won't like it anymore."

"Sure I will."

He looked at the sandwich again, and then back at me.

"That's what happens, though. First you do it because you love it. Then you do it because people expect you to. Then you do it because it's all you're good at. And finally," he said, raising his hands and letting them fall, defeated, to the table, "you realize you have to get a *job* doing it. And then you're finished."

I'm uneasy like always being inside the prison, sure, but also feeling, as I always did in his presence, like I'd stepped into a nice ray of light on a cloudy day, still feeling the burnished blush of that greeting hug. When he'd grip me in his arms I'd inhale the clean-soap smell of his laundered jumpsuit the same way Rolly would deeply breathe in the aroma of a new car and declare it good, knowing my dad had made a point to get his hair cut and shave twice to look good for me. The truth was that he *did* look handsome. On the bad chow he'd shed the little belly he'd once had, was doing two hundred push-ups and two hundred sit-ups every day, shoulders filling out his jumpsuit, his hair less gray than I remembered, off the booze, looking good to the point I sometimes wondered if the others in the visitation room ever took me for a younger brother rather than a son. He did look great, so long as you ignored what was there in the eyes. The eyes were the same old flat reptile eyes, and you felt the truth was in there only you couldn't translate it. You didn't understand what you saw there. But your blood did.

"How's your Uncle Rolly doing?" he asked.

"It's a good week. Eight sales this month plus maybe another plus I bought him a pool table."

"No kidding? With the scratch from this new job?"

"He loves it. Talks about having his friends over—"

"That was smart, getting him the table. That way, you know—"

He made a vague gesture.

"What?" I asked.

"Well," he said, "let's just say with that behind you, he won't go around acting like you owe him one."

"No," I said, "it—he's not like that. It was—I just wanted to give him a gift, say, you know, Thanks, pop. Thanks for looking out for me. For us."

"Believe me, kid, he makes out just as well. You know he claimed you as a dependent? Gets a tax deduction. Plus Zooey after him all the time about his eating, not giving him one minute of rest, you there as a little buffer. Mind you, he needs that attention from Zooey, Rolly does. Going to seed, last I saw him. That's how you identify the moment when someone's given up. You know how you can tell when you've gotten old?"

"When you hurt yourself in your sleep."

He shook his head and leaned in close.

"*When you're taking the same medication as your old man,*" he said.

"Dad, I—"

"What about this job?" He sat up suddenly, straight up, then rocked his head slowly around the swivel of his neck, taking in the room during a feigned stretch, then leaned down close again, his voice a full octave lower. "This new job I've been hearing about. Opportunity, opportunity."

"How'd you learn about it?"

"You think I don't hear things?"

The truth was I was a little uncomfortable that he knew. A certain kind of person, you give him a little opening, ask some advice, maybe, try and find out what he thinks, instead of offering up something useful and then leaving you to your business, what he does is this: He climbs right into that little opening and makes himself at home in your life. Every time you turn around, he's there, right up in your world and making himself a part of it. And that was Dad. He wanted to be the inside man on everything.

"I'm just surprised this got back to you," I said.

"Sounds like an easy opportunity. Pretty much there for you, being offered up."

"I guess. I guess. Maybe. Still, I don't want to regret it, later. Maybe complicate things for a few other people."

"Forget other people. Put yourself first for once."

"I haven't made up my mind yet. Maybe I'll think about it for a little while."

He let out frustrated exhalation of breath and shook his head, looked away, his knee bouncing up and down quickly like he had to take a piss call or something, and I could see it killed him that I was even considering not taking it. *Get the old life back, Jake*, Werner had said. Not just my life, but Dad's life. That was what he was envisioning, too, and I imagined the revenge he had planned: As soon as he gets out, have me bring him to the jazz brunch at Chime Creek, roll up in one of Rolly's Cadillacs after a shoeshine and a new suit, walk up to Werner and clap a hand on his shoulder and say, *Been a long time, hasn't it?* Let them know that he may have gone away for a stretch, but he'd won in the end.

"Kid," he said, "you don't ever want to let something like this slip away. When someone's offering you a hand up? You don't turn it down."

"You know how things get complicated, Dad—"

But he didn't seem to be listening. He was looking at the couple at the next table.

"That screw over there," he said.

"What about him?"

"He owes me twelve cigarettes. Hey, Junior," he said loudly, "you got that half pack?"

Junior and his wife turned to give us flat stares. My father met them halfway with his best high-wattage smile, the one I'd seen him give judges, policemen, attorneys, and whenever I saw it a little bit of the light seemed to go out in the room.

"How you doing today, miss?" he asked.

"Fine," she said.

"Later," Junior said.

"Twelve, Junior," my father said, his knee bouncing up and down. "Imagine, taking a week to pay up twelve lousy cigarettes."

"Forget it, Dad," I said.

"No, wait, kid, see, he owes me. Twelve cigarettes I won playing high-low, right Junior?"

"Right," Junior said.

"Dad, I have to go," I said.

"Hold on, sonny. I'm sorry, kid," he said, and turned back to me. "I just want to see you get ahead, I know how hard on you this whole thing has been. You having to pay my bills. I'm really—I really feel bad about that, kid. Why I'm so happy to see an opportunity like this come along for you."

"It's okay, Dad."

"So maybe this job thing—maybe it helps everybody out. Takes the weight off you, give you some cash in your pocket. And truth be told," he said, leaning down close again, so close I could smell the Listerine on his breath, the pomade in his hair, "truth be told, kid, it would help *me* out a little. In here. Understand?"

He sat back and looked at me with those eyes, and though I couldn't read the message encoded there, once again my blood seemed to understand it perfectly. My dad wanted me to take the job, all right. That had been made clear. As was the fact that he wasn't talking about the opportunity at the club. He was talking about the offer from Colonel Tom.

"I mean to say, Jake, that if you do it," he said, "you'd be smoothing things over for me. A couple rough spots here and there. A couple of old debts."

"I have to go, Dad," I said.

"You're going to do it, right, Jake? We're agreed?"

"I don't think you're listening to me."

And he wasn't. His body was rotated toward me but his senses were back on Junior and the ham sandwich his wife was unwrapping. It was after lunch and I'd have bet my car that he wasn't hungry for it, but I could see that he was hungry for the *idea* of it.

"Miss," he said, "miss, I see that you brought Junior here a nice sandwich to have during your visit. What if I was to make you an offer: twelve cigarettes for half that sandwich. No cigarettes for *you* of course. Cigarettes for your fine man here."

"This here sandwich is for *Junior*," she said.

"But still," he said. "It's an easy twelve. Half a day in the laundry to earn that much."

And I saw her reconsider.

"Fuck yourself, Asprey," Junior said, and took a giant bite, chewing indignantly.

"I have to go, Dad," I said, and stood up.

"Miss, you don't—hold on, sonny, watch me charm this lady right out of her sandwich—you don't have to give it *all* up. Just half, and save your husband half a day in the laundry with that one kind little act. You know how miserable it gets in there, with the bleach and the steam and the machines going around and around? They're going around and around, miss, but they're not *going* anywhere."

"Goodbye, Daddy," I said, and left him shaking down a con for half a sandwich and twelve cigarettes.

And then the horrible process in reverse, like a diver ascending through lightening pressures of deep atmospheres, and you sensed the risk of rising too quickly as you glided past the bored guard and through the steel door, every exit attended by a rotating lock, then metal detector, recovered keys, reclaimed wallet (with its identities intact), through the waiting room and checkout, year, make, model, license number of car, signature, another set of doors, then down the paved walk to the car against a running riptide of wind, the heavy love of Mother Nature weighing down until it seemed as if all the trees were bent forward weeping.

TEN

ROLLY'S LAMB BURNING—NO SURPRISE TO anyone, least of all to Zooey and me telegraphing mounting anxiety over the curtains of smoke rising from the grill. Dusk had swiftly descended, the pleasant weather drawing us outdoors barefoot, though how well the evening would play out was still anyone's guess, Zooey steadily drinking her "tea"—a weak mixture of bourbon and lemonade—and I had only a beer as consolation for the understanding that soon I would have to intervene. It was said of Rolly that he either had to become a better grill man or a worse person, because if he didn't improve someone was eventually going to have to just come out and *say* something to this kind, generous, untalented cook—which of course no one wanted to do: Because saying something would send him to pieces. It was almost endearing, the way he kept ruining meals, though it was also sad, in the way endearing things usually are, and I wondered why he'd picked tonight to present such a challenge for himself. I hid behind my beer as best I could, but when the dripping fat began to catch fire in leaping flare-ups I asked nobody in particular *Maybe we finish in the oven?*—and then I noticed Rolly's gaze rising past me, over my shoulder toward the hedge, and I turned to find Sally, framed by the lowered sun, walking toward us across the lawn. This was Sally outside of her chef's whites, making the moment count: beginning with the substantial onyx hair, at work always twisted and braided and pinned high on her head beneath a white scarf, a spectacular undertaking I imagined required an hour with a roomful of Hollywood stylists—now it had been released, to fall and divide around the scalene architecture of the shoulders and fine-boned throat, trailing halfway down her back. Also the favorite ancient jeans that had known her body long and well, the jade-toned tank top so casual and correct it had to have been one of the nicer things she owned, the kind of thing probably made her feel good to pull down off the rack, knowing she'd earned it. It was understood that her sandals had been purchased expressly to hide the minuscule tattoo of crossed knives on her instep, a mistake she regretted and didn't want Rolly and Zooey to see. I had kissed those crossed knives, imagining I could taste the sharpened silver, wondering why she wants to hide something that could provoke me so, only she insisted. This was Sally outside her chef's whites. For a moment she looked like someone else.

Who did she look like? Oh yeah: like herself.

"You're wanting radiant heat with this thing," she said, and striding to me plucked the tongs out of my hand and leaned over the grill. For a moment I was silenced by a glimpse of brilliant white underwear against Mediterranean skin, and then it was gone as she hooked the tongs into the grate and, incredibly, hoisted the entire rack *with* the lamb up with one hand, the cords of her muscles standing out along her arm as she took the metal spatula from Rolly and scraped the coals to one side, the heat causing Rolly and me to step back even as she leaned closer, Rolly grinning now with relief and amusement, Sally's hair trailing down as she chunked the grate back down and rolled the lamb to the cooler side of the grill with her bare hands, dropping the cover over it with the vent slightly opened. She reversed the tongs and handed them back to me, then dusted her hands off. "One hundred fifteen degrees in the center, chef," she said. "Then rest fifteen minutes in the open air. No more, no less. Okay?"

"You eating, Sally?" Zooey asked. "We've got plenty."

"I could be persuaded."

"What's the occasion?" I asked.

She extended her lower lip and blew a wisp of hair back out of her face.

"I happen to adore a rare lamb," she said.

"Really?" I asked, and managed to pack about nine syllables into the word.

"Actually," she said, "I thought I should check on that hand."

We all looked at my wrapped hand.

It looked like it was going to be okay.

"How about a beer, Sally?" Rolly asked.

"How about a martini, Rolly?" she asked.

"You know the way, sugar," he said. "Get me one, too, will you? This beer isn't getting me halfway where I need to be over an open flame."

"You want one, Jake?" she asked.

"I guess it's the thing to do."

She swiveled and padded inside, calling over her shoulder, "One-fifteen, Rolly. No more, no less."

The screen door whisked closed and slapped shut behind her. I turned back and found Zooey biting her lip and frowning at her crossword, Rolly lifting the hood off the grill to poke at the lamb for no reason at all. Both on the verge of an outburst of unalloyed hilarity, and only then did it occur to me that the entire evening had been planned, each detail carefully plotted by two people who had watched me return more downcast than usual from an especially trying visit to the Pennsylvania State Correctional Facility at Slippery Rock. Their restrained hilarity said: *Well, go on. Go on and get her.* I opened my mouth and then realized I hadn't a clue what I'd say, so I slapped the tongs into the handle of the grill—as forcefully, you could say, as a football player spiking a ball after a freak touchdown catch—and followed her inside.

Zooey's satellite channel broadcasting *Pathétique* through the little speakers on the window ledge above the sink, sweetly serenading the defeated fern, slumped and ready to quit. Basic elements for a drink were arranged on the counter—the cracked ice, the olives—and one martini, I could see, had been constructed and summarily one-quarter-drained. But no Sally. The door leading to the basement open, and I imagined I felt a draft of wind leading to it, a slipstream guide—as if the door leading down were an exit rather than a dead end. "Hey, Sally," I called, and followed the sound of my voice downstairs, into the pleasant aroma of whiskey and chalk and wood, the boards of the steps cooler than the grass had been against my bare feet. With no lights on, the room was awash in adulterous light, the setting sun pressing its last advantage through the small casement windows, transforming every object into a carved silhouette of itself—in the corner the squat black obelisk of the easy chair, beside it on the wall the spidery frame of the cue rack. Sally, too, was just an outline, revealed to the west in circumambient light as she circled the table trailing her hand on the green felt.

I cleared my throat and said, "You miss it?"

"Things are better already, with Kimber. Quiet in the house, you know, peaceful? I slept last night, Jake. I don't think I've ever felt so rested. So awake, you know? It was like the weight of the table had been lifted right off me."

"You used to play. Now and then."

"Saturday nights. We'd make popcorn, after my bath get ready for bed and Dad and I play downstairs while Mom made dinner. He'd let me steal sips of his drink. I always wanted his drink, not hers—she'd drink that ghastly crème de menthe, some sort of cocktail that looked like a Chinese medicine. I'm barely tall enough to see over the table, here I am playing in my nightgown, using the rake so I can reach, having sips of Old Fashioned. Maybe eat the cherry if he lets me."

"He'd let you win."

She hesitated.

"And it would make me so mad," she said. "Why would he do that?"

"Because he loved you."

She came around the final corner of the table and stopped before me.

"It seems like a funny thing to do with someone you love, doesn't it?" she asked. "Let her win."

I said, "What really brought you over? My hand is fine. They've asked you over before, you always pass. But to take a night off? It's not like you."

She stood there looking at the table for another long beat, trailing her fingertips over the felt, and then said, "I was at work. And I happened to overhear Werner on the phone. Okay I was like listening in, all right? Walking by, even Wendy's gone, I hear him talking about the job, so I stood there at Wendy's desk, I guess my heart beating a little too fast, listening to everything he said. And when I'd heard what I needed to hear—well, what I did was this: I walked back to the kitchen and told Juan I wasn't feeling well, said he was running the show tonight. And I rolled up my knives and left. Did you ever have a moment like that? When you just had to step outside yourself for a while?"

"Werner and the phone call," I said, and felt a cold drop of sweat roll down my rib cage. "What did you hear?"

"He said the job was going to be filled, that it was decided, he'd already talked to his pick about it. Just had to get the final okay."

"Sally," I said. "Sally—it isn't you. The pick. It's me."

Only I didn't say that. That was what I ought to have said, brought it out, along with the truth about my mistake in the car with Kimber—but the thing about Sally is, she isn't good at disappointment: She just can't do it anymore. That's why she gets things perfect all the time, so she won't have to deal with the results of imperfection. As one might understandably be in her situation. *Sally—it isn't you. The pick. It's me. And I made a terrible mistake with Kimber. I'm sorry, I'm sorry, I'm sorry.*

What I *ought* to have said. But I didn't.

"I'm going to get it, Jake," she said. "I've waited so long for this, showing up at that kitchen every morning six days a week, someone *else's* restaurant, getting everything *they* want right, profit going in *their* pocket, never doing it my way. Watching and waiting. A couple of years in the office, a few good bonuses, scouting locations, working on *my* menu? I'll have enough put away and the good credit to start my own place, people knowing my name. Something small across town, build from there. I've been waiting as long as I can remember. And now my time is here."

Now she was looking at me.

"I think I went home to celebrate, tonight," she said. "To mark the little moment. But there I was, at home, listening to silence. Kimber gone doing God knows what. And you know what I realized? I realized I didn't have anyone to celebrate with. That I was all alone. Almost like the news had never happened, like there was nothing to celebrate in the first place. I tried to make it work. I poured a drink for myself. Then I poured it out. Like an anti-celebration, like a—like a memorial. I got the news I wanted but I was alone in it. And it felt like the death of an expectation. I guess you know how that is."

"I do."

"Maybe that's why I thought of you. Of Rolly's invitation to come over. He called me at the kitchen office, said, *He had a bad one today. He could use a friend.* I was standing there washing my empty glass, and I thought of his invitation. I thought of you. I realized that you would be happy for me about the job. And that made *me* happy. And then suddenly it was like I couldn't get over here fast enough. Put on my favorite jeans, my best top, knowing you would notice."

The room did a slow fade to black, a film of cloud passing over the sun. One moment I could see her face, read what was there, and then she was gone, and she reached out and took my hand in both of hers, placed my palm flat against the center of her chest—and I felt the urgency of her fear matching my own, the rapid tap of her blood. Upstairs, *Pathétique* ended. A brief beat of silence, and then "Moonlight Sonata" began its patient melody, the chime of glass, ice cracking, and soon the click of a spoon, Rolly upstairs now, but she only held my hand more tightly against her chest.

"Why is it that I'm upset with you tonight?" she asked. "As if—as if you had gone and let me win at something."

I suppose I would have pressed my lips to hers, then, to let her know that I was nothing and no one to be frightened of, but before I could gather the courage I needed to step closer to her, the light switched on overhead and Sally squinted at me through her tears as Rolly called, "Kid, you down there?"

It was full dark by the time the lamb was finished and rested, a good meteor shower on offer as we sat down. Wine never came up—we just never got there, Rolly wading fearlessly into a second martini instead and bringing me along with him, Zooey enjoying her glass of "tea" and Sally sipping at her first drink, Zooey's radio playing piano sonatas through the kitchen window. When the cooler air descended from the trees I gave Sally my sweatshirt, hoping it would carry the faint scent of her perfume tomorrow. What was there between Sally and me seemed to have got into the air, sent out its vibrations, because Rolly and Zooey were sort of teasing each other in that manner married couples use to signal mutual interest, maybe something happening upstairs after lights out.

Something like that could have happened between Sally and me, too, I suppose—I think we were both surprised to find the moment there upon us, like a freak storm on an otherwise cloudless afternoon, the electric attraction of coming clean about emotions you don't fully understand, and I think we would have followed through with that kiss if the room hadn't suddenly brightened, if Rolly's innocent uptick of the light switch hadn't rinsed us in clarity and plain sense and the composure that we wanted people like Rolly to believe we possessed. She'd swiped at her eyes with the heels of her palms, and then we did something else for the first time, something we had never done before: We held hands in silence, facing each other, like a couple about to recite their vows. I think if he'd clicked the light back off, anything could have happened. But instead Rolly repeated his question, and when I answered, "We'll be right up," you could feel the spell lift—you could actually feel it leave us.

After we'd cleaned our plates, Rolly said, "Sally, best I've ever had."

We'd eaten in near-darkness, enjoying the novelty of the outdoors, the spotlight too harsh anyway and only good for nighttime croquet matches or maybe horseshoes. Overhead, past the light applause of the leaves blowing in the wind, Ursa Major and Minor, the big bear and her little cub, were obscured in turns by rushing sheets of torn clouds, the weather cruising by as if hurrying along to an important date, all around us a thousand armies of summer crickets dreaming their collective dream and sighing into the night.

"You ought to try it with some *raita*," Sally said, her mood warmed up by the drink and the good meal. At some point during the meal she had tucked her legs up under her for warmth. "Get some coriander and lemon peel over the lamb before you grill it, some good salt, too, for maybe two hours, then serve the *raita* alongside. You mix a little good yogurt, not the American shit on offer but the good Greek article, maybe add some lemon and cumin? And grate a cucumber into it."

"That with lamb?" Rolly asked.

"That's how you do it," Sally said. "The milk of the mother with the meat of the child. You make the connection there on the plate."

Zooey crossed her arms under her breasts to keep warm, and Rolly reached out to gently grip her elbow.

"Jake's mom used to tell me that," Zooey said. "That you could feel the connection whenever they got in bad trouble. You could feel the fear, she said, except you felt it where you'd fed them."

"Jake wasn't even a year old—" Rolly said— "one day he got his hand stuck in an elevator door. His mom ran him to the hospital, thought he'd mangled his fingers. While she was waiting for the X-ray she called me up, said, *Rolly, bring me a shirt, I'm plain soaked through in front. Everytime I think of his hand going in the door it just pushes right out of me.*"

And for a moment we were silent together, because we were all thinking the same thing, wondering where that connection had gone. "Do you suppose they know?" Zooey asked. "The ewes, when it's time for the lambs to go. They know what's going to happen?"

"How could they not?" Rolly asked. "A lamb, it looks like a four-legged meal. Just looking at them I get hungry."

"You would," Zooey said, and swatted him with her napkin. Letting him know it was a lock, something was going to happen tonight, maybe he shouldn't drink himself useless.

"I've been to the killing floors," Sally said. "They bring you there so you're forced to come to terms with the commerce of it. What you're doing for a living. You treat the meat with respect if you know where it came from. And you always see the same thing."

"What do you see?" I asked.

"They know," Sally said.

"I'd think they'd keep the ewes separate," I said. "From the lambs. Keep them penned up somewhere else, that way you don't have a scene."

"No, the parents keep the lambs calm," Sally said. "The kids, they look around and see the parents there, they think, Ah, there's Mom, everything will work out."

"How do the parents look?" Rolly asked.

"The steers look bored. They're thinking, *I can't do anything about it.* The moment they smell the blood, they go passive. They're thinking, *All right, come spring I'll just make another.*"

"What about the ewes?" Zooey asked.

"Mothers don't like the smell of blood," Sally said, and we left it at that.

An hour later I walked her down the driveway, and we stopped at her car and turned to look back at the house, hearing Rolly and Zooey laughing over some private joke as they carried the dishes inside, Zooey telling him, "Leave it, honey," and then the bright rectangle of kitchen light reaching across the lawn went blank.

"He won't be having any ice cream tonight," Sally said.

"I doubt he'll miss it."

"It seems like a good life."

"They match up."

"Almost forgot."

She slipped the sweatshirt over her head in a fragrant backdraft of her perfume, then held it out to me—except when I took hold of it she didn't let go.

Just like Werner in the coat closet.

"What do you suppose would have happened?" she said. "If he hadn't turned on that light just then."

"But he did."

"It's like the universe doesn't want us together," she said. "Like someone seems to think we're no good for each other."

That summer afternoon in Sally's basement—that afternoon it had been near-darkness, too. *I want to give you something*, she had said, gripped my arm, and I followed her downstairs as besotted with that green bikini as I had been all afternoon, feverish and dizzy, and after the hot white light of the pool deck I could scarcely see in the gloom, just well enough to realize what she'd meant by that remark when she turned and shrank back against the table, her chin lowered but her eyes raised.

I trust you, she said after, but to do what?

"We don't have to let anyone else decide," I said. "It's up to us."

But she shook her head and turned a quarter turn away, letting go of the sweatshirt, hunting for her car key. I'm twenty-five years old and realizing that this woman is my whole life. I lose her and I'm going to have to start all over from nothing.

"How many things are up to us," she said, "really? Your parents. My parents."

"Why did you cut me loose like that? Why wouldn't you *see* me? Did you *want* to mess me up? Because that's what you did. Eight weeks together, and you cut my fucking heart out. I never got over you. I'm still not over you."

She wasn't looking at me, just sat there looking at her keyring, count-ing through the little silver slices as if adding up pocket change.

"Your dad, Jake," she said.

"He told you to stay away. Called you from the cellblock. Delivered his sentence."

And she laughed, actually dropped her head back and laughed at the sky, except two tears squeezed out of the corners of her eyes and ran down to her jawline.

"I wish," she said. "Oh, Jake, I really wish that would have been what happened. Because I wouldn't have listened."

"Your parents. *They* wouldn't allow it."

"I wasn't going to let them know. What was between us. I didn't let *anyone* know. I just put it all down in my diary so I would remember every last detail. Eight perfect weeks. Because I never wanted to forget. But then Kimber found the key. And it all came out."

"I'm sorry."

"We're at the dinner table and she tells them what she read. And I remember feeling so—stupid. Not because of you, or because of what we did. Stupid because I'd actually thought that it would be safe, writ-ing it down. And my father wouldn't allow it. *His father is a thief*, he said."

I trust you, she'd said.

Translation, nine years late: *I trust you to keep this between us.*

"I understand," I said.

That being the summer her father had stopped using the topical anes-thetic before giving me the Septocaine stick. Wanting me to feel that little sting, too.

"They wouldn't allow it," she said. "Even after he was gone, I couldn't bring myself to go against it. It was like they always said, *Not while you're living in our home.* And when I heard Werner talk about the new job—" she looked up at me, "—when I heard him say that, I made a promise to myself. I said, *If I get the job, it's not their home any longer. It's mine. And then we can be together. Jake and me.*"

She opened the car door and stepped inside, belted herself in for the drive. The car reversed down the drive and paused briefly in the street, before changing directions to drive down the hill. Neither of us waved goodbye. Instead we locked gazes for three heartbeats, and I think she gave a little nod before putting the car in gear. As if we'd just agreed to something.

I'm thinking, *You can take the job Werner's offering, Jake. Or you can have the girl.*

But you can't have both.

I waited until she was gone around the turn at the bottom of the hill, then walked up to the house. Zooey had left the lights beneath the kitchen cabinets on for me, the television screen blank, and the night, pregnant with silence, seemed to sigh as I walked to the phone and dialed the number.

"This job," I said. "Tell me more."

And there was a little beat of silence as he savored victory.

"Come meet me," Colonel Tom said. "We'll have a little talk with an associate of mine."

I had once asked my father, *How did you do it?*—meaning, *Find it in you to go ahead and do those things, break the law that way?* He answered, *Easy as falling off a log.* And now I understood. What he'd meant was, it's not the *doing* that's hard. The doing's kind of easy, once you've gotten past what must come before, which is the *deciding*: the act of making up your mind that you have prescribed a future for yourself and now must do certain things to bring that future into being. The way I see it, your father is your flesh and blood. Which applies certain obligations—you protect your flesh and blood from the outer forces who want to *do them harm.* When I got back in my car after that phone call, though—when I pulled the driver's side door shut with an oily squeak and in that enclosed space found that Sally's perfume was all over me, like a sickness, like an antibody—when I inhaled the aroma of her skin, the word I kept thinking of was *family*. And you have much different obligations there. You protect your *flesh and blood* from others. But whom do you protect your *family* from?

Answer: from yourself.

ELEVEN

IN THE COLONEL'S TRUCK WE crossed beneath the last overpass, into the part of town best avoided. Two miles past the second trailer park he slowed and drifted onto the unpaved camp road: It unfurled into the dense birch forest toward the base of a limestone mountain, where, among the heavy timber, entire generations of families had labored to draw sustenance from the earth and, failing to find it, had been forced to seek goods and services downmarket. We soon passed a group of four men in overalls lowering the gutted carcass of a pig into an oil drum of boiling water. They paused in their work to watch us, four heads turning in unison to fix us with flat dead stares, the oldest among them offering Tom a brief nod that was less a greeting than an assent, permission that could be revoked at any moment. Ahead the road would divide and divide into a hundred divisions and subdivisions, forked paths composing factors of decisions and every one of them bad. I'd heard it said that the camps within actually preferred to leave the road in a terrible state of disrepair, so that John Law would never easily or quietly find his way in. In strange synchronicity with the earlier night, the Colonel had chosen this drive to reveal an interest he'd cultivated in the genre of music we call classical, and now plaintive Boccherini was broadcasting on a radio station from the college, the reception improving as the elevation rose.

He shifted into four wheel drive to climb across a rutted-out breakdown in the road, my window down to let my hand trail against the truck's steel hide and taste the cool night air—I suppose because I wanted to remember this moment, to have some tactile experience to nail it to, should I ever feel the need to revisit or regret, and smelling the birches and the rust and iron smell of the trout stream applauding alongside the road, I felt that I had somehow been here before, not this place but this situation. I was reminded of the first time my father had taken me hunting. You don't ever forget your first time holding a weapon. The hour was early enough that the *stars* were still out, an entire semester of astronomy class carpeting the sky overhead, God's ticker-tape parade, my breath smoking out in front of me in the dark as I waited on the cold stump, rump frozen against the wood, the startled noise and the blurred bolt of brown against brown streaking across my line of vision, and raising the gun into the crisis of sighting in I felt myself go sick at heart but fired nevertheless and watched one of the shapes go down. My knees were loose and weak as I walked toward the spot where it had fallen and, not trusting them, I had to sit down. That was how my dad found me, halted twenty yards from the only deer I ever killed, without the legs even to walk toward it. *You always were a great shot*, he said, and it occurred to me that just as talent can be used for good, so can it be used for more selfish interests. I did not know many things about my own nature, but smelling that trout stream now on my way into the deeper woods where I was sure some sort of test awaited, I did know two things: first, that I was not capable of killing ever again. And second, that the man I was traveling toward was. *I'm an associate of Colonel Tom's*, he'd told Sally, but I think Quinn Lightpainter, in that moment, was being modest. My guess that Colonel Tom was, in fact, an associate of his.

Rabbits zigzagged off into the dark ahead of Colonel Tom's head-lamps as he took another left fork, even in this capable truck Tom bouncing along at just ten miles an hour until faint lights showed between the birches. The emerging camp had recently been painted white, a deer suspended by its neck from a porch beam and twirling in the wind, looking every bit like a hanged man. Tom cut the lights early and rolled over the pine-needle floor to the open yard, punching the dash lighter as he stopped the car twenty yards from the camp, radio on, a Debussy piano sonata now, and turning his body slightly toward me he plucked a joint from his breast pocket, passing it once through his lips. When the lighter popped out he held the glowing coil to the joint and inhaled deeply, luxuriously exhaling the smoke through his nose, closing his eyes and seeming to take sublime pleasure in the music as he held the joint out to me between his thumb and forefinger. I pinched it and pulled the smoke into my lungs, the marijuana signals amplifying my senses instantly, the music somehow enriched and the mineral smell of the stream made cleaner and brighter. I tilted my head out the window and looked up through the high tops of the pines leaning to and fro in the wind, their branched tops swaying back and forth against the backdrop of moonlight, and the clouds hurrying along to their very important dates.

"Quinn Lightpainter," Colonel Tom said. "You know him?"

I ducked my head back in the cab and had a second pull on the joint—shit, already high as a pilot, feeling the seat comfortable behind me. I didn't want to meet Quinn Lightpainter. I wanted to go to sleep.

"I've seen him before," I said.

Lightpainter was a butcher—not a meat cutter but the genuine article working out of Zion in his bloody white apron, I'd seen him at work taking apart a side of beef, leaning over his table with a delicate foot-long boning knife, the point sharp as a needle going *tap-tap-tap* at the meat to loosen it from the bone, never slicing, always just a series of gentle *tap-taps* with the narrow tip. That was all he ever used, the hacksaw for the big bones, the boning knife to take what was left apart. It was scarcely a store, more of what you'd call a freezer with a cash register—he kept his store so chilly you'd plan ahead with a jacket even in summer, though he never did wear anything heavier than a T-shirt under his apron. The place had been a sensation when it first opened, some Native American butcher with a strange name and weight-lifter muscles and jailhouse ink up and down his exposed arms like colored sleeves, good meat here from distributors in New York City. In a sleepy town, sometimes that's all you need. Rolly used to go there, saying he had the best lamb. But even Rolly had stopped going. Quinn kept cutting up meat, and the store stayed open, but no one ever went there, so far as I knew, and gradually it became part of the collective knowledge that someone was using the place to wash a large amount of money.

"Everyone has," Tom said. "You don't forget him. That long black hair of his—"

"—in a braid going all the way down his back," I said, the smoke loosening me up, maybe that was his idea.

"Longer than any woman's in town."

"Women around the pool are always talking about his hair, wishing they had it. I've never seen a man with hair that long. Like he's trying to say something with it."

Tom held his hand out for the joint.

"Quinn's Cahuilla," he said. "He doesn't cut his hair unless someone close to him dies."

"You'd think he'd have lost his mother, lost his father—"

"Yeah, only they ditched him when he was born. They're already *gone.* State-raised, that's why he's such a bad apple, no family to look to, so he's got no one to cut it *for.* I said to him, *Quinn, you better hope you never go in the joint, they* make *you cut it in there, three inches maximum.* You know what he told me? He said, *Anyone wants to cut my hair, they're going to have to kill me first.*"

"I'd think your hair would be the last thing you'd worry about in there."

"In my opinion, you can trust a criminal who cares about his looks. You see your dad lately?"

"I saw him today."

"His hair look good?"

"It always does."

"See what I mean?" Colonel Tom said, and took another pull. "Now, Quinn, he takes good care of his looks, too, and that signifies something. I guess you could say that he's my best friend in the world. And if pressed, he'd most likely characterize me as *his* best friend. You know how I know? Because that guy saved my life. That's no small thing, to go around on a blue-sky day and think, *I'm here because of another man*, but that's exactly how it is. We were doing a jewelry store in P-town, I've got the security guard, and this fat old fuck starts gripping his chest. I get him on his face and I holster my piece, tell him to lay still, and smash the first counter and go to shoveling, figuring by helping Quinn do the cases I'm cutting sixty seconds off our exit time. Except something goes wrong. I know this because I hold up a fistful of chokers and I see the worst thing in the world. I see Quinn pointing the shotgun at me."

I closed my eyes and lay my head back, feeling the Debussy notes stirring in my groin.

"He's going to put you down," I said, "let your dead body take the fall."

"Exactly. There's like half a second of silence as our eyes meet, and then *boom*, he fires. Only I'm not hit, and I turn around and see that he put a round of buckshot in the wall over the security guard. His aim wasn't so true and he got the guard with some of the shot, and the guy's blinking away blood dripping down from his hairline. He ain't clutching his chest anymore but he's gone milk-pale, and I see that the backup revolver he'd kept in his boot is now spinning dropped on the floor, and when it stops spinning I see that it's cocked, because he was about to point it at my back and say, *Freeze, cocksucker.*"

He took another pull on the joint.

"Now, I know myself," Colonel Tom said. "And in that moment after he said that, I'd be thinking, *I'm not doing time, no matter what.* That's always been the rule with me. Do *anything* to avoid going inside. Anything. So even though that fat old fuck had the drop on me, I'd have tried to pull on him and put him down. And I'd never, ever, have gotten that piece out in time. Which means I'd be dead. That's what I think of when I think of Quinn. So now I owe him one, just about the biggest thing one person can owe another. Anyone ever messes with Quinn—well, I guess that pretty much means they're messing with *me*."

I considered the clean white camp, yellow light burning in the windows.

"Is he in there?" I asked.

"He is," Tom said.

"I guess we better go in," I said, and, looking back to Tom, was astonished to see him holding the black Smith & Wesson out to me, grip-first, a look on his face that suggested amusement but probably was anything but.

"Hey, Tom," I said, "Why so serious? Not like I'm going in there to knock over Fort fucking Knox."

"It's just to show him you mean business. He'll probably take it off you, maybe pat you down. Either way, you don't want to go in there naked. It'll give him a bad idea about you, he pats you down and finds nothing."

"What kind of idea would that be?"

"That you're too trusting. People who trust too much, they get sloppy."

"You keep it. He'll know you're carrying."

Tom shook his head, exhaling smoke from his nose.

"You go alone," he said.

The wind kicked up and that deer twirled around as I came up the steps, man, it gave me a fucking *fright* when it spun a half turn and stared right at me with those doll's eyes, onyx with a bright little chip of moonlight there in the center, its tongue hanging out the side. I took an unconscious step backward, then froze when Quinn, off to my left, said, "I'm having a special on that tomorrow."

Quinn, the way I remember, somehow possessing the presence you imagined a glacier would have, or a tiger, malevolent pitiless things that traveled and moved and did as they wished. He sat in the shadows of the porch drinking what smelled like a bitter tea but probably was not. The tilted slats of the louvered window revealed the orange radiance of the potbelly stove inside, his face barred with colored light, the features unexpectedly sad but eyes bright with understanding, the eyes knowing and seeking and searching. You imagined that when he directed his gaze your way he was assessing the architecture of your muscle and bone, in his mind taking you apart nerve by nerve.

"You get it yourself?" I asked.

"A neighbor out here owed me, he paid me with a deer. I get good money on wild meat, maybe a little extra on the chops. Maybe make some jerky for hunters want something to eat in the deer stand. I haven't made my mind up how I want to carve it up yet."

"Too warm to hang it, though."

"Yeah, not near cold enough. When it's down around freezing, you hang wild game maybe ten, maybe fifteen days no problem. Grouse, too, game birds, I've seen them go twenty days, though by that point you're eating rotten meat. Why it's so tender, once things have gone by they're sweeter. This I'll break down after you go, we have venison burgers flying out the door by noon. I put some sage in them, some pork fat so the meat isn't dry, you grind it together? Maybe even a little dusting of ground-up juniper berries or some coriander. Your friend, the chef I met, what was her name?"

"Sally."

"Yeah, Sally. You tell her I have good venison, she's going to want some."

"I don't think she's allowed to change up the menu. She has to cook what they tell her to cook."

"Maybe she ought to try and change things up. You get something good, you got to make the most of it."

I sat down on the chair opposite his, Colonel Tom's piece uncomfortable against the small of my back, the naked steel still warm from his grip and the thumb safety imprinting itself in my skin. Across the yard, Colonel Tom's truck lay in a liquid pool of moonlight, the ember of his cigarette the only thing visible inside the cab. I sat listening to the wind high overhead in the trees, determined to wait for Quinn to speak, but when ten heartbeats had passed in silence I said, "I never did like to eat anything I got myself."

"How come?"

"You can taste the fear."

"Yours or theirs?"

"Theirs. You can taste it in the meat."

"You get your own?"

"Just once. After that," I said, "I always missed on purpose."

"Why you keep hunting, you don't like it?"

"Because so long as my dad took me, I knew he'd always give me the first shot."

"And you'd miss, thinking the deer's getting away because of you."

"Something like that. Eventually he wised up and stopped giving me the first shot. And then I had to taste that frightened meat again."

"I always thought it was funny," he said, "animals panicking when they smell blood. Whenever I see blood I calm down. I get in a fight in a bar, I'm scared until it starts. My glass always chattering on the bartop when I set it down that last time. Then the first head butt comes and everything's clear to me. What's about to happen."

"Every time I see a fight I just get scared. Want to run. You're lucky, being able to come at things that way."

"I don't know," Quinn said, "there's only so much blood to go around."

"Are you scared right now?"

"You some kid from town with a father doing twelve years up in Slippery Rock, maybe you have a bone to pick with me I don't know about. Maybe your dad raised someone has it in him to do me some harm. I see the way you're sitting funny in that chair. You're packing something, right?"

"Tom's piece."

"That's what I mean. Maybe you have reason to come up here to put my lights out for something I don't even know I did. So I'm sitting here in the dark afraid of you."

And I wanted to laugh—nearly did, really—because that seemed sad to me, Quinn saying he was frightened right now. Quinn telling me that I was something or someone of consequence.

"We're just here for business," I said. "No trouble. We keep it simple."

"No, it's never simple. Colonel Tom, he's good like that, he gets people interested, tells them how easy things are going to be. Except he's not smart. My closest friend, but I don't let him do the plan. I do the plan. Are you smart?"

"Not really."

"See, now I have to be smart enough for all three of us. He comes to me with the idea, knows he can't pull it off alone. So I'm sitting here in the dark thinking up how we do it."

"You want my keyring. I hand it over. When you're finished with it, you hand it back."

He shook his head.

"That's why I have to think for all three of us," he said. "You some new employee, just weeks in, father up in prison, a young kid with no sense. Who you think they come at first? They pull you in, sit you alone in an interrogation room two hours to soften you up, then they polygraph you. Two hours later I'm getting booked, have to cut my hair."

"What is it you're after?"

"Better you don't know. I just tell you that this is the kind of job you wait a lifetime for, they got something worth more money than I've ever seen, only they don't know it. And they not even going to know we *took* it. That's why we're doing it, like we pull a job but there never was a job and all you got to do is be quiet about it. Get in, get out, that's the end of it, only you a lot richer."

I lifted my keyring out of my pocket and dropped it on the table between us, but he raised a scarred boot heel to shove the ring back to me.

So it would be his thing, from start to finish. His way, his terms.

"We got to take it off you," he said.

"How?"

"Better we don't tell you that, either. That way you surprised, don't have to act. Maybe tomorrow. Maybe next week."

"In public?"

"Yeah, in public. You're the problem, the one they come looking for they *do* find something. So me and Tom, we give you a true story to tell how a couple of guys took it off you unexpected. We do it in public, there's no doubt attached, you just a guy who was a victim. Tell them, *Officer, I don't know what happened. I had the keyring. Then I didn't.* And that's the end of it."

"Why get me involved? Why not just take it from me for real?"

"Because," he said, "we got *two* doors to get through."

And once again I'm getting twenty-twenty vision on things. They wanted my keyring, sure: elementary enough. But they wanted something riskier in the deal: They wanted an inside man.

"The second one is really bad," he said. "They got a buried bolt on the inside, take you too long to cut it, too noisy."

"A buried bolt," I said. "You're talking about the supply closet."

"Yeah, you be there all night making noise cutting through a buried bolt, and the whole point of it to get in and out they don't even know where we *went*. The second key you going to get for us. You going to get it from your friend the chef."

"Hey, Quinn," I said, and tried to bring a laugh out of my chest, "we want to leave Sally out of this. Right?"

"Have to have the key. That's the way it is."

"Have Kimber do it," I said, thinking: *Keep these guys away from Sally however I can.* "Take it off her at home."

"The chef," he said, "she keeps her key in the safe. At *work*. Every night locked up."

"Why are you so sure?"

Quinn allowed himself a little tired smile.

"Your chef friend," he said, "I've tried to sell her a little venison now and then."

I pictured it: Quinn there in the office, talking about hung venison and knowing he's not going to get the sale. Knowing that and not caring, because he's taking it all in—the room, the bolted supply closet, the open safe, the receipts, the little keyring there on her desk.

"When do we do it?" I asked.

"Don't worry when. You just go about your business. What matters is what comes after. You know Mo-cot?"

I shook my head.

"The Creator. Not the nice one, that boojwa Christian bullshit, white beard and rays of light and shit. Mo-cot, the Creator, he's not a nice man—rules heaven and earth. But he makes a big mistake. What he does is this: He teaches mankind about warfare, thinks they'll do a good job of keeping each other under control, but you know what they do?"

"They kill him."

He showed his teeth in the moonlight, pleased with me.

"That's right," he said. "So now the Creator, he's dead. You understand what I'm telling you? No one running the show anymore. Because the things you make come back to you. That's why you'd better think ahead before you say *yes* to me, because after you say *yes*, you can't say *no*. You understand now?"

"I do."

"I see blood I calm down. Right now, you and Tom here to see me, a gun on you, no blood in sight, I'm scared as a rabbit. I see simple meetings like this go wrong all the time. Have to drink some peyote tea just to stay cool. We go ahead with this, you show me you the sort of man can handle himself, not get spooked and start talking, maybe I calm down. But we go ahead and people get crazy, start talking, I get nervous. And only one way left to help myself calm down. You probably sitting there feeling good that you made me nervous, right?"

"I guess."

"See, that's how stupid you are. You think it's a good thing I'm feeling scared, puts you in a position of power. Problem being that it makes me want to bust your head against that wall so I can see a little blood, feel better. You going to keep me feeling this way, nervous? Because I look at you, I see a guy maybe who likes to talk."

"I've got an old man up in Slippery Rock, and I never said a word on him. You think I didn't know what was going on? Even as a kid I knew. But I never talked. I could have named names, maybe lightened his sentence, even though I was just a kid. But I never did."

"Yeah, but that was your old man. No, I see you as a guy who starts to talk the moment they get you in a room. Sweat be jumping right out of your skin. So you do me a favor. You take that deer with you and go back to town. Just unhook it, drag it back to that truck there, and load it in the back. In the morning you have your pretty friend break it down for you, she knows how. And have her cook something nice up for you, on me—have her cook up the heart *en brochette* with a little paprika. Tom tell me I'm crazy to give anything away, but I know it's a good buy, because for one lousy deer I'm saving myself from having to walk you into the woods some night. You know what we do, we get in the woods? I take that gun you're carrying and I put one here—" he touched his temple "—and one here—" he touched his breastbone, "and then I drop you in a hole. Have to dig it myself. I don't think either of us wants that. No, you take that deer, and you bring it to your pretty friend, and you and me aren't having to deal with any holes off in the woods."

He stood up, picked up his mug of tea and began to walk inside.

"Thing is," I said, "I don't like venison. And I need this job."

I was trembling—partly from the cold and partly from something more primal within me, grateful for the smoke Tom had given me. Everyone frightened of everyone else, dosing up just to talk it through. Quinn sighed fatalistically, wiped his hand over his face, reached up with one finger and gave the deer a little twirl.

"Where did Tom get the idea?" I asked.

"Don't worry about the idea. Just remember that all you got to do is get the second key tomorrow morning, carry both with you everywhere you go next week."

"And then stay quiet. After."

He reached up and gave the deer another light turn.

"Man," he said, "maybe you smarter than you think."

TWELVE

"THE TURN'S HERE," ROLLY SAID.

I'd left work over lunch, my backup, Ginny, agreeing to spot me for a few hours while I helped out Rolly. He said his acid indigestion was really kicking up today, the crazy heat and cruel sun bothering him more than usual, has him dizzy only he didn't want to tell Zooey and make her worry. We're in one of the big loaner Caddies, a real boat, bringing it back from the airport where the owner had dropped it on his way out of town for a week in Bermuda, Rolly in the passenger seat because he's not up to driving it alone.

"But the dealership's over there," I said.

"Other way. I want to show you something."

So instead of left it was right, off toward the quieter north end of town, the public golf course that wasn't anything like Chime Creek but not too bad from what I understood, plus the little hippie colony of failed painters living together in open marriages among a few galleries, more divorces than you might expect, and just beyond the only restaurant other than Semaphore that could rival what Sally was putting on. I'm already seething about being pulled away from work, Werner bound to find out somehow and dock my pay, I've got a stolen key burning my hip pocket and now Rolly wants to go on one of his classic sidelights, thinking, should I be staying away from Rolly in case Colonel Tom decides to show up? But no, It takes Colonel Tom an hour just to get out of bed, nothing's going to happen today. Maybe some nerves there, sure, some buyer's remorse, but nothing I can't handle. Sally would put her keyring back in the safe tonight, and wouldn't know that one of its number was missing until tomorrow morning, when she tried to unlock the supply closet.

And then what?

We're both sweating but Rolly won't turn up the AC, saying it dried out his sinuses, and I'm too exhausted to argue. I'd been up half the night, too jammed to sleep despite the half joint I'd smoked during the ride home, laying in bed wondering about Quinn and Tom and what they had planned. *Better you don't know*, Quinn said.

But better for whom?

"Up here," Rolly said. "The entrance right here."

Left and slowly up the curving drive, in under a few nice-looking alder trees and a clean landscaped lawn swooping down on the back nine of the golf course. Nice white condos lined up along the fairway, and a few older couples sitting outside having tea and crabbing over the heat and the crossword. Crabbing nice, though, like they were keeping each other amused. SYLVAN HILL, the sign said. I recognized it as the name of the little retirement community Zooey and Rolly talked about now and then.

"What's the story?" I asked.

"Here, kid," Rolly said. "Cut the engine."

I stopped the car and switched the engine off, my forehead quickly glossed with sweat. Rolly turned his whole body to face me. He'd sweated through his shirt in patches.

"That gift you gave me," he said. "The table."

"It's nothing, Rolly. I wanted you to know how much I appreciate you guys—"

He held his hand up to silence me.

"That gift," he said. "It got me thinking. You know, Zooey and me, we never could have kids. It's not easy for a married couple, something like that coming along, like a tornado touching down, only this tornado doesn't break up your house, what it breaks up is all the plans you had for the future. We decided, better not to find out who has the problem, that way, you know, the one who can have kids doesn't start getting funny ideas about starting over with someone else. We don't know who has the problem, we're really in it together, you know?"

He lifted a white handkerchief from his pocket, mopped his face.

"Then you come along," he said. "Nice kid, I know you love your dad, he'll always be your father, but he's poison. It hurts to even say it, but it's true. I think you know that, and you know that I'm enough of a grown-up to understand that you can love someone and be disappointed by him at the same time. Your father, if he called me in the middle of the night and said he had a flat tire? I'd get dressed and go help him. If he needed a kidney, I'd give him *mine*. But I wouldn't loan him one nickel. You understand?"

"I understand."

"Then you come along. And maybe you don't see this, but you're good for Zooey and me. We were scared to make that offer to your dad, but we knew it was the right thing to do. And here you are, suddenly this life we believed we'd never have—well, we got it. Suddenly we have a fourteen-year-old kid sleeping in the back bedroom. We go to bed at night, you know what we talk about? We talk about you. Because you sort of became the kid we thought we couldn't have. You've given us that. Which is a better gift than anyone could ever give."

"I'm sorry about the other night. With the table."

"It's all right. Afterward I was laying in bed thinking, Well, this is what having a kid is all about, you live out the full range of emotions every day. You feel gratitude, you feel disappointed in them, all in the space of an hour. It's all there, which I guess you would call a full life. And we have you to thank for that."

He mopped his face again.

"So," he said. "Zooey and I've been talking. We planned to sell the house in about five more years, maybe eight, and move here. She's already got a few friends here, I'll have two friends retiring here in a couple years. And we were thinking, Well, maybe we do it now, the housing market really up like this? Prices what they are, we make a pile of money on it. More than we ever dreamed we'd make on this place when we bought it—what? Twenty-seven years ago. We paid less for that house than you'd pay for this car."

"You want to move now."

"We sell the house, we can buy ourselves one of the little condos here and have a mint left over. Enough to never worry about money again. Enough coming when we sell it," he said, "that we can afford to spend what we've got now in savings, send you back in the fall, Jake."

I never have been one who went in for crying much. I think that's because I never had a talent for it, the shedding of tears—because having a good cry doesn't make me feel better, the way a good cry should. The only thing that having a good cry makes me feel is that I want to have *another* good cry, and then another. Whenever I feel any tears working their way up, what I do is this: I cancel them out. But this time it wasn't up to me. Something irresistible pushed them up and out— maybe an understanding of just how far off the rails I'd gone, that stunt I pulled last night, sitting there with Quinn, Tom's cannon against the small of my back and pretending I had any right to be there. It's that easy to make a mistake you regret forever. I suppose everyone has his particular Grand Mistake somewhere inside, but it's people like Rolly and Zooey who keep you from making it—because you don't want to disappoint them. I sat there with my vision swimming, looking out over the steering wheel at the alder trees, not daring to look at Rolly, I guess wanting to take off my belt and slide across the seat to give him a hug, but I just couldn't do it, and finally he said, "I'm going to go inside, kid, pick up the paperwork, give you a minute." He got out of the car, blew his nose on the white handkerchief, then walked inside and left me alone looking out at the hard sunlight.

When I'd got myself together again I lifted my cell phone out of my pocket only the battery had run down again, the charge funny ever since the long trip at the bottom of the pool, almost like it had tired itself out for good shining and shining in the dark that way, so I pocketed it and walked to the main building, air conditioned and clean and bright inside, a library off to the left where a couple were sitting and reading, a television room to the right, a nice bright dining room ahead, not a cafeteria but an actual dining room with waiters, people seeming pleased to talk with the residents.

"Is there a phone?" I asked the receptionist.

I followed her directions down the hall, past a wall of windows that overlooked a garden where residents were tending plots of tomatoes and herbs, dropped coins in the pay phone and dialed the number. The girl who answered in a bad mood, sounding inconvenienced by the call and not afraid to let me know it.

"Colonel Tom," I said.

"He's out," she said.

"Yeah, but when's he *back*?"

"Back tonight. You want I should leave a message?"

"Tell him," I said, "that Jake says it's over."

"What's over?"

"He'll know. Just tell him Jake said that's it, the whole thing's over, he can forget it."

She was quiet for a moment.

"The Colonel," she said, "doesn't much like people telling him to forget it."

"He's not a Colonel."

"What?"

"He's not a Colonel. If he has a problem," I said, "he can call me."

I hung up the receiver, turned, and sagged back against the wall shaking—I suppose the way you would after a near-miss with another car on the highway. A long shuddering breath that says, *Look what almost happened to me. Look what I almost did to myself.* When I'd got myself together again, I dialed the second number, the one I knew by heart, and fed quarter after quarter into the machine until it was sated, until it announced that it was willing to connect me.

But this was summer: She was away, and only the machine there to receive me.

"Dean," I said, "it's Jacob Asprey. I'm coming back. You'll have what you need before I arrive. The bill's been paid."

Rolly was waiting in the car, looking over the contract. I sat behind the wheel and turned the key in the ignition. At work I would walk upstairs, find Sally at the tail end of the rush and step into the office, slide her supply closet key back on the ring, and she'd never know how close she'd come to being a part of this thing. The rush over, maybe I'd sit down over a cup of coffee with her, tell her I was going back to school. Then take her hand and say, But maybe I come back on weekends and visit you. In your home.

"Rolly," I said, "thank you."

But he wasn't listening. He was too absorbed in reading the paperwork.

"Get this," he said, grinning, and held up a floorplan. "It's got a basement. A *basement*. For the pool table."

Still no air conditioning.

Let's put it on, I told him, but Rolly's still complaining about his sinuses, he snores and Zooey kicks him out, makes him sleep in the guest room, though we're getting some good airflow in the car as we're driving the long straight stretch past the airport when a beat-up black Econoline van shifted into the passing lane and accelerated alongside, the muffler rattling and roaring, and I nearly drove off the road when I had a glimpse of the driver and passenger both wearing black knit ski masks, just eyes and teeth showing. The passenger turned to look at me and his eyes were dead, dead as those deer's eyes even when he grinned at me through the mouth hole of his balaclava. I looked back to my right. Rolly reading his contracts out loud over the roar of the wind, though he stopped and looked up as the van accelerated hard, hurtled fifteen yards ahead of us, and then came halfway back over the double line as the driver jammed on the brakes in a loud squealing sideways slide that left four smoking tracks of black rubber on the pavement. I stomped the brake to the floor and the Cadillac, suddenly gone grace-less, foundered in my hands, the big boat of a car juddering and chirp-ing to a stop just a few feet from the van, Rolly leaning forward bug-eyed and white in the face, both hands splayed on the dash in front of him and the contracts a confetti mess on his lap and the footwell. The van doors burst open and two men stepped out, each with a sawn-off shotgun in his hand, dressed in army-fatigue jackets and pants with the knit masks, looking like a couple of Balkan terrorists on the job.

"What the *fuck*," Rolly said.

I put both hands up in surrender.

"Wait," I said, "I made a call—"

And then the shorter of the two men reached the car and, coming around to Rolly's side, chopped the barrel of the shotgun into the cen-ter of the windshield, the safety glass exploding in a spiderweb of frosty cracks but holding together. Both doors pulled open and I could smell the fear in the air, that electric note of sweat and tension as shotguns appeared inside the car, the sawn barrel abrading my cheek, the men yelling, *screaming* themselves hoarse for us to *Get the fuck out*. I tried to get out but couldn't. I kept trying to stand up but couldn't get out, kept trying as the one to my left is shouting he's going to blow my fuck-ing *face right the fuck off*, I don't get out, going to do it in *five seconds*, and I hear, almost in a whisper, "Kid. Hey kid."

I turned. Rolly, half out of the car, his two hands raised in surrender and his face white as a fishbelly, said, "Your lap belt, kid," still in that near-whisper, and he reached down and pressed the button. The seat belt slipped liquidly up and off me and suddenly I was free. He was still watching me, pale but his face deadly calm.

"Be cool, kid," he said.

I stepped out into the hot sunlight, the two cups of coffee I'd had before lunch boiling in the back of my throat. The other guy was Quinn, a little bump running down the back of his ski mask where he'd tucked his hair down into his collar, and I watched him pushing Rolly over to the van with the butt-end of his shotgun and telling him *Hands on top of your head, you old fuck.*

I looked back into Colonel Tom's icy eyes.

He said, "Here we go, Jake-O."

As calm and quiet as I could, I said, "Colonel, I made a call."

"Did you now?"

"Colonel, I made a call. It's off. All of this."

His teeth showed in the little mouth hole.

"No, kid," he said, "it would seem that it's very much *on,* wouldn't it?"

We looked together at the van, Rolly around the front of it, and through the windshield I saw that he had his hands up on the hood. A hundred yards up the road a white car idled at the crest of a hill, the driver having realized something bad was happening and unwilling to come closer.

"Colonel," I said, quietly, "I called the bar. I told her that it's off. I'm going to walk away. You take what you need, maybe get this car for your trouble. Do what you want. But I'm not going along with it."

The little mouth hole filled with teeth again.

"Sorry, kid," he said. "You had your chance."

"I'm not going along with it."

"Hey, man," Quinn yelled. "This guy's not looking so hot."

"Two minutes," Tom called back, then looked back to me. "Understand, Jake, it's too late to back out. That'd make problems for me. Which means I got to make problems for you."

"You can make all the problems you want for me. I haven't done anything. I'm out, Colonel."

"Hey, man," Quinn said, his voice sounding tight, "he's not looking good at *all.*"

"Sure, you think you're out," Tom said, "but, see, Jake, it's not just guys outside I know. I know plenty who are *inside*. Know them well. Unpleasant guys who have very little to lose. And one of them might just take a shine to your dad, you pull some stunt like you're talking about here. Were I to tell one of them that maybe you had done me wrong. Okay?"

I licked my lips but failed to bring any words up and out, and he seemed to read assent in my silence.

"By the way," Tom said, "I am *so* a Colonel. Just not in their army. And after this job I'm going to make General. You begin to have any doubts tomorrow, start thinking about changing your mind? You just remember what I said about your dad."

"Hey, man," Quinn said, his voice rising, "this guy's *down*."

But Tom never looked away from me, kept cool, his eyes level on mine. Then he stepped back one step and seemed to give a little nod. Preparing himself for something. And I realized, just a beat too late, what it was he was preparing himself for.

"Sorry, kid," he said. "Here's how we keep it real."

And although I had time to spot the blurred stock of his shotgun flicking my way, saw it in drawn-out slow motion—although I saw it coming so clearly I could read the twelve-point Helvetica inscribed on the stock, I couldn't get out of the way as it clubbed the side of my face. A thousand flashbulbs crackled and I lay down over the baking double yellow line. I had one dizzy moment to notice a piece of quartz stuck in the tread of the van, the pavement hot against my cheek, before the day did a slow dissolve into nothing.

THIRTEEN

U.S. MARSHALL RAYMOND TIBBENS WORE a blue suit like a true G-man, but he also wore a white Stetson cowboy hat and handmade cowboy boots, the sort of clothes you'd expect to see on a wealthy Texas oilman in the business pages of a newspaper. I remembered seeing those boots approaching me as a fourteen-year-old in the Palmyra, New York, police station, feeling that they announced the arrival of a new and wilder paradigm, something I was unaccustomed to, that a frontier of sorts had been met and crossed forever.

When he saw I was awake, Tibbens removed his hat and smoothed back his hair.

"How bad's your pain?" he asked.

"Not bad, if I don't move."

"Where are you?"

"The hospital."

"What day is it?"

"Thursday."

"What's your name?"

"Jacob Cameron Asprey the Second."

"Your father being—"

"The Asprey doing one hundred forty-eight months up in Slippery Rock on fraud, conspiracy, obstruction of justice, witness tampering, and flight from sentencing."

"Also Jake."

I said, "You're the one who brought him in from Palmyra. I guess you ought to already know everything there is to know without asking me."

"I guess I ought to. But a person takes a knock on the head like you did, he may not know it himself. How do you feel?"

"Rolly," I said, and lifted myself up on one elbow, though it fired a thunderbolt of pain down my neck. "Marshall, what about Rolly?"

I'd had a glimpse of him just after the EMT's loaded him into the ambulance, Rolly sitting up on a stretcher with his shirt off and a blood pressure cuff on his arm, an oxygen mask over his mouth and nose, his face white, about to say something to me when they slammed the rear doors to the ambulance and peeled away with the siren broadcasting at full volume. We followed in a second ambulance, no siren, the first one already unloaded in the ER bay when we arrived, the EMT walking me in and giving me an ice pack to press against my cheek while I waited to see the doctor. She whisked in quick, wanted to know if I needed a CT and stood before me with a penlight, checking my pupils and asking, *What is your name* and *Where are you* and *Do you know why you're here?* In the end she said I was fine, they wanted to watch me for a few hours, would give me something for the pain and allow me to lay down, maybe dinnertime I can go home if I sleep and wake up okay, though first the police want to get the details of what happened. But she wouldn't tell me about Rolly, would only say that he was fine in a way that did little to convince me.

Now Marshall Tibbens, leaning forward, elbows on his knees, balancing his hat lightly between two palms, said, "He had an atrial fib, the EMTs thinking maybe he was having a heart attack."

"Is he alive?"

"He's fine. Already complaining about the food, which I guess is a good sign. He'll be okay if he doesn't have any other big scares today. Your aunt's with him now."

"Raymond," I said, "why are you here?"

"I was doing a security detail at a district court in Philipsburg. I heard about this and thought I'd drive over."

If I lived to be a hundred years old I'd never forget that moment, Dad and me in the upstate New York jailhouse, Dad's hands cuffed to the chair behind him, when Tibbens walked in looking like the same oil-man he did today, came right across the room to us and said, *I'm here to bring you in.* Except that day I'd thought he was saying it to me, thought he was telling me that we were both going to jail, and in a strange way I was glad, knowing that I'd at least be with my dad for the rest of the day. And even in that I'd been wrong.

"You wanted to know was I okay," I said, maybe sounding a little ungrateful.

"Something like that," he said. "I know you've had a tough go, and sure, I guess I feel obligated make sure you're okay. I don't have any problem with your dad personally—the man's his own problem—except he gets his son mixed up in his messes, and that's something else entirely."

"I guess this time neither of us can blame him."

"You know what it was all about?"

"Just two guys. They stop us in the middle of the road—"

"Armed pretty good—"

"A couple of shotguns. Like they were going to knock over a bank."

"I don't make it," Tibbens said, not sounding like he's questioning me or trying to catch me in a lie, just seeming genuinely confused, frowning down at the hat balanced between his palms. No wedding ring. "Two guys armed like that, only they don't take the car? After something else, then. What did you say they took off you?"

"I didn't. All I'm missing are my keys and my money clip. I guess the same from Rolly."

"Anything valuable there?"

"The master key to the dealership."

"I mean on you."

"A few closed-out credit cards, maybe forty bucks—"

"The keyring?"

"Car keys, house keys, the key to the gate at work—"

"What's work?"

"I'm a lifeguard."

"What," he said, "like a swimming pool?"

"Exactly."

He sat looking down at his hat for a little while, still seeming confused, and said it again, "I don't make it," then put his hat back on and stood up. "Sorry about the scare. I guess maybe a couple of hardcases mistakened you for folks carrying some money, maybe a bank run for the dealership or something? They get pissed off when they find you've got nothing, let you have a tap in payback. Your uncle's going to be all right." He started to leave, hesitated. "You see your dad lately?"

"Yesterday."

"How is he?"

"He was shaking down another con for twelve cigarettes."

"Cigarettes going to kill that man," he said, and left.

Twenty minutes later an orderly walked me down the hall to see my uncle. Rolly was sitting up in an inclined hospital bed, Zooey beside him holding his hand flat between both of hers and looking about as worried as Zooey can look, which is plenty worried. Rolly bitching that he's *fine*, just wants to go home, though you could see the experience had put the whammy on him, he won't be sneaking those late-night dishes of ice cream anytime soon. A clear oxygen tube hooked over his ears and running under his nose, better color in his cheeks now but still looking ghosted, though I gathered I must have been the one who looked messed up because they both stopped talking when they saw me standing in the doorway. Zooey was out of her chair and crossed the room to hug me as tightly as she dared, saying, "My God,

Jacob, I was so scared for you two when I heard. I thought I had lost both my men."

She made me sit down in her chair.

"I guess I'm okay," I said, and heard the words catch in my throat. The enormity of what I'd done, how deeply I was caught in the quick-sand, arrived in a vivid rush, and suddenly the room was too bright, too hot, a cold slick sweat on the back of my neck. It was downright *physical*, the sensation of watching all your alternatives and options close down, doors locked and bolted forever and leaving just one out-come on offer.

Jacob Cameron Asprey. You are now a criminal.

"What about you?" I asked.

"They're checking my enzymes," Rolly said, "gave me an EKG and a blood thinner. You get a concussion, kid?"

"I don't think so. The doctor said I can go home for dinner."

"They told me the guy belted you right across the face with that shotgun."

"He got me pretty good."

"He give any reason why?"

"No," I said, "he just stepped back and gave a little nod and that was it."

Rolly shook his head, unable to believe something like this could happen in *his* town, more like something you read about going on down in Philadelphia, maybe Pittsburgh.

"They must have wanted the dealership key," he said. "They didn't even take the Caddy. Couple of numbnuts, they think Monty isn't over changing the locks right *now*?"

"Maybe they thought you had a cash delivery for the lot," I said.

"Guy gets mad, me not having the money he thought he was going to get," Rolly said. "So he takes it out on you."

"Will they let you go tonight?"

"He's staying," Zooey said.

"They said *maybe* I get to go," Rolly said.

"He's staying," she said, looking at him sternly. "I'll stay right here with him. Sleep in this chair."

"I'll take care of Coop," I said.

"Horrible to think those men are out there," Zooey said. "You think they live around here?"

"I doubt it," I said.

"They'll get caught," Rolly said. "Guys willing to take a risk like that, don't even take the time to figure out I have the money belt on me first? They're going to make a mistake."

It may have been the painkiller, or just the queasy afterglow of violence, but I began to feel shaky and sick, not sure of my stomach, and walked into the bathroom to put some cold water on my face and neck, Rolly and Zooey bickering about whether he could get some takeout tonight, maybe some Chinese, the Moo Goo Gai Pan he liked, and she's saying, "Rolly, you just don't get it, do you?"

The sight of the stranger in the hospital mirror—framed by antiseptic white light—silenced me. The wrap-up wasn't so bad, really just two butterfly bandages, the first behind my left ear, the second over my left temple, but in both places the skin had split, black blood and Betadine crusted around the bandage, still more spattered on my collar and my left shoulder, maybe more than you'd expect from small cuts like that, and I remembered what Werner had said when I told him I bleed a lot.

Fuck him.

Let him take the stock of a shotgun stock in the face and see how he does.

Another woman in the room now talking with Rolly and Zooey. I stepped out of the bathroom wiping my face on a towel and was introduced to Detective Lisa Solo, maybe thirty? Nice Hispanic looks, thin and a little shorter than me, black hair pulled back in a clip, wearing a lightweight, slim-fitting dark charcoal suit and white shirt open at the collar showing a little more up front than you'd expect, her badge weighing in her breast pocket, talking to Rolly and writing details down in a little notebook. The fingernails bitten down. She asked

Would I like a glass of water, something from the machine before we talk? I said I'd rather we got to it, my heart going a little too quickly, gripping the armrests to steady my hands. I had lied to a cop before. This wasn't my first time. But the last time happened when I was fourteen years old.

"So Mr. Asprey here," she said, consulting her book. "He was telling me two guys by the airport road. Black ski masks, army fatigues—"

"One taller than the other," Rolly said. "The shorter guy with me. Wide, though, like strong, a weight-lifter."

"My guy sort of heavier," I said. "You could see under his jacket he had a little extra weight."

"You get any positive ID on eye color?" she said. "Maybe even hair color?"

"Not me," Rolly said.

"Blue eyes on mine," I said, "I looked right into his eyes. Cornflower blue, I think they're called."

She wrote, saying "Uh-huh."

My heart beating faster now, I turned to Rolly, even though it hurt to do it, sent another good head-clearing jolt of pain down my spine, and said, "And light blond hair on your guy, right, Rolly? When he was pushing you toward the van, some of it curling out under the cap at his neck."

In my mind's eye Quinn shoving Rolly toward the van, the little bulge of his braid showing under the cap where it tucked into the collar of his green jacket.

Rolly frowning at the bedsheet now, trying to think.

"Like your cousin Deena, when she was a baby," I said. "Little bright curls showing under the cap at the neck—"

My dad talking in my head now, coaching me on how to talk after the cop pulled us over for the taillight, convince him to let us go with a warning: *You make him see it, Jake. Don't tell him. Show him. Mom sick in a Toronto hospital, the fever, the doctors frowning at the results—show him, and he'll see it so real in his own mind it'll be like it really happened.*

Lisa had stopped writing and was watching Rolly, listening with what seemed real interest until he looked up at her, clear-eyed.

"Yeah, he's right," Rolly said, nodding, and he looked up, his expression rinsed of doubt. "That was it. Blond hair on my guy."

"You're sure?"

"Just like my cousin, when she was a baby. And big, like a weight-lifter. I could feel how strong he was when he pushed."

She wrote in her book.

"Age?" she asked.

"Could have been anything," Rolly said. "Twenty or forty, I don't know."

She looked at me and I shrugged. Being sure to meet her gaze.

"And they take off you exactly what?" she asked.

"Just what we had in our pockets," he said. "Both of us are down, they go through our pockets and rob us. And then they're gone."

"Your guy say anything to you?"

"He has me around the front of the van, pushing me up against the hot engine. I'm feeling sick, it's so hot already today. I'm scared witless, my ticker really funny, I start to speak, what does he do? He pushes me harder, the black paint over the engine so hot through my shirt it nearly burns me, those waves of warm air rising from the engine block? I say to him, *I'm gonna be sick, you keep shoving me into this.* I try and turn to look at him, he pushes me back against the hot car again, harder this time though, *wham*, and then I start to see all the little fireflies that are circling around us."

"Only there aren't any," I said.

"Only there aren't any," Rolly said. "And it was about five seconds later everything starts to go a little fuzzy. Like there was cotton in my ears, my heart trying to push its way up out of my throat. Not really what you'd call pain, more like—something going wrong in there. I don't think I fell over all at once. I just remember hearing this buzzing sound in my ears, looking at the pavement, on my hands and knees and hearing buzzing, like crickets in the grass."

She wrote and wrote. And then she turned to me.

I could see right away that she had a special interest in me, this Lisa Solo, with her good suit and no-fuss hair and predatory cleavage. This woman had been delayed because she'd been reading up on my dad's file, knew that I was raised rich, the way she probably wasn't, rich by way of fraud and conspiracy, and that this trail had ended with me sitting in the back of a police cruiser outside Palmyra, New York, my dad handcuffed and the lights going with no siren, Dad telling me a story about Granddad shooting the strikebreakers' dog while the cop called in the busted taillight and found that he'd struck gold, a fugitive from a federal sentencing making for Canada. She knew that this was in me, this history, and while I didn't see any suspicion there in her eyes, I did see a level of curiosity that made me more than a little uncomfortable.

"You took a real knock," she said. "I got one of those once, right here?"

She stepped close and turned her head away, revealing a little scar high up on her jawline.

"I have a perp down in an alley," she said, "my knee in his back, I think I'm safe, he gets hold of a brick and lets me have it. I didn't hardly know my name for a couple hours. He warn you or anything?"

I shook my head.

"He just stepped back and nodded," I said. "And then he did it."

"That's what's got me confused, them just stopping you and taking you both out. I make this as a smash and grab, two guys go in a little hotheaded, wanting to get something and get out quick. You think maybe Mr. Asprey, your uncle here, is right about the lot-keys? Your guy ask about a money belt or anything, maybe some cash from a sale?"

"Nothing," I said.

"You provoke him at all?"

She was smiling now, going sly and even a little twinkly on me, inviting me to let her in on my secret, how I'd fucked up in a tense situation on a hot afternoon, nearly got myself and my uncle killed. Maybe figuring I was a little embarrassed to come out with it.

I said, "Maybe I like got a little mouthy when his partner said Rolly wasn't doing so well."

"You mouthed off to a guy carrying a shotgun?" Lisa asked.

Not criticizing me. Sounding genuinely impressed, actually, wondering how I'd found the balls to do it. Wishing she'd been there to see it. And just when I needed them, at the moment when I would have been entirely unable to manufacture them, there they were: more tears, there for the second time that afternoon, and this time no less real than the first. I was crying again. But not for the reason they thought I was.

"Rolly had just had a talk with me," I said, not bothering to swipe my face. I must have made quite a picture, and I felt a little piece of me assent to Colonel Tom and his plan—Jacob Cameron Asprey II, bandages on the side of his face, the victim of a freak outbreak of violence with blood all over his collar and tears rolling down his face. I could see it myself, and the picture held together. "He told me they had decided they would sell the house, give me a loan so I could go back to college in the fall. I'd been stuck here until he told me that. And I guess in that moment, the guy shoving Rolly up against the van while he's looking sick—I guess I was feeling protective of him."

"What did you say to him?" she asked.

Still looking surprised.

"I said, *You assholes don't let him sit down in the shade, give him some water, this is going to turn out a lot worse than a robbery.*"

"No shit," Rolly said, sounding impressed.

"I couldn't help it," I said, and leaned forward the way Tibbens had, put my elbows on my knees and my face in my hands. "My stupid mouth."

"You see this kid?" Rolly asked her, and the tone of his voice wrung a little wince out of me. "The kind of kid tries to do the right thing even when it means a belt in the mouth."

Lisa scratching in her book now, getting it all down.

"Van's most likely stolen," she said. "I bet we find something missing nearby this morning. Maybe they even gave it a little hillbilly paint-job, they tape the lights and use a couple of spray cans in a garage. Let me get a make on that, see what I can turn up. We get lucky there's a security camera somewhere spotted them doing it, maybe someone saw something when they were picking it up. You can get them all kinds of ways." A beat of silence, and then: "Jake."

I looked up.

There I was, *the victim*: cried-out eyes, blood on my collar, bandages. She was holding her card out to me, all signs of amusement gone, just a ferocious interest there in her eyes, she wants to get to the bottom of this.

And all at once I knew she was my doom.

"You think of anything, you call me. And next time," she said, "don't be a hero."

"I won't," I said.

Coop hungry, Coop *starving* and even a little frightened, all but saying *Where you been*, thinking he wasn't going to get to eat tonight with all the lights off in the house as night fell, night putting the real fear in him, that hunger-fear.

I switched all the overheads on, tried to make the house cheerful, even found Rolly's dance show on the television, the same guy leading the show, only this time down in Miami Beach, and he's got his shirt off in the sunlight, girls in bikinis and bare feet on the white sand around him, I'm shaking my head as I dish out Coop's food bowl and pour three fingers of Rolly's bourbon into a glass tumbler, drink half down, step over to the sink and dip my head under the tap, run it cold until I'm shivering a little, stand up again and slick my dripping hair back with my fingers and just let the water run down my neck and collar. Then carry my drink over with a chair to sit and watch Coop eat from a safe five feet. He went *at* the food, arched his back over it to warn away anything or anyone even *thinking* of moving in, but something provoked me—the events of the day, I guess, the heat, hard sun overhead, the smell of blood all over me still, my neck and head aching, sick at heart for putting Rolly in harm's way like that—and I slid my chair a step closer, saw his teeth bare a little even while he kept eating, slid another step forward, two more and I was sitting right there behind him, Coop tense and cocked as a catapult. I had a big drink of the bourbon and reached down slow even as he began a low rolling sound deep in his throat through the eating and snapping at the food, placed my bandaged hand squarely on his back and felt his body humming like a live wire. But he didn't bite me. He went on eating and eating, making that rolling low sound in his throat, and I suppose I would have begun to stroke his fur, except the phone clattered awake, echoing the chiming ring all through the quiet kitchen and empty rooms of the dark house, and even Coop had raised his head and stopped eating.

"I don't make it," Tibbens said.

"Marshall," I said, and switched the phone to my right hand, pressed the chilled glass against my sore left cheek, the cold helping to numb the sensitive cut on my finger. "I had a shotgun pointed at me today. Got knocked out, was in the hospital all afternoon. I've got blood all over my shirt. Just about lost my uncle for good. And to be honest," I said, and meant it, "I'm already feeling a little drunk on this—on this bucket of bourbon I poured for myself. Maybe now isn't the time to talk."

He said, "Anyone out there have a bone to pick with your old man?"

"Every creditor here to Erie."

"Not legitimate, I mean cons. Him consorting with them the way he was at the end, with it all coming down around his ears. With the loan sharks."

"Raymond, to this day I hardly even know what my dad's business *was*. Much less have any sense of the people he was mixing with. If he had some business left open, I'm guessing these people recognized that it was finished from the moment he walked through the gates at Slippery Rock in bracelets."

"Not with debts, though," Raymond said. "Debts, it doesn't matter who with—they go on and on, people wanting to collect half a lifetime later."

In the background I heard the sound of a juke, the low murmur of bachelors on the make, and realized he was out, just like the rest of us trying to find someone to sleep next to at night, except he was fucking it up by thinking about his work. I pictured him with a first marriage somewhere in his history, maybe even a kid, something that didn't work out because he was always away, distracted even when he was around because he couldn't let the day go. And that worried me, that he couldn't let me go.

"What if you had a talk with him?" Tibbens asked. "Maybe visited him, asked if there were any outstanding grudges there—"

"I see him Wednesdays, he gets one visitor a week."

"I could get you in there," he said. "Tomorrow."

"It can wait."

"Truth, Jake?"

I tipped the glass back and had a long drink.

"Sure," I said. "Why not?"

"It bothers me when I see how the kids get involved. Every door I walk through, there's an unhappy kid on the far side. Just last week I go in a house in Yountville in my windbreaker, a pump shotgun in my hand, two men around back. This tubby kid is sitting on the couch eating Froot Loops and playing a video game. He freezes with the spoon halfway to his mouth. I say, *Where's your daddy?* He hesitates. Says, *Dad's down in the basement.* We stand there looking at each other for a moment, and I hear *tap tap* on the back door glass, the rear team wondering if they need to come in yelling. I say to the boy, *If I go downstairs and he's really upstairs, you buying him time, he might get it in his head to run, and I might have to use this.* And the kid says, *He's upstairs in bed.*"

"You have to admire the kid."

"See, you're missing the point. This boy's eating cereal, playing video games, and his poppa the bank robber is upstairs. The kid doesn't lie because he's trying to protect his dad. He does it because he's wondering who's going to take him to school if I take Dad away in the back of a squad car. It's not loyalty, Jake. It's *fear*."

"Leave it alone, Marshall," I said.

"You think I *want* to be this way?"

"It was a one-time thing," I said, "what happened today. A robbery."

"I don't make it."

"You already said that."

"I make this having to do with your dad. And I'm sitting here trying to have a beer and instead I'm thinking maybe I could help you out, help you get beyond this. I think what happened today had to do with some old business that never got settled. We find the ones who did it, maybe we help you put it all behind you."

"Trust me," I said, "it's behind me."

"I can get you *in* there, outside normal visiting hours," he said.

"I bet you can," I said, and hung up on him.

I remained at the counter for a moment, my hand absently resting on the phone. Something not right—no, worse, something just plain *wrong* here. I reached up to snap the switch beside the television on. The bright floodlight drenched the elm tree and the table and chairs in its fluorescent shimmer, revealing no one.

I'm alone.

Only something's not *right*.

Coop shrinking away from me now, his tail tucked in and his ears back on his head as he backed away. Retreating from the cellar. I turned to address the door—gapped open a crucial inch or two—and moved one step closer, then two, moving as carefully and deliberately as I had when I put my hand on Coop's back a moment ago.

Down the stairs in the dark, pulse surging in my temples, hearing each quiet footfall on the dry wood stairs, the house groaning and sighing and settling. At the last stair I reached up to flip the light switch.

The naked bulb bright overhead revealing the Magician sitting back in the easy chair in a tailored black suit, squinting into the burning bulb, a glass of bourbon over ice in his hand, his legs crossed and his hat dropped over his right wing tip.

FOURTEEN

HE KEPT HIS GAZE LEVEL on me as he swirled the ice in his drink, had a sip, then set his glass down on the side table. With nimble fingers he plucked a cigarette from his breast pocket and offered me one.

"It has been a long time, Jake," he said.

"I didn't know you were out."

Tico lit his cigarette and lay his head back, breathing out smoke, watching me. The hair had lost some of its color but otherwise he looked the same—deeply tanned no matter what time of year, hair slicked back like an Italian gangster from the twenties, oil-black waxed chevron mustache, tall and gone just a tiny bit to seed but the cut of his expensive suit bringing him a long way back.

"Good behavior, you know," he said, "it is making a difference in my sentence. I rehabilitate cons, show them how to do their taxes, give classes. In Starke I am not the Magician. In Starke they are all calling me the Professor. I have it good there, help the bulls with their retirement funds for free, maybe a five-twenty-nine for the twins, and they are making money off me, they don't let anyone mess with me, make sure I don't have to smoke anyone's cigar. I wonder, does your father have it so good?"

"I guess you figured you'd see yourself in."

"I call a friend at the hospital, he tells me you are released, your uncle staying the night with his wife, I figure it's a good chance we should talk."

"We could have met somewhere."

"You should be locking your door. So trusting, these suburban neighborhoods, thinking there are no criminals out there who want to do them harm. In stir I am learning the value of a locked door. You can't get out, sure. But then also no one else can get *in*."

"Tico," I said, "how did you get past Coop?"

He shrugged.

"Your Coop," he said, "I take one look at him, right away I can see with him it is food. There on the other side of the glass, baring his teeth at me but glancing now and then at his food bowl. Wondering *where is my Jake, when will I be eating next?* He is showing his teeth but what he is saying is, *Let's make a deal.* So I have the driver take me to the corner market, get him an entire box of bones. I expect it to take half the box before we are friends, but you know how many it is taking, Jake?"

"One."

Tico clapped his hands together once and laughed at the ceiling.

"I offer him one and it is all over," he said, "we are agreed to be friends. I give him the rest of the box as a favor, show him how it is with us."

"Just don't pat him while he's eating," I said. "You may be surprised."

He reached over his shoulder and tapped his cigarette ashes behind the chair, the con reflexes still ingrained, a long time before he will unlearn them.

"You and me, Jake, we should be friends, too," he said. "We throw each other a bone, why any need to be fighting, maybe some bad blood in the past but what is that to us now? I never spoke against your father. Your father never spoke against me. In this way we demonstrate that everyone is friends."

"He'd have served no more than twenty-four months if he testified against you."

"And yet he didn't. A man of principles."

"Some might say a stupid man."

De Soto shrugged, adjusted himself in the seat.

"Once you decide to become a criminal," he said, "all you have is your word that you won't talk. It's why life is hard in prison for people who talk. How is my friend Jake?"

"He looks good. I saw him Wednesday."

"And he is the same?"

"Yes," I said, "exactly the same."

"Credit to a man, he goes in the hole and emerges as himself."

"He'll be different when he gets out. No more of that business."

"I am wishing I could agree. But your father—he is beautiful, a true specimen. He took the matter as far as anyone would have dared. And then he carried it further. To bring him out and tell him to walk the line—like telling a thoroughbred she cannot run anymore. You can tell her, but will she listen?"

"He's seen where he'll end up."

"And yet he cannot help himself. The true nature makes itself known. As with you. In your business with Colonel Tom and the butcher."

I leaned against the wall, my legs suddenly gone a bit unsteady under me.

"How much do you know?" I asked.

He seemed surprised.

"How much do I know?" he asked. "More than you, Jake. More than you."

I considered this for a moment, and felt the need of my drink, the glass perspiring now on the upstairs counter.

"Wait," I said, and walked upstairs to retrieve my glass.

Coop lay in the center of the kitchen floor, muzzle flat on the ground, splayed out like a well-fed dog ought to be, and nothing but his eyes moving as he guiltily watched me cross the kitchen. I might have been angry with him but the truth was that I understood. I felt like telling him things were tough all over.

"I hope it was worth it," I said.

Found out, he whined once, gulped and swallowed and made sad eyes. I poured the two fingers of bourbon and padded back downstairs, sat across from Tico in the same folding chair where Rolly, defeated, had watched me run his table.

"Tell me what you want," I said.

He lay back his head and blew a perfect smoke ring. Enjoying himself, warming up.

"Everyone is going to make a lot of money off this," he said. "And after the money is made, some old debts are finally canceled."

"You owed Colonel Tom?"

"You have things backward."

"Colonel Tom owes you."

He nodded.

"And your father owes Colonel Tom," he said.

"He told me that debt was paid."

"Well sure," Tico said, "he *is* a terrific liar."

"What was it for?"

"I lend Colonel Tom thirty thousand dollars," Tico said. "He tells me it is for a personal loan, a man he knows is good for it, a man can be trusted. I don't even ask who, I wish to God I had." He lay back his head and blew another smoke ring. "It would have saved me plenty of trouble. Because if I had learned who it was, I would have known this man was never going to pay the money back."

"He blew it all? Trying to ease the way with a few bribes to witnesses, get them to recant—"

"No," Tico said, "even better. Jake, he is deciding that he is wanting to give his son a chance at a real life, not a father in prison but a real life, school, everything, so instead of using the money to make the bribes, what the man decides to do is this: He splits and tries to start over in Canada."

"Except this man," I said, "he has a busted taillight. Being penny-wise."

"Too fucking cheap to fix it, figuring he can charm his way out of a fix."

"And a bored cop in Palmyra spots it, pulls him over—"

"With thirty grand in his trunk and a warrant out."

"It was fifteen. I heard Colonel Tom say he was only going to get fifteen."

"Yes," Tico said. "That was the agreement, he gets fifteen, and then, if Colonel Tom sees a few months later he is having luck with it, he gets another fifteen. The problem is that on the way out of town he is breaking into the shed in the woods behind the bar and he is stealing that second fifteen. Punch the glass, smash and grab, and an extra fifteen large of my money is riding on his hip."

"Right," I said.

"So you see the problem," Tico said. "We've got fifteen gees plus fifteen gees stolen plus vigorish on the entire thirty with interest over the lifetime of the unpaid loan and anyway the insult of it all."

"It's a lot of money."

"But we're all friends, here. Everyone understands everyone else. We make dispensations, everyone goes home happy. The problem is just what comes after, everyone wondering if you are your father's son. He made a mistake, but he kept quiet after. I am wondering if you understand the value of staying quiet, too. Everyone here is wondering if you can do the kind of silence we need."

"It was stupid of you to involve Kimber. She's a child."

He shook his head, amused.

"Jake," he said, "you know so little."

"Say it, Tico. It was stupid. Unwise."

"Jake," he said, "this is not our first job with the girl. Okay?"

Sally, your sister is in trouble. Take it a step farther: *And now I am, too.*

"Kimber, she has already proven herself," he said. "Colonel Tom grooming her slowly, showing us that we can trust her to be silent for this job, for that job. Perhaps too eager to be paid, but that is to be expected. Even so, she knows next to nothing with this one, Jake. Because this is our best and brightest job. She only knows that we will give her five large if she uses what she has at hand to convince you to work for us. This is enough. Like all children, all she wants is the bright shiny car, the new life somewhere else, maybe convince herself someday she will be a television star."

He set down his drink, plucked his hat off his shoe and rose to his full height, adjusting his hat over his eyes. I lay back in the chair and looked up at him, the naked bulb behind him casting him in hard silhouette, just his cold blue eyes showing beneath the hat brim.

"So," he said, "we are agreed?"

"Yes," I said, though I had no idea what I was agreeing to. It didn't matter, anyway, because this had all been decided. It was going to go forward all on its own, now. "I can—I can do silence."

"Good boy," he said.

I watched him ascend the stairs, heard the thump of Coop's tail on the kitchen floor, heard the Magician's murmured approval, and then the oily click of the latch as he closed the door behind him.

FIFTEEN

A FREAK THUNDERSTORM AT SUNRISE: Through the window I'm watching big sweeping ocean liners of storm clouds on the way to Iceland, the weather gods giving them a festive send-off, bottle rockets and Roman candles and sparking pinwheels, cleaving the air with their bullwhips and camera-flashes. Intensely awake, dry-mouthed and wretchedly hungover, the entire left side of my face tender to the touch, I watched an inch of rain boil the yard in fewer than ten minutes—and not five minutes later the clouds are stepping aside, gutters running rainwater, and the driveway edge a surging stream with the sky dawning an astonishing postcard blue overhead.

It was strange being downstairs in the kitchen alone, no Rolly having his endless argument with the newspaper headlines, no Zooey talking him down from his high-cholesterol ledge. Rolly would be okay. He'd come home from the hospital, life slipping back into its familiar groove, but I sensed that I was forever changed. And it felt like a parting, a sundering of sorts from my old life when, wincing at the first sip of coffee, I activated my tired cell phone and discovered that I'd missed three calls from Kimber. She's just a kid, and what does a kid do? She keeps hammering at something until she gets what she wants.

Or she keeps hammering at it until it breaks.

The warm damp must have been terribly inviting to those things that do typically avoid the dry heat of day, because I counted three different snakes making quick silent whips off into the high grass as I padded up the slate walk to the pool. Word gets around fast: fast enough that someone knew I'd be without my keys today, had unlocked the place for me. Guardhouse, too, and not five minutes into skimming the pool surface of leaves, sun diamond-hard overhead now, Kimber called a fourth time. Speaking on a cell phone while on duty was strictly forbidden. But then so was smoking, and I was already breaking that rule, finishing a Winston from the pack I'd picked up on the way to work.

"They haven't paid me," Kimber said.

"Tough luck," I said.

"Oh, sure, the three of you like an old boys' club. Just like last time, the time before that, the time before *that*. Months before they get around to paying me."

"Kimber," I said, "they haven't paid me a dime either."

"Maybe we ask the Colonel about it—"

I pictured Rolly reaching down to unclasp the belt trapping me in the car.

Watched it slip liquidly up and away in my mind's eye.

Be cool, kid.

I said, "He's going to tell you the same thing I'm telling you."

"Which is?"

You see how I have to spell this shit out?

"Which is," I said, "to sit tight and relax."

"Thing is, Jake, I've got my eye on this shiny black Camaro. And I'm worried it's going to get bought right out from under me. Now wouldn't that disappoint me?"

Noise now off to my left, someone shouting on the golf course.

I dipped the ember of my cigarette into the pool and pitched it over the tall hedge that divided the deck and the West Gate parking lot—the back lot, where a decidedly downmarket array of staff cars were hidden from public view. "We're all going to have to wait. You, me, Colonel Tom. Everyone's going to have to wait until it's all played out. That producer you're going to find at Formosa? He'll still be there next week. And if he isn't, there'll be another one just like him stepping in to take his place, with a little gold lighter ready for your lonely cigarette."

I'm thinking: *Anyway, Kimber, you can't even fucking smoke in bars in Cali anymore. So what does that say about your dated dream? It says that your time has already come and gone. It says that even your dreams are sad and underimagined.*

More noise off to my left, down the gentle hill, someone shouting again, one of the groundskeepers near the sand trap on the seventh hole waving a mechanic on a golf cart over. The mechanic stopped his cart by the trap and hopped out to have a look, even from this distance their body language telling me they're unsure of what to do next. Two men who use their hands all day, fix cars and put in fences and change oil, men who aren't afraid to get their hands involved, now they're standing back in perfect mirror image of each other, looking down at the sand trap rubbing the backs of their necks and afraid to touch a thing. The groundskeeper shrugged and pointed up to Werner's office, his body language saying, *Get him, tell him,* and the mechanic nodded, went back to the cart and picked up a walkie-talkie, spoke briefly into it before hearing a crackling squawk back and returning to the sand trap to rub his neck and look down at what was there.

"I hear you, Jake," she said, "but thing is—"

"This is exactly what Colonel Tom was *talking* about. You give them any sign you're anxious, in a rush? They're going to get *worried*. You don't want people like that worried. You don't know what they're capable of."

She was quiet for a long beat, and for a second I feared I'd lost her, it had all unraveled that quickly. She'd call up Colonel Tom and say *I want*, and we'd have a problem. Because it's that easy for the little seed of doubt to get planted good and deep.

"All right," she said. "I can wait."

I hopped up on the lowest rung of the white fence but still couldn't see what the men were looking at.

"You're going to be the first to get paid," I said, trying to make my voice soothing now. "Everything nice and relaxed until then, yeah?"

Thing is, I wasn't feeling relaxed, either. I was already feeling like I'd need another cigarette to get me through until it was time for the next cigarette.

"You'll call me up?" she asked. "Let me know."

"I'll let you know."

Kimber quiet for another moment.

"Two nights ago," she said. "Sally came back late. I'd thought she was at work but she was dressed in that lucky green shirt of hers, tipsy. I said *Where you been, the Oscars?* And you know what she said?"

"*Out,*" I said.

"Exactly. *Out,* she said, and then she went upstairs."

The groundskeeper down on his hands and knees now, peering into the trap.

"She look angry?" I asked.

"No, she looked relieved, far away, like dreamy? And as soon as she left the room, I actually said it. I said, *She was with Jake.* And she was, wasn't she?"

"Yes."

"What happened that night?"

Werner and Hippolyte, the head greenkeeper, walking down the hill now toward the sand trap, Werner buttoning his coat like he was getting ready for an interview, Hippolyte looking like he needed a drink more than usual. I identified.

"That's up to her to tell you," I said. "Or not."

"What happened?"

"Kimber," I said, "drop it."

She paused, and I felt it happen: all sense of control leaving me, a sensation that exactly resembled that moment in the car with her when, at the touch of her hair, all strength had left me.

"Tell me," she said quietly, "or I'm going to the Colonel today, let him know I'm getting nervous about getting paid."

So that was where we stood. Kimber not afraid to take the whole thing down, or too stupid to understand, even if she was just trying to get her way. I guess I would have been frightened if I weren't so wide open to what was coming my way. Because I'd just realized how it worked, when you joined another person in a crime: You were in it together, like some blighted marriage with no love but all the same mortal stakes at play in every remark, every glance.

"She told me," I said, "that your father wouldn't let her see me."

"Why not?"

"Because my father is a thief."

"They paid me five grand to soften you up, get your heart on a stick," she said, her tone acid. "And it wasn't even me who got you. It was Sally. Always Sally, the one the boys want. They want to fuck me, but she's the one they want to fall in love with. They want to go to bed with me, but she's the one they want to wake up with in the morning. And you're no—you're no different than the rest. You're in love with her, aren't you?"

"Yes," I said.

"Well," she said, "ain't that just fucking *sweet.*"

The thing about cell phones is that no one hangs up on anyone anymore—the punctual *click*, the *crack* that used to announce that the conversation was over. Now they're just with you one moment, gone the next.

She was right. That was how cross-purposed I was. I wanted Kimber in my bed, but I didn't want anything else to do with her. I think it hurt her to know that love was out there, that others could have it, whereas her only recourse was to poison it, to cancel it, to make it gone.

Werner looking down into the sand trap now, more composed than the others, though I was guessing he was merely disguising his unease as impatience. I walked around the pool and climbed the ladder to the lifeguard stand and shaded my eyes, but even from that high perch I couldn't see what they were looking at, so I left my phone on the chair, climbed back down, and hopped the fence.

"Just leave it as it is, gentlemen," Werner was saying as I reached them. "Just wait for the authorities, we don't want to complicate or confuse things."

"What's this?" I asked.

All four heads turned to me in unison.

"Break-in," the groundskeeper, still on his hands and knees, said.

"What," I said, "we were robbed?"

"As of yet," Werner said, "we haven't found anything missing."

"How did they get in?"

"Through the kitchen," Werner said. "They would have been after the safe."

I'm thinking, *But no, Werner, what you couldn't know, what I know, is that they were after that buried bolt leading to the supply closet. Which opens at one end into the kitchen, the other into the grounds wing. But that's where things go dark for me, too. Because I don't know what someone would want down there. I don't know what they'd be after.*

I stepped closer and peered over the edge of the trap—and I was entirely unsurprised, I was almost *comforted*, when I saw two loose keys resting there in the sand, partially embedded in the trap by the heavy rain that had run through. The first one mine. The second one Sally's. As if the person in possession of them had run out of uses for them and had decided to leave them for whoever came next.

"These being the keys they used," Werner said.

"Whose?" the groundskeeper asked.

"Mine," I said.

"Were you in on it?" the groundskeeper asked, and looked to the mechanic with a grin, the grin saying, *Because his dad—he's the one who—his dad is—*

"You want me to kick your teeth in?" I asked.

"Gentlemen," Werner said quietly, "how'd you like to be docked a day's pay?"

I turned and walked away, not up toward the pool but following the slight curve of the hill to the right, around the squat elm toward the West Gate, where the lot opened onto the course and the staff carts came through, the groundskeeper saying something behind me under his breath, too quiet for me to hear, though I guessed it was rooted in the same subject as just about every other cheap insult anyone ever bothered to send my way.

Coming around the elm I'm seeing that *this* is where the snakes I spooked had come to hide out from the humid heat—here in the cooler shade of the elm, where the grass had been allowed to grow ankle-high—because for a moment it seemed as if the grass had come *alive*, so many quick curling lines whipping deep into the bluegrass, even the snakes running from me as I'm striding up toward the opened gate, this being the spot they would have come onto the grounds: no cameras. Colonel Tom and Quinn would have padlocked it on their way out, a groundskeeper probably having opened it back up coming through on a cart first thing in the morning. I stood there in the shade, my skin prickling into goose bumps, it's like I can *smell* them here, and taking a knee in the grass I can see tire tracks in the wet grass where ordinarily there would only be signs of the narrow wheels of the carts going in and out. I gave the tracks a rough kick and smear with my flip-flop, swept the grass up and over itself, then reversed direction, turning back around quick and ducking out from under the elm onto the lawn. Two police cars cruising slow up the main drive between the alder trees, bright-colored rollers going but no sirens, headlights on high beams even in the heat of day, as if they were driving toward a funeral. I glanced back toward the West Gate before I hopped the fence to the pool, relief slowly threading its way through my blood like an anesthetic.

They don't even know how you came in.

A call I had to make up ahead of me: something I didn't much feel like doing, because it was going to set so many other problems in motion.

But I had to make that call, because *not* making it would set worse problems in motion. I removed the card with the number from my money clip, then climbed the ladder to the lifeguard chair to retrieve my phone. Two more police cars rolling up the long curved drive now.

She answered on the first ring.

A muffled *boom* rocking the sky as across town they dynamited the quarry.

"I know why they robbed me and Rolly," I said.

SIXTEEN

"SO THEY WANTED YOUR KEY," she said. "Not Rolly's key, *yours.*"

"For the kitchen entrance," I said.

Half an hour later, Lisa sitting across from me up in the dining room, the place taped off and being photographed, the forensics team in the back dusting everything down. No mere breaking and entering smash-grab, these had been professional thieves who had left only the ghost of an entry behind—not one hair, not one print. Her notebook out only she's not writing anything, her coffee gone cold in front of her, dressed the same way, the smart slim suit, the white shirt open a little too much below the vertical architecture of her throat. And let's agree on this— that the extra button she'd left open was a test, and so far I had failed to draw a passing grade. The thing about cleavage is, it's a full-time job. Going around all day not noticing it, or pretending not to notice it, is work, and it's murder. And we don't even know why we like it.

"The key," I said, "it's good for the West Gate, the pool gate, the guardhouse, the kitchen."

"You ever use that entrance?"

"Never. I just unlock the pool gate and open the guardhouse and I'm in business."

"Why does your key work on the kitchen?"

"They must have installed them all together, bought one round of locks for the help and figured, *Well, it's easier to manage one set of keys.* No reason to separate us. The West Gate, the pool, the kitchen. That's how all the lowest level employees come in, where our parking lot is. The guys who do grounds maintenance, the janitors."

"And you."

"And me."

"You're not allowed to come in the main gate?"

"No, we have our own back drive and everything. They don't want the members feeling like they have to mingle with the staff coming and going. Us coming up that nice alder-lined drive over there in our shitty cars. Which I guess would complicate the exclusivity or something."

"Sounds pretty fucking aristocratic," she said, "if you ask me."

I was dressed in my red trunks and the white T-shirt with the red cross over the heart, flip-flops on my feet, my phone in my pocket in case Zooey wants to give me an update on the tests Rolly was getting today. In other words: looking like I was staff. There had been a time when I'd been proud of the lifeguard emblem on my breast. But that feeling had passed. Now this was just another uniform.

"That's the whole idea," I said. "A Bentley parked next to a Camaro—it's like a category error. Each shaming the other."

"The West Gate is a back lot—"

"Where the trash Dumpsters are, trucks for moving heavy stuff, the staff carts are supposed to go in and out through there. That sort of thing. Hidden from the pool and the seventh hole by a hedge. The staff always going there to smoke cigarettes, even though they're not supposed to. We maintain it for ourselves, so nobody from management even looks in there—"

"Let me guess," she said. "No cameras."

She slid her coffee cup around on the linen for a moment.

"So they walk in the staff drive," she said, figuring it out. What would Bethenny have thought of Lisa Solo—this beautiful woman with her loaded weapon and her cleavage, her chummy solicitude? Bethenny would have said she admired her. And then she'd have tried to seduce her, and in the morning would slag her out. "A couple of guys. Maybe park down the road. Help me see it. They have good cover there?"

"Excellent," I said.

"Then unlock the—"

"The West Gate."

"Yeah, the West Gate, walk around the front of the pool. Still no cameras, because the dumb fucks trained them all on the main entrance, thinking they're protecting the rich ladies from having their jewels snatched. Then maybe use your key for the kitchen? You know Sally, right? The chef?"

"Since we were kids."

"What do you think of her?"

For a moment I thought she was asking me the same question Kimber had asked earlier—I thought Lisa was asking, *Do you love her?* And then realized that wasn't what she wanted to know. That wasn't what was on her mind at all.

I said, "Why do you ask?"

Lisa shrugged, though she seemed to have a clear idea what she was after. And suddenly I'm not feeling so hot.

"Investigator tells me they did a quick account of everyone who is supposed to have keys granting access to this door," she said. "Like you said: you, the staff. And one other key comes up missing. That second key you saw in the trap: It was Sally's."

"Her key to the kitchen door?"

"No, to the supply closet."

"Somebody took it off her."

"Yeah, but she doesn't have a *story*. You take a shotgun butt to the face in broad daylight, that's how you lost yours. I asked her, *How did you lose it?* And she doesn't know."

"If she knew how she'd lost it she wouldn't have lost it."

"You know how *you* lost *yours*. I asked her again, I get the same thing. She said she locks that key ring in the safe every night, gets it out in the morning to get into the supply closet, use the smaller key on the same ring to unlock her desk drawers. The rest of the day it's sitting there on her desk. Every penny in that safe was still there this morning, which tells me they didn't get in and get the key that way. Even the most principled criminal will take what he can get, even if he's after something else. No, they took it off her, only she doesn't know how or when. Isn't that funny?"

The twinkly look back now, she's inviting me to participate, take the bait, agree with her that it's a little strange Sally doesn't know how she lost it.

"The way she talks about you," Lisa said, "I can tell there's something there. Maybe something serious. I'm not *too* worried about it. But then sometimes I'm thinking, well, a girl like that—I mean a real beauty, Jake, don't you think?—a girl like that, maybe you'd feel obliged to go the extra mile to protect her."

"She hasn't done anything wrong."

"Then why does it sound as if you're protecting her?"

I'm sweating now, despite the frosty air conditioning, the calm conversation.

"It doesn't matter what it sounds like," I said. "Not if what I'm saying is true."

"But her story doesn't hold together. *Where did you lose it? I don't know.*"

"You're telling me you think she was involved?"

"Hey, I didn't say that, Jake—*you* said that. But let's just suppose— let's just go ahead with that little thought of yours, that Sally was involved. When it comes to the subject of drug dealers—a subject about which I happen to know a very great deal—what you do is you begin with what you know and build from there. Break it down into simple facts. Do you know, Jake, what the number-one day job is for a male narcotics dealer looking to set up a fence? He works in construction. You know what the number-one job is for a female narcotics dealer?"

She dipped her head toward the kitchen, as twinkly as ever.

"The hours, the fringe types—" I said.

"That's right," she said, nodding, "kitchen work."

"Not as if she's a fucking line cook, detective. She runs the place."

"Right. So we're assuming the whole thing is a misunderstanding, your idea that she was involved. We asked her if it was all right if we go over a few questions. And the answers she gave pointed to a whole lot of nothing. The answers were a whole lot of *I don't know*. And we didn't like that."

"Who is we?"

"We?" she asked. "Well, we is me."

"You're involved in this now?"

"Yesterday, what happened to you, that was my bit. But two felony crimes within twenty-four hours, so close together, I'm inclined to see them as connected. So this business—I'm making it my business."

I looked around at the taped-off room.

Get this: The cops had brought *in* cups of bad coffee.

Be cool, kid.

"What felony? There's no felony here," I said. "Werner himself said nothing's missing. A couple of strung-out teenagers walk in with my key, thinking they'll try Sally's key on the safe. The moment they're in they see it's a dial entry, their plan's fucked, and they walk out. They're probably back in Trenton already, working on their next job."

Lisa shaking her head before I'm even finished.

"These guys planned out a job," she said, "knew who you were, what you had, how to get it. Not afraid to break a few bones to do it. Knew where they had to gain entry, knew the lay of the club. Even knew where the cameras were and were not, how they have to walk in so they don't get a positive ID, walk in the—in the West Gate, around the front along the course, up around and into the kitchen with your key. You don't pull a job like that unless you've got a clear idea of what it is you're after. You don't do a break-in this way if what you want is what's in the cash register. For that, you put a piece on Sahib down at the Uni-Mart."

"You know how lost you sound? Telling me Sally has *anything* to do with this?"

"I hear this all day long. This piece of shit who liked to choke the baby whenever his girlfriend left for work? Yesterday his mother tells me, *He's a good boy.* And I sympathize with her, Jake. Because I think she really believes that, that he's a good boy. I understand you have something for Sally. That I'm not questioning. Like I said—tall, green eyes, long dark hair. Built like a clothes model, maybe goes one-ten and five foot eight. Lost her parents. Can cook like an angel, from what I understand. It makes you go weak in the knees just thinking about it. Jake, *I'm* weak in the knees for her, and I don't even go in for women, mostly. I'm not saying the girl you know did this. I'm just wondering if you know her as well as you think you do. I'm wondering if the girl you *don't* know had something to do with this."

"I don't get it. You're supposed to be helping me."

"I am helping you, Jake. I'm your best friend. I'm helping you gain a little perspective."

She stood up, closed her book and placed it in her breast pocket. Those nails bitten down so far they told a second story, a story of worry and sleepless nights, of an understanding of the forces she could and could not control.

"Truth is," she said, "any fool can see Sally wasn't in on it. Not that she knew of. But she may know more than she believes. They wanted her key, thought it would get them something after they were in with *yours.* Maybe they were just mistaken, thought it was for the safe, I don't know. But that's relevant. That's *important.*"

"Where is she now?"

"In the back," Lisa said. "You want to see her?"

Then the slow trip through the dining room into the back, my eyes focused on the back of Lisa's head as she padded ahead of me up the carpeted center aisle and through the double doors, into the high bright antiseptic light of the kitchen, cops everywhere, photographers' strobes crackling every third or fourth second with the fizzy flashes of old-time cameras, the air stinking of cop humor and cop boredom and the lazy zeal of cop tenacity, moving slow but knowing they were going to get you in the end, and in the back office where she always did her receipts Sally was sitting with a cup of water forgotten in front of her. Only she wasn't sitting in *her* chair—she was sitting in the low folding chair beside the desk, the staff hot seat she used when she brought someone in to tell him he was dogging it. She looked at me, and for a moment I saw no recognition in her eyes at all, and I realized immediately that she *got it*, that she knew there were people of consequence present who suspected her.

"Sally," Lisa said, "I brought your friend Jake from way back here to say hi. He was just telling me you all have been friends since kindergarten. And you look like you could use a friend right now, all this uncertain stuff hanging over you, these things going missing that you can't explain."

It was relevant, too, in that moment, that Sally was more attractive than Lisa. Sally did effortlessly what Lisa was working to pull off daily. Two women in a room: Matters of personal power are always going to come up. With men, they just size each other up and immediately know, and the matter is solved. But with women the warfare is conducted in subtler ways, and the outcome is always uncertain. Only Sally wasn't participating. Sally was just staring off into middle ground, the light of the desk lamp revealing her bone structure in pale fluorescent shades.

"Hi, Jake," she said, "I guess they had my supply closet key. She tells me it's outside in one of the traps. I just don't know how they got it off me. I had it yesterday morning, today I pull the ring out of the safe and it's gone."

She looked around the office, then back at me, her gaze settling on the bandages, the bruises, and I felt a poisonous satisfaction as I measured the impact of my damage, realizing once again that Colonel Tom had been right. I felt an urge to call him up and say, *Thanks. Thanks for the beating.*

"What happened to you?" she asked. "Your *face*, Jake."

"Two guys," I said. "They stopped us on the airport road. Me and Rolly, yesterday."

"He took a shotgun butt to the face," Lisa said, leaning against the doorway, a clear note of approval in her voice. "I guess they wanted his key, too. To get in the side door."

"Rolly's all right?" Sally asked.

"He'll be fine, had a good scare but okay," I said. "He stayed in the hospital last night."

Sally seemed to retreat back into that middle ground again.

"This is nuts," she said, sounding numb, almost drugged, looking into her cup of water. "This makes no sense. What were they after, coming in here?"

"We're still figuring that out," Lisa said.

"What," Sally said, "like they didn't rip anything off?"

"They haven't found anything missing," I said.

"I'll let you catch your breath," Lisa said, "maybe come back in a while and we talk, try and figure out just how you lost that key, when maybe it happened? That's really what we need to figure out. These people knowing the lay of the place, I'm wondering if any new staff leap to mind. I'll speak to Werner about recent hires, try and get a bead on someone may have had some trouble in the past, maybe could have handed a job along to some friends?"

She stood there in the doorway for a moment, expecting some sort of response from Sally.

"Thing is," she said, "what's bothering me is why get *your* key, Jake? These are people who clearly knew the lay of the place, knew what key went where. So I'm wondering—yes, I'm wondering why they get your key for first entry, when it's clear our Miss Sally here has everything they need. Both keys, I mean. Isn't that funny?"

I licked my lips but before I could answer she gave a little nod, no connections there yet but clearly something forming, and then she ducked out of the little office, leaving the two of us alone, the sound of her heels retreating down the center aisle toward the main office.

"This is nuts," Sally said again, and picked up her water but only looked into it.

"Don't let them make you nervous."

"Nervous? No, Jake, they don't have me nervous. They have me wondering if I'm going to prison tonight."

"Don't think that way."

"Guy wants me to go down to the precinct, answer questions. I told him, *Hey, maybe I'm supposed to have a lawyer around for something like that,* and you know what that fucker said to me? He said, *Hey, we can whistle up a lawyer for you, if that's how you want it to go down.* And then he smiled, like we were talking about the weather."

I sat in the desk chair, took the glass from her and set it down.

"They know you had nothing to do with it," I said. "Lisa herself just told me that. A couple of lowlifes took the key off you, same as they took one off me, only they didn't have to crack you in the face to get yours."

"Like the thing with Werner, though," she said, "the kid drowning last month. It wasn't his fault. But people are going after him anyway. Because they want someone to pay."

She went away again, then seemed to come back all at once, leaned over the desk and held my chin in her fist just like Zooey, turning my face off to the right so she could study the bandage on my temple.

"And look at me," she said, "going off the rails when you're the one who went in the hospital. When you're the one who got hurt. Look at your face. They could've killed you."

"At least it was quick."

She took my hand in both of hers, my palm up, tracing the lines there as if trying to read my fortune, and the little office, with its humming fluorescent lamplight and no window, seemed suffocating and close, a notch too warm, and I realized that I was scared of her, I was *terrified* of her and how close she was to finding me out, wanted to get out of there and get away. Except it wasn't the space or the light or the heat that was suffocating me—it was the weight of dishonesty, and only one way to unburden myself.

"Isn't it strange?" she said. "How all these awful things keep bringing us together?"

"Things that are out of our hands."

"As if there's a design to it. Maybe we're unlucky people. Or maybe we bring it on ourselves."

"Neither. We're not unlucky people. We don't invite it in."

"Maybe it's me, bringing all this on you. I always wondered about that, I lose one parent, then the next, think I'm bad luck. My therapist says, *No, that's just you trying to impose order on things, thinking somehow there's a reason behind it. That's easier than accepting that bad things happen to good people.* I thought I had a handle on it all. But look at you. Look at your *face.* Someone *I* know, trying to get in here. I bring the bad luck. But you're the one who pays."

"Sally," I said, "it's got nothing to do with you, with me, with luck. And it's over now. They came in, they got what they wanted. We'll never hear from them again."

But now she seemed confused, the smooth brow knitted, and she eased back in the chair and crossed her arms, Lisa's heels returning now, walking our way with purpose. Reminding me of the sound of Bethenny coming up the stairs, and now as then I felt that the moment was pregnant with possibility, only I didn't know if that possibility was good or bad.

"Something's not right," Sally said.

"I know it. I know it."

"That's not what I mean," she said, and turned to look at the cops outside, then back to me. "Why do I feel that same way I felt two nights ago?"

"Like the universe doesn't want us together."

"No," she said. "Like you've just gone and let me win at something. Not being totally honest with me."

Rap rap on the door frame, Lisa standing there looking confused.

"Werner's sure of it," she said. "They didn't get anything."

A moment later, I was back in the high bright light of the kitchen, silver and clean chrome framing the scene, the activity of law and order all around me. Sally staying back in the office wondering what was going to happen next and how she got involved, second-guessing her choice of kitchen crew, guys she thought she trusted, because they were the only ones who could have got it off her. No crew in today, Sally having already called to tell them the place was closed for a couple of days, though you could bet the cops were paying *them* a visit right now, checking with immigration and making certain everything was signed and stamped. The supply closet already open, Sally usually the one to open it because she's in first, someone else closes it up because the janitor is the last one to leave, only without her key someone else would have had to do it this morning. I imagined that I could feel a tide of air propelling me forward as I strolled toward the supply closet, all the rumors of intent leading there, as if what was there were a way out, and I suppose I *would* have whistled a little tune to fake nonchalance only I couldn't seem to hustle up the spit. In the long, narrow supply closet, naked bulbs overhead flickering and humming, bare wood shelves were piled neatly with everything from bleach to buckets to boxed glassware to staff uniforms, here a pile of tablecloths and, in clear plastic bags, ironed stacks of washed linen napkins. And strolling down the line, I was trailing my fingers along the shelves, the supplies getting more and more earthy, darker and damper and more organic as I passed bags of potting soil and mulch, the aroma of kerosene and lamp oil as I neared the end where the far door opened into the grounds wing, the small hangar like a locked down, very clean, very well-swept warehouse for: parked golf carts with trailers behind them the staff used to carry cut-down branches and such, rows of rakes and racks of shovels and picks and piles of sand, tarps for heavy rains, the console of flow-control units for the fertilizer tanks outside, the console marked with skull and crossbones, beside it a red chart of emergency call numbers in twenty-point type, the east bay open now to let in the bright white light of day. Hippolyte stood at the entrance to the first open bay smoking a cigarette, with his shaking hands, waiting until it was time to have his first drink of the day.

"Can you spare one, Hippolyte?" I asked.

He fished a cigarette out of his breast pocket and handed it over, lit it for me, and I struggled to keep the unfiltered smoke down.

"Sorry about the, ah, the remark out at the trap," he said. "Sometimes my staff, they say things—" he twirled a trembling finger beside his temple, "they are being too smart. My grandmother taught me not to be saying smart things when I was a boy. I say something like that, think I'm funny? *Psh.*" He swiped the back of his hand across an imaginary face.

"I sometimes wish my father had hit me like that," I said.

"He is hitting you with a belt or something?"

"No" I said, "he didn't hit me at all."

"Why you want him to hit you?"

"I guess because it would have helped me get ready for what came later."

Because that was really what the first blow was. The first blow was there to prepare you for the second. And the second to prepare you for the third. *This hurts me more than it hurts you*, parents are known to say, though I'm inclined to think they're coming at it wrong. *You'll thank me later*, they ought to say. When you get hit later in life you'll think: That wasn't so bad. Because it's the wounds we receive from those we love that truly harm us. Consider Sally, her right hand a road map of scars where the left had a slip. She's got a picket-fence of burns on the tender flesh of her wrists. But ask her about pain and she'll tell you the same thing. It's love that really hurts.

We smoked in silence until I said, "We needed that rain."

Thinking that Hippolyte is a man who understands what it means to be dry and require rain. Thinking that maybe this is why Hippolyte is so in demand, because he spends his entire waking life in a daydream of thirst, and knows what it means to stare at a clear blue sky and pray for relief.

"I was thinking we were going to be using the sprinklers," he said, "but with the drought maybe the township aren't liking that so much."

"Maybe you run it at night, they don't know it."

He exhaled smoke through his nose, shaking his head.

"Last summer," he said, "a hippie lady from the art colony is camping out all night to *catch* me. We are paying a good fine on that one, the witch."

"I remember."

"Not this time. I am telling Werner, tough shit, we're letting the grass go brown, see how they like it. Property values go down they are *begging* us to water."

"It must be a bitch keeping all that green."

"Yeah, you aren't even knowing it. The rich men playing golf, it's not enough that the grass be watered. They blame me for their score it's not even. No, it's got to be the right cut, the right color."

"The right color?"

Hippolyte straightened suddenly, sliding into his famously knowing imitation of Werner, even summoning forth the voice and intonation and accent, and slid his hand down an imaginary lapel to smooth it.

"The grass must promise *immortality*," he said in Werner's clipped, correct manner. "The grass, Hippolyte, must be making them feel young with every stroke or shank or slice."

"That's nice, the grass makes them feel young."

"Yeah, but like you are saying, it's a bitch to be keeping it. One hundred forty-six acres, Jake." He picked a flake of tobacco from his tongue, flicked it away into the grass. "I don't know how we keep up."

"You have any funny stuff back here to make that happen? Expensive equipment—"

"A couple of carts, that's all."

"What else you have back here?" I asked.

"The time clock for punch-in. A break room. The flow control for the fertilizer tanks. Some mowing equipment—"

"A fridge of cold beer."

Hippolyte licked his lips.

"Yeah," he said, "that's about it."

I scanned the room while he tried not to think about a good cold beer. And again I'm not seeing anything of consequence here, except maybe the flow control on the tanks. Otherwise it's just fucking picks and shovels and I can't see what they'd want back here.

I said, "I've heard you can make bombs with it."

"What," he said, "beer?"

"The fertilizer."

He tapped his ashes.

"No, man," he said, "you are using the ammonium nitrate on that. We are having the compressed stuff. We use anhydrous."

"What can you do with that?" I asked.

He said, "Melt your fucking face right off, you aren't careful enough."

"You ever burn yourself?"

He held up his right hand and showed me. Just like Sally, little red lines of scarred skin near the wrist. What would Bethenny say about those? You become a doctor to heal yourself. You become a teacher so you can learn. So why become a greenkeeper?—always tending the fallen garden, always raising riches from dry earth. Answer: because you're thirsty.

"Way back, I have my own operation and try and manage it myself. Learning the hard way. You ever work with anhydrous," he said, "wear gloves and a mask, man. Wear a fucking diving suit."

So that was where it led. A few golf carts, a fridge of cold beer, a flow console, picks and shovels. That was it. And standing there smoking with Hippolyte, looking out at the baking grass and feeling like I'd arrived at some sort of dead end—I mean, nowhere else to *go*—I wondered if it really was possible they hadn't got anything. Like it was all over. And I was relieved. I was out.

As if in reply, my cell phone chirped once in my pocket, and turning away from Hippolyte I lifted it out to answer.

"Asprey," I said.

The sound of rushing wind, Mahler playing in the background.

"Do you want to get paid or what?" Colonel Tom said.

SEVENTEEN

"NIGHT FISHING," COLONEL TOM SAID over the roar of the wind, "is one of my favorite pastimes. They're more apt to bite at night, it gets too hot during the day and the fish won't rise, not even for a good fly, one you've tied by hand. A lot less *wasting time* going on at night."

The sun had been down more than three hours. Night doing its night thing, thinning the herd with sleep, dividing us into classes of those whose hungers retired easily and those whose hungers did not. At this hour, our limited company on the streets composed an entire genre: noirish and countrified, armed and willing, and charged with all the necessary urgencies. The production values of the rural Pennsylvania night are high. With a cupped white moon overhead, placid barns bolted against predators, and the star-frosted grass gliding by in fields of cindery lunar shades, it is beautiful out here in the Big Empty. But the players?—they were strictly low-budget, extras propelled into leading roles of their own making. The vehicles growing more menacing after we passed the last Amish farm stand and crossed into the truly wild hill country, the blacktop winding among birches until the Colonel eased off the road, parked, and stepped down to unlock a padlocked chain burnished silver by his powerful headlamps. Soon we were swaying and dipping our way up a narrow lane, the undergrowth so tight on either side rosebay and ninebark are brushing the hide of the truck, a bright sickle of moonlight leering at us through the sheltering canopy overhead.

"I've never heard tell of anyone fly-fishing at night, Colonel," I said.

Sharing a joint now, the heady fumes of a lucky break and money propelling us along.

"Kid," he said, "trust me: it's the best time. We'll both be eating pan-seared trout for breakfast, put a little wild fennel in that pan you've got something *good*. Miss Sally, she'll fall over herself she sees you've got fresh trout packed in fern boughs in her fridge."

"Never mind her."

"You ever hear of your dad going night fishing?"

"Not once."

Tom rubbed his beard.

"Funny," he said, "I went night fishing with *him* once. And it was quite an eye-opener of a trip, if I do say so. Yes, we learned a *lot* about each other on that particular trip."

He dropped the truck into low gear as he rolled down an easy bank to a line of trees, cutting the engine but leaving the headlights on high beam, the good halogen lamps breaking everything down into hard shape and shadow, penetrating the tree line and revealing the quick rapids of a wide stream beyond. With the windows down I could hear the fast water and smell the coppery cut bank through the trees, probably watercress along the stream edge, thinking maybe I'd pick some for Sally to go along with the trout as I stepped down onto damp ferns and joined Tom at the rear fender of the truck, the fly rods already in his hands.

"How do you expect them to see the flies in the dark?" I asked.

"The trout look up, they see mister fly laying on the surface against the moonlight. Like a sweet little dream. And they go after it and swallow it down. You know what someone's hungry for, you know how to get him."

We had to push through grabby damp ferns and hawthorn and a couple of sticker bushes that didn't want to let us by, prickly seeds clinging to my shirt fabric once they did relent, snakes on my mind, those glossy quick whips I'd seen on the pool walk earlier. The air was cooler down the bank alongside the water, a little bit of mist rising with the mineral smell of the quick rapids, some white water farther down you wouldn't want to cross on foot. Three boulders were strewn across the broad reach before us, the granite stark and white in Tom's shimmering headlights, here and there jewels of quartz glittering in the lined strata, below them black slow turning pools of water where the trout would hide from the heat of day. Come here at evening and drape a perfect cast right into that pool, you'd have dinner in minutes.

And damn sure you'd be able to taste the fear in it.

"Here's what you want to do, kid," he said. "Take this little coil of line—just leave the rod, you won't need it. You want to wade out there with the line and climb up on that big rock right over there—that one, about fifteen feet out—then drop the fly in on the back side with a good bit of noise. That way mister trout knows it's there and comes up after it."

"Why don't I just cast?"

"You going to lay that itty-bitty fly in just the right spot in the *dark*?"

"Yeah, but—this hardly sounds like fishing to me."

"It ain't fishing. It's *night* fishing."

"I'm not going out there. *You* go out there."

But he just sat down on a rock and lifted another joint from his pocket and lit it. This being the kind of pointless male code criminals maintained—you don't get paid unless you seal the deal—so I kicked off my flip-flops and rolled my jeans up over my knees and stepped out into the stream. The water so cold it made me shout, yell at the moon as I stepped out over the sloping sandy bottom, nothing too tricky down there, the rocks my bare toes encountered a bit slick but kept clean by fast water, the current something you noticed right away, nothing to laugh about with it persuading me off to the right. Soon the water over my knees with the bottom of the stream still sloping down, and with no choice but to go ahead I was wading up to my waist with my jeans soaked, my teeth chattering, seriously wondering if I'm going to get dragged down, the water sounding anxious out here—like it was in a hurry to get someplace, or at least get away from here.

"There you are, kid," Tom called, voice flat over the rushing water. "Right up on there."

The rock showed at least three feet of its mass above water. A couple of good rough handholds and I hoisted myself up shivering and dripping, wondering how long I was going to have to play along.

"Right," he said. "Oh, just lovely, Jake. Now you get up top and drop that line into the water good and loud."

I crouched down on my hands and knees and peered into the pool on the far side of the rock. The water was turning slow, sheened with a skin of silver moonlight. I dropped the line in, watched the expanding circles trouble the mirrored surface, and gripped the thin thread double-wrapped around my palm in case something there gave a good quick pull, whistling an old Carl Perkins tune my father loved—"Honey Don't," maybe—and thinking, I get out of here soon enough, I call up Sally and say, *I have something for you. I could bring it over tonight. Thirty thousand. Forget school: I give it to you. You start your own place. I'll work for you for free—wash the fucking dishes, if that's what it takes. All I ask in return is another chance with you.*

But then she wants to know where the money's from and the money's the problem.

Nothing happening down below.

Night fishing, I thought.

Night fishing?

I looked up at the bank expecting to find the Colonel doubled over laughing at me, just one of those tricks men play on other men, and heard the whistle dry up on my lips when I spied Tom standing silhouetted against the hot white beams of his headlamps, the rods forgotten on the bank, the dark slash of his Smith & Wesson in his hand pointing at the ground.

I licked my lips and said, "Colonel, what's the joke?"

His voice somber.

"No joke, Mr. Jacob," he said. "Nothing funny here."

"Colonel, the job's done. Like you said. They don't even know what you got. They don't even know where you were."

He shook his head, not in the familiar way I'd known half a lifetime ago, the cocky old Colonel Tom who'd snort in amused disgust when you beat him at cards or when you tried to inhale off his cigarette and coughed it out—this time he shook his head and looked at the ground with what seemed like true sadness, doing it the way you would after losing a month's pay on the other team heaving up a Hail Mary with a second on the clock and somehow bringing it down good. Like it was out of your control and always had been. Like the gods didn't like you today and probably wouldn't tomorrow, either.

He raised the piece and used the barrel to scratch the back of his neck.

"Jake," he said, "we have two problems, and I'd like to talk to you about both of them."

"Why don't we go sit down over a beer, Colonel?"

"I'd prefer to talk here, on our little night fishing expedition. That all right with you?"

I said, "Whatever you want."

"The first problem," he said, "is that our friend Mr. Lightpainter has stopped taking my calls. Unaccounted for, can you believe it?"

Tom shook his head, scratched his neck with the barrel of the gun again.

"He came to see me this morning, said he wanted my Kowa scope," Tom said. "He brings it back after breakfast-time looking grim. I make a joke, ask if he was hunting some cross-county pussy or something, he just hands it back and takes off like he's on *business*."

"Maybe he took off to celebrate, Colonel. Down to—off to P-town."

"*P-town*?" He turned his head, hawked and spat on the bank. "I visited his camp tonight. Shutters folded, place packed up. The sort of thing you'd expect to see if he was going away on a long trip. I climbed up on the roof and put my palm on his chimney, and, Jake, it was *cold*. You make so much as a cup of tea, that thing's going to be warm for hours. That boy is gone, knew he was leaving when he brought that scope back to me, and I'm wondering where he got *to*. He come looking for you at all, maybe try and give you ideas? Maybe work something whereby the two of you take everyone's share?"

"I haven't seen him since you took that key off me."

"I'm thinking it's not such a good thing, that boy pulling a serious job with me and then just plain going *missing*. What don't add up about it is the product is still there. It would've made sense if he crossed me and split. That I can—that I can *understand*. But I went out and checked on the product myself, after I got back from his camp, and everything was there. And that don't make any sense to me."

"He'll turn up, Colonel."

"Funny," he said, "how you take a shine to calling me Colonel all the sudden."

"He'll turn up."

"All right," Tom said. "Maybe he did figure he'd go alleycattin' for a weekend, blow off some steam after a job, figures it's in the bag, his share. Maybe. But then we have a second problem. The issue being that the authorities seem to have taken an interest in me regarding these events of late."

"They asked me about fifty questions today. Not once said your name."

"Oh, but they're *thinking* my name. And that's got me wondering what you told them."

"I didn't give them anything. Not a thing."

"But someone's talking. Someone's vanishing, and someone's talking. Otherwise how come they're so interested in me? Is it because you're talking more than you think? See, that's why I have you out here, kid. Because I *need to know* if I can count on you to keep your trap shut. Are you the sort to go talking, Jake?"

"Colonel," I said, "are you loco?"

He casually raised up, just like one of the gangsta brothers from a rap video on Rolly's television show, his piece sideways, a hard bright camera-flash and a metallic clap and a thousand hornets of spattered granite seemed to leap up and sting me on my face, my arms, my hands, my neck. A pair of crows burst out of the trees cawing, and I fell over backward, damn near overbalanced down into the water, scraped my elbows bloody catching myself. And suddenly cold logic arrives and I'm wondering if I need to swim. Suddenly I'm wondering if I'm going to make it home at all tonight. I glanced down at the slow turning black pool and thought, *How far to that bank in the dark, Jake? How many strokes?*

"Jake," Tom said quietly, "I'll ask again, and this time I hope you answer civilly, not accuse me of being loco, or my aim is liable to improve. I do know loco, after all. I know that one of us has that loco gene—in your blood, in your milk. Your mom, she was loco, and she was also a little too brave. Thinking she could give up the pills were helping her out of that depression for her kid, afraid they'd get in your milk? And then do it that way, with a rope? You got to be *seriously* wrong to do it that way. So I need to know, Jake, if you're thinking you're going to crazy your way through this one. I need you to tell me true. Are you the sort to go talking?"

I licked a metallic taste from my lips and said, "I haven't let on a word."

"Then why did I get a visit from Raymond Tibbens tonight? Sat in my very kitchen. You know what he asked about?"

"He would have asked about my dad."

"That's right. I gave him coffee, played it a friendly visit. He said, *You have any unfinished business with Jacob Asprey?* And it damn near stopped my heart, Jake, when he said that. Because for a minute I thought he was asking about *you*."

"He came to see me in the hospital. That afternoon with Rolly. Called me later, asked me the same thing, said, *Anyone out there have a bone to pick with your old man?* Thinking that's what the robbery was, just some bad blood someone putting even again."

"You think he's got any sense of the plan?"

"He couldn't put it together. Kept saying it, *I don't make it.*"

"What led him away?"

I said, "I did."

We watched each other for a moment as he decided if he believed me, and I saw a terrible clarity resolve itself in his features, thinking, *How do I get away?* Again the simple answer: *Swim.* And then: *But that's what he's waiting for—to see if you try and get away. Because that will justify what he's thinking he's got to do.* I sucked in a breath and held it until I became aware of tugging on my left arm, powerful and steady, and looking down I saw that my numb hand, gripping the fishing line, was being pulled and pulled with urgency down toward the dark turning pool.

"My word, kid," Tom said, "are you lucky or what?"

Back in the car, a fourteen-inch trout gutted and washed and wrapped in newspaper between us, my right arm streaked with dried blood, nobody else out and the cab nearly dark, he said, "I've pulled fifty jobs with Quinn and never once did he go and vanish after."

"He'll show up in three days with a hangover and case of the clap."

"He better. Because I don't *like* it when things vary from the *plan,* you dig?"

He smoked and thought and then looked sideways at me.

"You want to go see it?" he asked.

"See what?"

"What we got."

"No," I said, "I don't even want to know what it is."

"It's awfully pretty. Fifty thou sealed up in a little white present. My little magic trick. Just a little walk into the woods."

Now that he's decided he trusts me he's dying to tell me what a genius he is.

Wants to show me this thing that's going to change his entire life.

"I don't want to know," I said.

"You change your mind, want to have a look, maybe celebrate with a line or two, you come to the bar tomorrow night. I have some business in Lock Haven but you want to see the product I could put it off another night. Band playing and everything. I mean, there shouldn't be any hard feelings about tonight, right?"

"You told me you went night fishing with my dad once," I said.

He took a while to answer.

"Sure," he said, "Just one time. Most go once. The important thing's to avoid going *twice*."

He held the joint out to me, the wind blowing through the cab whipping the tip into a bright red ash, Mahler playing on the radio.

"You're not going to pay me, are you?"

He rubbed the back of his neck, actually seemed a little uncomfortable.

"That check you wrote for the pool table," he said. "I had Kimber tear it up before Sally could deposit it. Thinks she lost it, I guess she's too embarrassed to ask you for another. Funny, huh?—Sally didn't even get a dime for it. So that one was on the house. I mean, you got a pool table out of it, right?"

"You're not going to pay me."

Mahler playing quietly over the whipping wind.

"Look on the bright side, kid," he said. "You've paid your dad's debt to society in full. You're now the man of the house. Jacob Cameron Asprey—from here on in, that's *you*."

Back home I walked through the backyard and heaved the fish into the woods.

EIGHTEEN

LATER THAT NIGHT, A GLASS tumbler of bourbon perspiring at my elbow, hair wetted beneath the kitchen faucet and slicked back again, I squinted into the fluorescent rectangle of the laptop screen scaring the quiet house with my typing, something preventing me from making the tightrope walk upstairs to sleep. Maybe the crystallized image of a weapon raised and pointed in my direction, the shutter in my mind's eye preserving a snapshot of Colonel Tom's cruel features above the camera-flash of the barrel in high definition, in autozoom and preselect. The first tumbler of bourbon had been to rinse myself of that image. And so had the second. With those out of the way I addressed the next obstacle to sleep: the uphill climb—the mountain, the Everest—of money promised and denied, the recognition that all along I'd been designated the sap, the fall guy. But no, with yet another tumbler down, enough bourbon to stun an elephant, the iced anesthetic and the joint I'd smoked earlier surely enough to neutralize even the bile of those revelations, I found myself still acutely, intensely awake. And it was gradually becoming clear what was keeping me from my bed: the fact that I had no measure of self anymore. My identity slipping through my greedy grasp.

I didn't know what I was involved in.

I didn't even know what I had done.

Here is what we do know.

Chime Creek, at last count you had 462 members. My father and I were once members. And members we ceased to be. This happened after Jacob Cameron Asprey, Sr. was convicted of tax fraud, obstruction of justice, flight from sentencing, conspiracy and witness tampering, and subsequently sentenced to a minimum 148 months in the Pennsylvania State Correctional Facility at Slippery Rock.

Chime Creek, the average net worth of your primary members is nearly two million dollars. The average salary of your primary members is just north of three hundred thousand dollars. The car most commonly driven by your members is a Mercedes, followed closely by a Cadillac. Many of these were purchased directly from Rolly Asprey, brother of the disgraced Jacob Asprey.

You are eighty-two years old, Chime Creek. Your age is beginning to show around the edges. It shows in your worn wood and tired rugs, in the way you cling to the past. Even you, Chime Creek, wince whenever you look in the mirror these days.

You have sixty-six employees. Nearly half are immigrants with work papers. Fourteen of these employees are charged with tending the grounds.

Your dining facilities include a restaurant, two bars, and a banquet hall. Unlike the overwhelming majority of country clubs, your food and beverage service actually brings money into the operation. Much of this profit is attributed to your executive chef, Sally Godstreet, whose talents are occasionally cited by local real estate brokers as a reason to move to the area, and who has been profiled in numerous food magazines. These food magazines typically accompany their articles with a full-page photograph of Sally in her chef's whites, apprehending her in a beautifully lighted moment of tasting a sauce with her index finger, as if all the editors and photographers were in collusion to capture her frankly sexual appeal.

Chime Creek, you have a pool with a maximum depth of twelve feet and a shallow end of three feet six inches. An eleven-year-old boy drowned in this pool earlier in the summer. The lifeguard on duty, who was in the guardhouse smoking marijuana at the time of the accident, now has two attorneys working full time on his behalf to keep him out of the very same prison where my father now resides.

"I have no words," the mother of the drowning victim was quoted as saying. "There are no words."

No one is arguing with that.

An older, more experienced lifeguard was hired as a replacement. This lifeguard is me.

You have an eighteen-hole golf course, Chime Creek, an old-style "parks" course comprising a tricky turn on the seventh, a *par* four on the back nine that pros characterize as "interesting," and 146 acres of land.

Here I looked up, contemplating the vastness of this number, the strange wondrous wasteland of it all, the same course with all the same problems you must confront again and again. Beat it one day, it's still there the next, undiminished—such beautiful symmetry! I imagined it now: the pulse of crickets in the brush, each blade of grass carved in sharp relief by moonlight, soothing silver shades burnishing Mother Nature's work.

With a little searching, we soon learn this, too: That the Environmental Protection Agency says a properly cared-for parcel of earth has forty-six thousand blades of grass per square foot. One can only imagine that Chime Creek's acres are all properly cared-for parcels of earth. Every square foot ought to have it so good as these.

And now we're zooming in—if this were a film, we would be approaching the subject, moving in, beginning to draw in the fine details. Such as:

The calculator tells us that there are 43,500 square feet per acre, which adds up to just over two billion blades of grass per acre. This further implies that upon the course there are some two-hundred ninety-two billion blades of grass, and that each must be maintained to a level of deep green greenness that carries within it a promise of something special, something unattainable even by great wealth and power—the general manager of Chime Creek says this operation prizes the idea that the grass itself must promise *immortality*, and do so with every stroke and swing and shank and slice.

The grass must make you feel young.

This elusive green color—some may recall it as matching the color of a bikini Sally Godstreet wore nine summers ago, during a formative moment of my life, the moment I learned that love is not enough—this green color requires vast amounts of nutrients to maintain its vigor, its youthful appearance. The vivid spark of life it possesses is therefore manufactured by chemical means.

The fertilizer Chime Creek has chosen to supply these nutrients is anhydrous ammonia.

And now we're here, we're zoomed in all the way. Here we confront the juddering heart of the thing—because a few simple searches into all the various visible objects to be found in that shed have revealed a startling fact: that anhydrous ammonia, interestingly enough, is a primary ingredient in the production of *N-methyl-1-phenylpropan-2-amine*, otherwise known as *desoxyephedrine*, otherwise known by the less formal names of Christina, Chris, Christy.

Otherwise known as Tina.

Otherwise known as crystal methamphetamine.

The DEA tells us that the street value of anhydrous ammonia can be as much as twelve hundred dollars per gallon.

Chime Creek, the Internet tells me that an outfit your size would be in its rights to have well over two or even three hundred gallons of anhydrous on hand at all times.

Pull back now, the reverse zoom, because now we have the specifics—now what we're seeking is the *big picture*.

But the numbers are too vast.

Only the calculator is able to compile such numbers. Only the calculator is able to bring it all together, to make everything clear by telling us that the white steel tank on Chime Creek's grounds almost certainly holds something around a quarter of a million dollars of street-value anhydrous ammonia, untraceable, and requiring nothing but access to the flow control in the locked grounds wing and an alternative tank loaded into a truck to transport it off into neverland forever. Certainly only a portion of that amount was removed. But whatever the amount taken, with dependency hinging on the accounting of one hopelessly disorganized, withdrawn alcoholic, unclear if they're ever even going to realize it's gone *missing*.

You may as well print the money yourself.

And how many kids will end up like me—with a dad in prison or worse—because of it?

The bourbon tasted as thin as water now. I stood at the window watching a light rain fall, and I imagined Hippolyte standing at his own window, a tumbler of vodka in his trembling fist, and always the question in his mind, *How will I make it through tomorrow?* I considered the number on the calculator face and, with a sense of interior free fall, asked myself: how many lives? How many families lose a son, a daughter so the Magician can get rich?

I suppose you could say a plan had begun to form in my mind. *I have no words,* the mother was quoted as saying. *There are no words.* And I think I understand—I think I get it, that some events carve their initials into you so deeply they change the shape of you forever, words beside the point. I will be responsible for those laid to waste by this theft—the sons, the daughters, the mothers, the babies.

My plan is much simpler than the plan constructed by Quinn, by Tom, though it is no less important that I enact it undetected, because I have no doubt that with so much money at stake, the punishment would be the ultimate penalty.

And I can do silence, Magician. Just listen.

PART THREE

✚

FAST EDDIE

NINETEEN

IN THE LIVING ROOM WITH Rolly and Zooey after breakfast, a second glass of milk in my grip, my joints full of ground glass, not the worst hangover of my life but easily close. Alcohol is poison, every hangover the evidence of a botched execution. When you're this sick, what you require is diversion, and today that diversion from the paint-stripping hangover was Rolly: He'd got himself dressed in chinos and a sport shirt, but he'd nicked himself shaving and he occupied his corner of couch looking dumbed-down and fazed, looking *cuckolded* by life, wishing he were back in his element at work in that sharp leather chair that told customers you were ready to play. All these doctors probing for weakness, hunting down the places where he was disintegrating. He was broadcasting the spooked vibrations of a man genuinely engaging notions of mortality, a man trying to maintain perspective and failing. He was good at what he did, Rolly. But like most people who were good at what they did, he was no good at anything else.

"Forget the results," Rolly said, "I feel good. I feel *fine*."

I'm thinking: *And this is how* you *fall, Rolly.*

"He's going to be taking some time off," Zooey said.

"Away from the dealership," I agreed, the way she'd coached me to at the breakfast table earlier, maybe help him get used to the idea. "How bad is it?"

"The same old noise," Rolly said. "The same things they've been telling me for years. My cholesterol too high—"

"*Much* too high," Zooey said.

"My ticker a little funny, the high blood pressure—"

"So they want him going easy for a few months," Zooey said, talking patiently to him and holding his elbow. "Bring all the numbers down, no stress, stop eating fast food at his desk. Then he can go back to work."

And I'm trying to find some good in this, fixate on the turnabout of Rolly getting his numbers down, finally. I'm trying to spin this disaster into something I can live with. Because right now I'm picturing Rolly slumped down on the hot pavement just before Colonel Tom cracked the shotgun butt to my face. I'm trying to conjure up some good in all this, because that image of Rolly taking the fall along with me: I can't live with it.

"I'm not feeling so hot," I said, looking down at my glass and realizing I'm going to have to drain it or Zooey's going to ask why I was off my food.

"I'm going to go off my nut," Rolly said. "They think it's good for me, home all day with nothing to do? Eating *oatmeal?*"

"We'll go for walks," Zooey said. "Take Coop. It's good for your numbers."

"It's a bad time for this," Rolly said. "I had big plans for the winter, the cruise—"

Rolly having a hard time just sitting here now, being the center of attention.

"I'll tell you, Jay," he said, his face pained, "it sort of changes things with the plan. What I was telling you about with going back to school."

"It doesn't matter, Rolly."

Little beads of sweat had gathered on my forehead, and the room a notch too warm even though Zooey had the air conditioning churning icy air through the house.

"Not that it's gone," he said. "It just slows things down a little. Zooey didn't want me to tell you until we were sure. I should have listened."

"It doesn't matter," I said, needing the conversation to be over. "I'm just glad you're okay."

"Maybe in another year, I get back, have a good winter—"

"Rolly, it's the last thing on my mind," I said, and I realized this was the truth. I was never going back. I had made a separate peace and, anyway, the education was now complete, had been completed for the cost of a shotgun butt to the face. Someday I would construct my own university—tuition-free, open to all, and based on a singular philosophy: the Symposium of Pain. You exit limping, sure. But the beating is worth it. The beating teaches you one valuable lesson: that you never want another one. "I just want you to take it easy," I said, "get better."

Zooey gripped his hand and smiled at him, and I felt another wave of that terrible sickness, the nausea deeper now, more pronounced, more present tense.

"I could learn to cook some new things," Zooey said, "make that fish recipe from Martha Stewart."

"At least I can still have red wine," Rolly said. "Thank Christ. But the money's going to be different without the commissions."

Behind him on the wall what I'd always thought of as the Jake Shrine. Before I'd moved in they'd hunted down the shoebox that held all my old swimming medals, had a bunch of them mounted in a nice frame, a black matte setting off a pentagram of five gold medals with bright blue ribbons, and at the center of it all a good-sized photograph of me at age ten, I'm standing on the pool deck with my hair in a wet whorl and the sun setting behind me, my warm-up jacket zipped to my chin against the evening chill. I'm grinning and holding up the medal that's around my neck, the one I got for setting the freestyle record at summer districts, the medal itself mounted just to the right of the photograph. They'd put the frame together because they really wanted me to feel at home, knew that was a happy time for me, before everything went strange. And looking at the old me, the quick swimmer, I was thinking that people make the wrong associations all the time—they think just because you can swim fast and over a great distance you somehow know how to save a life. I've no business wearing that lifeguard shirt, the red cross right over my breastbone. Because I don't know how to save a life. I damn near took one a few days ago, the life of the man who took me in at age fourteen and wanted to give me money to finish college, a man who thought it would be a nice idea to dig up my old medals, maybe give me something to cling to my first night here. That's the kind of lifeguard I am.

"Money's going to be fine, Rolly," I said. "I've got something going."

He left that one alone, his brow gathering into concern, Rolly knowing that I'm my father's kid and he's heard that phrase before and knows what it signals—the cheat, the scheme. To let off steam he turned toward Zooey and began arguing about what to have for dinner, Rolly saying after the hospital food he was in the mood for fish and chips and Zooey saying, "Rolly, it's going to be *baked*, maybe a little olive oil and wine and a green salad alongside," and I took the moment to make my escape.

Coop laying on the kitchen floor in the same spot, still full from that fucking *smorgasbord* he had two nights ago.

"You damn near ate your weight," I said.

He yawned and lay there panting, looking pleased and ashamed, thinking he really did make a new friend, maybe the Magician will be back someday with some fresh treats.

"Next time," I said, "don't be such a sap."

I was halfway up the stairs when my cell phone chirped.

Tibbens said, "What I don't get is, how did they get Sally's key off her?"

I brought the phone into the bathroom, told him to hold on a minute and cupped a palm beneath the cold tap, dipped my face into the icy sluice. Feeling as if I'd taken too much of my own medicine to abate that craving for a cigarette.

"Marshall," I said, and spat the taste of pennies taste into the sink, "there's a detective already on this. Lisa Solo, asked me about fifty questions already. She's going to get it worked out, eventually. So there's no reason for you to be worrying about it."

"Turn it around: Who would have been able to get it off her?"

Water dripping off my chin onto the marble.

"What about her crew?" he asked. "How well did she know them?"

"How well do we know anybody?"

"And the other thing troubling me. If it was someone in the kitchen, able to get her key—well, why do they need *yours* to open up the kitchen? It doesn't make sense. Don't they have keys themselves?"

"Ask her. You know the number for the club."

"Yeah," Tibbens said, "but she's not there anymore."

Lawmen, in my experience, enjoy moments like this one: when they bring a bunch of disconnected facts into terrible alignment, get you to understand that something is *serious*. I spat the awful taste again, sick now and trying to will it away.

"How?" I said.

"That quiet guy, her boss—"

"Werner."

"Yeah, Werner. He told me she's suspended while they're figuring things out."

"Where does he get that?"

"On account of Werner finally getting wind what kind of man her uncle is. It doesn't look good for the club, suddenly members are seeing in the press this Colonel Tom's history, realize the person cooking their meals is one degree away from a guy like that. After what happened earlier this summer he's already spooked."

I lay my head forward against the cool mirror, but the moment I closed my eyes the room went sailing away from me and I thought I might get sick, the sensation standing me straight up, wide awake.

"We're all spooked," I said. "How long is she out?"

"As long as it takes," Tibbens said. "Maybe I can help her, too. I want you to know, Jake, that we're going to work this out. I'm not going away without getting this made."

"I *want* you to go away, Marshall."

"You think I could do that, even if I wanted to? You think I *want* to be this way?"

"I bet you tried that same line on your wife."

No idea why I said that. Maybe it was the sickness boiling in me, or maybe I just wanted to piss him off so badly he had no choice but to hang up.

"Sure," he said. "I did. Tried to make her understand."

"Did she go for it?"

"She took my son and went to Vegas. And now," he said, "she lives with a punk."

"Thinking maybe she'd gain a little perspective out there."

He didn't answer.

"It doesn't feel good, does it?" I asked. "Having someone dig around in the places you already hurt. Even if they are trying to help."

Like Kimber, no *click*, no *crack*—just there one moment, gone the next. Except he wasn't going to stay gone. He was going to keep digging around until I could find a way to stop him.

I set down the phone, put more water on my face, and lay forward on the counter, my head on my arms wishing the room would stop rolling underfoot, Rolly and Zooey downstairs arguing over dinner, Rolly saying they should save money, Zooey saying they spend more on better quality food, like an investment in his health?—and there was no stopping it, suddenly it all came rushing up and I kicked the door shut so they wouldn't hear me. It was over quick and I flooded the sink with fresh water to wash it down and then ducked my head under the cold sluice, slicked my hair back dripping, and felt the good cold fresh water running down my neck. No time left to stop and think, it's clear as blue sky what's got to happen, so I picked up my cell phone and dialed the number.

When he answered I tried on the voice for the first time—the voice that sounded like a suit with money behind it.

"This is Jake," I said.

"And?" Werner asked.

"You're not giving me this job because you want to. You're giving it to me because you have to."

He was silent for a moment, and I pictured him easing back into his chair in a pantomime of cunning: fingertips steepled together.

"Good," he said. "Then you understand the first rule of running a business. *Keep the customers happy.* And that's what we're doing, giving you this job. Because someone, somewhere, really wants you to have this job, though why they'd want the son of a two-bit thief like Jacob Asprey in our business office is beyond me."

"You told me it was to make amends."

"And it is, in a way. I give you this and I'm done with you forever. Because once you have the job, it's on you to make it work. You don't, fuck up a project, blow a big client by saying the wrong thing? You'll be back poolside within a week. And my debt's paid. I'm done with you."

"You're wasting the job on me. It should go to Sally."

"Of course it should. She's demonstrated she deserves it. Running her own profitable outfit, her own hiring, payroll, making money. I mean, you know how rare it is for a country club to *make* money on its food?"

"Give the job to her, then."

"I can't, any more than you can refuse it. That's what I like about this. That you're on the hook, too."

"She'll quit if you don't give it to her."

"Juan will move up. He's ready."

You know you're sick when you can't quite hunt down your eyes in the mirror. As if you have a blind spot at the center of your vision, your eyes unable or unwilling to seek themselves and capture the organism in its own feedback loop. Water's dripping down my collar and Rolly is downstairs arguing about the price of cod, only I can't find my own face.

"We'll need a new lifeguard," I said.

"Why don't you leave it to me?" Werner said.

A shiny black Camaro in Sally's driveway.

Kimber's dream car finally here, where she wants it, the thing's going to carry her out of here, down to Formosa, where I had the feeling she was going to learn a great deal about herself.

I parked behind it but remained in my car for a moment, my hot engine ticking, I'm gaping at the car's glossy curved rump, thinking, *No wonder girls get hot looking at them,* I'm *hot just looking at it.* It looked like a sculpture whose subject was a youth that *might* have been, and watching it, not sure how to feel, really, I thought, *Was she stupid enough to go to him, give Tom a hard time about being slow in paying her? Or maybe he paid her off to keep her quiet.* God protecting drunks and babies and people too stupid to know just how bad the risk they're taking is. I was reminded of that first night at Bucknell, that pimped and primed Swedish automobile whisking my roommate and his new friends by in the opposite direction, *those fuckers,* and here it seemed almost as if that car had returned to me, the way things sometimes do when they linger in the mind. I think I did envy Kimber in that moment, preparing herself for escape velocity, her mind already mapping the way, which was any road that pointed West, and at the terminus of the trip the white HOLLYWOOD sign telling you that you were at the end of America, or the beginning, depending on what was seeded there in your heart, the letters wavering over the brushfires rising from the Valley and seeming to dissolve into the trembling blue air. People like me never get there. Because they won't let you in unless you have a car like that.

A strange impulse visited me in that moment, and against my better judgment I honored it—I suppose because I knew I was in over my head, outclassed by the situation, and I was willing to accept whatever help I could get.

I still knew her number by heart.

"It's Jake," I said.

Bethenny was quiet for a long time. For a moment I feared the connection had been cut: I didn't have the courage to call her a second time. Then I heard the musical *click* and *snap,* the faint crackle of burning tobacco, and realized that she was simply medicating herself for the encounter ahead. As with that moment with Kimber in the car, I sensed that I was somehow aligned with Bethenny. She wasn't my friend. But she was the enemy of my enemy—she was the enemy of the Jake who can't get his life together—and that meant something.

"I've started smoking again, myself," I said. "A few days ago."

"Who could blame you? There are so many reasons to begin again."

"And so few to quit."

"Anyway you can't keep drinking milk in the morning like that, Jake. People will talk."

"And say what?"

"They'll say," she said, and exhaled expansively, "that you have a complex."

"Where are you?" I asked.

"Bryant Park, by the library. It's a lovely day, I'm sitting here with a clipboard taking names. A fashion internship. But it's such a horrible place, Jake. It's like a big, beautiful nightmare."

"You should go home, give it up."

"Haven't you heard?" she asked. "They're not letting anyone leave. I'm stuck here."

"I'm going to do something stupid tonight," I said. "Later."

"Are you asking my permission?"

"No," I said, "I wanted to apologize. In case I don't get another chance."

"I burned your letter. I'm the one who should apologize."

"I think you helped me, burning things down like that. I think you taught me a good lesson with that one. And you're right, you know?" I said. "With that tattoo. You're right on the money with that one. Supposing truth *is* a woman. What then?"

"Then," she said, "you give up on ever owning it."

"Sometimes I think you know so much. More than me, anyway. I wonder if we could've been happy together."

"But you love that girl from home," she said. "What was her name?"

"Sally."

"I wanted to go to bed with her. Can you believe that? What a time we could have had. If I'd convinced her. But it never would have happened. She saw me coming from ten miles. She knows I'm just a tuning fork. Rap me ten different ways, I always play the same melody."

I heard the scrape of a heel on pavement.

"And that's the end of the cigarette," she said. "I accept your apology. I'd apologize for burning your book but—Jake, you know, I did you a favor."

"You read it?"

"Of course I did. Whenever you were out, worked my way through a page at a time."

"Was it any good?"

"You were convincing when you were writing about Sally. You had me all wrong, though, Jake. I'm not the villain. I'm more like the other thing. People who burn books are always being misunderstood. I just wanted to save you from yourself."

"I'll get it right next time," I said.

"Was that all true about your mother? What she did to herself?"

I leaned my head out the window and looked up at the awful blue sky. The silver slivers of two jets at altitude glided toward each other in perpendicular flight, trailing tiny white lines. For a moment I was terrified for them—they would collide in midair, send four hundred souls tumbling down through that high windy space—but the planes somehow crossed over each other's paths and continued safely through, the white lines forming the shape of an angled cross.

"Every word," I said.

"I'm sorry to hear that."

I licked my lips, craving another cigarette and a glass of milk in equal parts. Bethenny lowered the phone and spoke briefly to someone next to her—*one second*—and I experienced a panic attack of loneliness: She was about to hang up.

"It's time for me to go," she said. "Have fun tonight, Jake. With whatever this stupid thing is you're going to do. If you come back to school you'll have to tell me all about it."

"I'm not coming back."

"Good," she said. "We'd probably end up together again. And what would be the point of that? We have nothing left to teach each other."

No *click*, no *crack*—just there one moment, gone the next.

I leaned on the doorbell for five minutes, then stepped off the slate walk onto the grass and padded around the shaded side of the house, somehow affirmed in my decision to come here by the discovery of a perfect symmetry: Kimber there, again dressed in the lawn-green bikini, same chair, same sunglasses. Same bottle of bourbon on the table beside her, now half-empty, prissy pink bow still in place, along with a glass and an ice bucket.

"I guess you fucking well got paid," I said. I never have been much of a speechmaker but this time the words were there for the taking. "Oh, sure, you're just a kid who doesn't know any better, or doesn't have to, anyway, with the rest of us lined up to dry your eyes when your dollhouse goes up in flames."

She turned her head to look at me, and even through the oil-black sunglasses I saw that her face was distorted in confusion, and as she lifted back the sunglasses and I noted the raw, red eyes, the lines of experience on her face, the little horizontal burns on the inside of her wrists, I took a step back and sucked in a pained breath.

Sally said, "You approach a lady this way the day she's canned?"

"That wasn't meant for you."

"You really know how to sweet-talk, Jake."

I stood there unsure of where to look. Somewhere down the block someone gave a few halfhearted pulls on a mower starter, without luck.

"I think you should know," Sally said, "that I'm quite buzzed. And it's hardly breakfast-time."

"That wasn't meant for you."

"But I received it just the same."

"You looked like Kimber to me."

"I'm not so drunk I believe *that*. Why don't you sit down, Jake? Have a drink and sweet-talk me some more? What's the occasion, anyway?"

"I just heard about work."

"Oh, that. Can you believe it?"

"Yes," I said, "this being Werner."

"The snake. Do you know he once made a pass at me? He did. In his correct little Bavarian manner. You know how it goes—the two people alone, the boss sidling up behind for the back rub. Who would've guessed he had any id beneath that suit?"

"I'm not surprised."

"It was on his mind when he called me in to tell me. Worried I was going to go to the papers or something, but what would be the point, am I right?"

She lifted what was left of her drink, I was guessing her third or even her fourth, but she poured it back a little too aggressively and the ice rolled up against her face. She set the glass back down rubbing her nose with the back of her hand. I sat down on the end of the lounge, and when I placed my hand on her shin she looked steadily at me with her cried-out eyes, her sunglasses pushed up to hold twinned waves of her hair back.

"I must look ridiculous to you," she said. "A ridiculous silly nothing of a girl."

"Never."

"Why do I feel so ridiculous, then? Is it this bikini?"

"It's lovely on you."

"I put it on for you. Should I be embarrassed to admit that? Well, I've drunk just enough that I'm not, though I'm sure I'll regret saying that tomorrow. I got up this morning and thought, *I'll just waste the day by the pool, see how the other half lives,* and somehow I knew, Jake—I knew you'd be over to see me. That you'd hear and come to see me. Like the opposite of the night I came to you, with everything turned inside-out. That night I had everything and I wanted to share it with you. Today I've got nothing and I feel the same way. And this bikini—I opened my drawer and there it was, right on top, like a—like a gift, even though I haven't worn it in years. And I realized, when I saw it, that I wanted you to see me wearing it. How ridiculous is that?"

She rubbed the back of her hand over her nose again.

"Then I came downstairs and found that car in the drive," she said, "and I had the strangest thought. I thought, *Jake got himself a new car and he's come to pick me up and take me away from here.* But then I thought, *Well, that's silly, because where would he get the money for something like that?*"

"Let me get you some water."

"Why did I do that to you? Sleep with you, eight weeks with you, and then turn you away? Despite what my father said. Where did loyalty get me?"

"You did it because he used to let you win. Even if it made you angry when he did that, you loved him."

"I think I know why I did it, asked you to come downstairs with me at that pool party. I did it because I had realized that I was in love with you, and I knew I'd have to tell my father, eventually, that I wouldn't be able to keep it secret forever. He was going to figure out how I felt about you, anyway. And I wanted us to have something between us before it was all taken away. So we had eight weeks, at least, before it all came spilling out."

She had another drink.

"Oh, it was such a dreadful mistake, sleeping with you," she said. "We weren't even any good at it, were we? But every one of them since then has been so bloody awful, no matter how good it was. Even the good ones I regretted, because I was comparing them to what happened with you. They were all nice and fun but I hated them all and I wish I hadn't had any of them. It would have been nicer if I'd been with someone else first, because then I would have had that over you, instead of you having this power over *me*."

I gripped her shin lightly and she looked away.

"Don't," she said. "I want to feel badly today."

She lifted the bottle unsteadily and poured herself another drink, slopping some over the edge as she dropped in a fresh fistful of ice.

"You'll end up sick," I said.

"Where did she get the money for it, Jake? A car like that."

"You'll end up sick."

"What could she have done to earn money like that?"

"Sally," I said, "Werner's giving me the job."

And this had the desired effect. It caused her to freeze with her drink halfway to her lips, her line of thought atomized.

"Rolly has to take time off work," I said, as quietly and evenly as I could, my hand steady on her shin. "His doctors are worried, want him minimizing stress, focusing on himself. Money's going to be tight for them for a few months. Which means it's something I have to do."

"When do you start?"

"Monday."

Sally considered this in silence for a long moment, then turned and cracked the drink down on the table, a fragile smile on her face. She wiped the moisture from her hands and raised herself to her feet, stumbling just a little, and stood over me so that I had to lean back to look up the shining length of her body, Sally gazing down with her raw eyes, hands on her hips. She was a tall woman. But somehow in the moment she seemed even taller—as tall, even, as the women who had once lorded over my teenage dreams, imperious and unattainable and somehow possessing the terrible power to cause you to tell the truth.

"How long have you known?" she asked.

"Long enough."

"But you weren't going to take it."

"No."

"Because you wanted me to have it."

"Yes."

Her eyes beginning to swim now, the sickness playing its terrible bebop in my head, and the crickets buzzing in the hedge as loudly as the roar of the mower going down the block.

"Why would you do that?" she asked.

"Because I love you."

"You do?"

"I always have."

"But we're not allowed to be together."

"It depends on what you think is right. They've been gone," I said, "a long time."

She shook her hair.

"I promised him I'd stay away from you," she said, "and promised myself I'd never go back on that, not so long as I was in *his house*. It was going to be my house once I got this job. But now I'm not going to get it. Nine years I followed his request, stuck with it. But I'm so tired, Jay, so tired I feel like I could just lay down and sleep for a week. It's so wearing keeping your promises to someone who's no longer around. It's harder than anything, and I can't do it anymore. So I want you to do something, for me. You will, won't you?"

"Yes," I said.

She ruffled my hair, and I'm wondering if maybe she had *five* drinks.

"Jake-O," she said, "Jake-O, chum, here's what I want: I want you to be me."

"You're drunk."

"I want you to be me, and I'll be you, and you can be the one who breaks her promise today. You can be the one who lied to her dead dad when she promised him *for always*."

"I'm no good at lying."

"Sure you are," she said. "You're a terrific liar. You lied to me all along about the job. See how good at it you are? Kidding. But not really. What else have you lied to me about, Jake?"

I said, "Sally, I should go."

"Then we're agreed," she said, and took my hand in a sloppy handshake. "You'll be me, and I'll be you, and you can be the liar, and there in the dark we won't know who's who and it won't matter because we'll still be together."

"You're making a mistake. You don't want this. What you want is a friend."

She leaned down and took my face between her palms.

"Jake," she said, "poor Jake, do you really think you're my friend?"

She reached down and gripped both my hands in hers, her face kissing distance from mine for perhaps five heartbeats. Then she pulled, pulled *hard* until I was standing, and drew me weaving toward the pool house, her eyes steady on mine as she walked backward ahead of me, still gripping my hands.

"That's what I want," she said. "I want you to be me. I want you to be the liar."

"This is nuts."

"It's what I want," she said. "Will you refuse me?"

At the threshold of the pool house—cool and dark as a mineshaft inside against the hot bright sunlight of the deck, the couch beckoning, a fan turning lazily overhead—I lost my nerve and resisted, held back, but then she slipped free of my grip and backed into the room, so dark inside against the glare of the day that she was merely a silhouette. The silhouette made wings of its arms, reaching behind its back, then lay the bikini top on the smooth wooden floor, stepping easily out of the bottoms and laying those beneath, the two pieces resting on the wood floor in perfect position, a disappearing act, the silhouette retreating farther to the couch and raising its arms to me. After that I couldn't have resisted with all the strength in the world, not even if I'd wanted to.

And then she was on top of me, hot skin slick against mine, both of us collapsed together and breathless from the sprint, limbs trembling, the lost time we'd tried and failed to make up for in a single frantic go, and she put her face into my neck and cried.

"You bastard," she said. "Why did it have to be *you*?"

I lay there pressing the heel of my palm against my mouth, not knowing if she meant the job or the lost virginity or any of the thousand other histories we shared, though I guess it didn't matter. I wasn't able to answer any of those questions. Because I was crying, too.

"I know it was Kimber who took that key," she said. "I know she took it and someone paid her good money for it, thinking they were going to land something at Chime Creek, maybe get in the safe. It's been worrying at me, how all this happened, and when I came downstairs and saw that car this morning I was actually glad. I knew she'd been paid off, my own sister. You know what that's like, to think that about your own family?"

"I do."

She stopped crying and lay there quietly for a moment. I was terrified that she could feel the beating of my heart.

"It couldn't have been her," I said, thinking, *And from there it's only one step to Colonel Tom. And from Colonel Tom it's only one step to me.*

"It had to be her. And in a way I'm glad, Jake. I'm *glad* it was her, my own sister." She swallowed hard. "All along I've been thinking that if it wasn't her, if it wasn't her, Jake—it was you. Because you needed money, too."

I was happy her face was on my chest, averted.

"I guess taking the job proves it," she said. "That it wasn't you. And this is how grateful I am."

"You've been drinking all day," I said. "You should sleep."

And I did feel her breathing slow, her body relax into mine.

I said, "Are you going to call her on it?"

"I just want her gone. She told me she's leaving inside of a week, moving out to become another cautionary tale in West Hollywood. For the price of a key I'm rid of her."

She relaxed against me more.

"I'm going to quit, Jake," she said.

"I told Werner that."

"I'll bet he said Juan would move up. That he'd be just fine without me."

"He said he couldn't do without you."

She slid her hand up and rested it on my throat, her fingertips draping over my pulse. Down the block the mower cut out.

"You see?" she said. "You're a terrific liar."

TWENTY

THERE WAS THE POOL HALL, at night, with its squalid cement-block architecture, like a shelter from an urban war still to come. Electric lights in patriotic colors adorning the perimeter, bright neon vibrating into the darkness and reflected by the silvery pools distributed among the pitted ground. Rows of trucks in glossy greens and reds and blues had filled the lot, motorized candies starved for attention—but the windshields were all smoked and mirrored glass, as if the passengers were assassins, or celebrities, set on moving anonymously. Crossing the uneven ground toward the pool hall a hoarse voice whooped off to my left, the quick response a chime of glass breaking and, in the gapped stall between two trucks, the sudden stamping, panting dance of two men grappling in a fight. Huddled packs of threes and fours muttered and coughed and sipped Mason jars of sticky clear liquid, passing pinched red embers of burning herb, some singing along with the country music echoing from within the bar, flat reptile gazes communicating all the urgency, all the cocked and hair-triggered nature of the night, with its implied threat of violence and pain. This was why you got drunk outside, before you went inside: so that you could stand being inside—where everyone was drunk.

I had come here for none of what waited within: the savagery, the altered perception, the uncertain promise of a fight or a fuck. What I wanted was out back—in the woods, somewhere deep in the birches. In the fearful clarity of the quiet afternoon, Sally asleep beside me, I had arrived at a simple understanding: *It's not enough to walk away from the mistake.* The morning's nausea had by then subsided, receding like a flagging tide, but a dreadful sense of purpose had flooded in to occupy its place, the intent as urgent as the heartbeat tempo of the band thudding now up through the earth. Alone in the back lot among the parked cars, the rear fire door gapped to invite in a smoke-clearing breeze, I paused for a moment with my eyes closed and my face upraised to the sky, allowing myself the luxury of pretending any other outcome was possible—and then, turning my back on the bar, strode into the forest along the same path my father had walked while I waited in the truck, escape on his mind and larceny in his heart.

The weak light of my cell phone showed the way, a path winding between hawthorn and fern, the trunks of the birches reflecting cindery lunar shades. Each branch and leaf cast a gliding shadow against the stirring backdrop, until it seemed that the forest itself were coming alive. The light losing heart, draining dry, and when it seemed that my phone might soon quit entirely I switched it off. Another minute of moving with hands outstretched in the dark, the music from the pool hall fading some, I sensed a great mass ahead of me, and halted when I spied the black prow of a roof angled against the glittering canopy of sky. My seeking fingertips touched rough wood, exposed nailheads, flaking paint. I retrieved my phone and switched it on, the milky light casting its glow onto the walls of a painted shed just large enough to hold a parked car, two padlocked double doors to the side and a window whose glass had been removed.

I gripped the sill and hoisted myself up through the window, crouched briefly on the frame with my heart beating rapidly, then dropped lightly down to a dirt floor. I'm smelling damp earth and sawdust, gasoline and ganja, too, as I stood up, wincing when I walked into a spiderweb.

The sticky strands clung to my face, and when I'd plucked them away I lifted my phone out once again and powered it on, watched the perimeter of the room take shape in the pixelated light. Cobwebbed corners, floor to ceiling, a pair of rusting pitchforks whose tines were stained a sticky, inky black, more cobwebs in the rafters overhead, there a small safe, squat and black, the light losing heart again, a few bags of cement and a wheelbarrow tipped up on its side, and, in the center of the shed, jarringly clean and freshly painted, a large white tank on a rolling sledge hooked to a four-wheeled off-road vehicle, a valve on the top with a silver handwheel, the sort you'd expect to see on a propane tank for a gas grill, a black tube leading from its mouth down to a dented bucket. I collapsed the phone again and placed it into my pocket, the weary transistors warm against my hip.

Melt your fucking face right off, Hippolyte had said, but no time to go back, no time to revisit or reconsider, because the plan had always been that there was no plan. Knowing if I allowed myself even a moment to consider what I was doing and what it meant, who I was betraying and what the price of discovery would be, I would have lost my nerve. Knowing courage wasn't a renewable thing; you had to use it when you found it. I stepped forward reaching into the darkness until my palm found the cool hide of the tank, raised my foot and edged the black tube out of the bucket, lifting it casually over the side to let it fall in the dirt. The handwheel cold in my grasp but my palm warming the aluminum and, experimenting with the moment, I turned the wheel an eighth of a turn, heard and felt nothing, still nothing and more nothing, then nothing, waiting and nothing and no signs, and another fractional turn, then another, and still nothing, then nothing and more nothing and still nothing, another quarter turn, still nothing until my indrawn breath seared the insides of my nostrils, burned them, *flayed* them with the sharp sting of ammonia, eyes tearing with caustic fumes, my next breath a hiccupy hitch and gag in my throat, the skin of my face cold and tight, and rearing round I fell heavily over my own feet, on hands and knees on packed earth discovered clearer air at ground level, and realized the noxious stuff wasn't draining down, it was *rising*—it wasn't seeping into the ground like spilled seed but going aerosol, it was inside me but I couldn't find the fucking window to get out and get *air*. I couldn't find the way out and it was inside me, the poison, flesh of my lungs peeling back like old paint. No light!—a single spark and the air would ignite, transform the shed into a bomb and torch half an acre, each panting exhale sounding like *high* or *my* as I slapped around the walls trying to find the window, *where is the way out*, good riddance to me but not like this, and then my hands found the rough wood frame and shouting I hoisted myself up and out of it, my shirt caught for an exquisite instant on a sill nail, and then I tumbled heavily onto thick swatches of sweet soft fern blessed by the fresh clean good, good air, oh sweet air, unable to run for a few seconds, unable to crawl, unable to do anything but lay there coughing a thick gruel of my supper onto the ferns. On my feet again, I began to lope toward the sound of the music, my shirt pressed over my face and one hand held out before me. As if I hoped to ward off the terrible blow that nature surely wished to deal me. I didn't stop running until I reached the back lot to the pool hall, and crouched down panting beside a white van, waiting for equilibrium to return.

For a moment I imagined that the shouting and whistling and stomping from within the bar was for me. But no, I was just a boy who had made a man's mistake and, in undoing it, had opened his world up to other men who would do the boy harm. I considered the rear exit door, pictured the swirling tide of dancers within, feet going *quick-quick, slow, slow,* the men turning the women as they stepped with two hands exchanging positions over their heads. Then I looked back at the woods, starlight bright now and the clouds broken, as if shooed away from this terrible sight, Ursa gazing down at the quiet trees, Big Bear and her little baby, and all the coy stars leering down at the comedy below.

How far to that shed, Jake?

A few hundred yards? What if the wind blows it this way?

If it leads them to Colonel Tom you go down too.

But this was how it had to play out. That poison, rising into the air and carried this way by a single innocent breeze—what would it do to a trapped roomful? I imagined the moment of crisis, the band falling off wind and, in an instant, fifty people down, one hundred. The image got my feet moving again. I spat once more in the dirt, strode to the back door so overcome by the fumes that I missed my first attempt to grasp the door handle, and pulled the fire door open to peer inside. The exit alcove was empty, up the doglegged hall two cowboys lashing a piss-trough with the evening's beer and shouting along with the music, thudding percussion coming up through the floor as I turned to the wall and punched the glass face of the fire alarm.

Time to swim, Jake, I thought, and yanked down the white handle.

I came awake past three with Coop roaring at the back door.

The evening's events crowding in on me: It was the Magician, they'd realized what I'd done and were here for me, creeping toward us through the forest out back, and when they were through with me I'd be at the bottom of Sayers Dam.

Coop had made friends with him, though.

If it were the Magician, Coop would be pawing at the glass and thumping his tail, whining to get out there, thinking he was going to get an extra meal.

Rolly was downstairs ahead of me, at the sliding door, with his index finger hooked in Coop's collar and peering out the glass door. Both of us dressed in boxer shorts and looking as if we'd run some hard miles in the last few days.

"A bear down from the mountain," Rolly said.

You could tell when one was around because all the dogs in the neighborhood would act crazy, pissing on the carpet and scraping doors down to the bare wood—even biting through their cages, though it wasn't clear if this was because they wanted to get at the bear or get *away* from it. Sometimes you had the impression that even the dogs didn't know. We'd had trouble with bears before, back in seventh grade one of them killing two farmers' goats, tore up a rabbit hutch or two, and just as it was getting so people wouldn't let their dogs out alone, a state trooper ran up on it in his car and put the bear down with a tranquilizer gun from his trunk. The next morning the game warden brought it around to the middle school, the bear drugged inside an enclosed trailer that had tiny airholes punched out of it with nailheads. The teachers marched the classrooms out one at a time and had us line up, each kid filing by the trailer to peer in through one of the airholes. I moved up on it for my turn feeling like those dogs, not sure if I was curious or terrified, my senses telling me in equal parts to go see and run away—but everyone was watching, and fear of shame was the weight that tipped the scales toward courage, or at least an outward show of what would look like it. I leaned close and peered inside. It was dark in there. An earthy smell emanated from the space—not a stink, not really, something more like what Quinn was getting at with his hung deer, a gamy rot with a queer undercurrent of sweetness. What was inside was breathing heavily, sighing humid breaths under syrupy snores. What was inside sounded like a sleeping giant you would never, ever want to wake—and yet I kept moving closer. I knew what was inside was dangerous and that was why I wanted to see it. I suppose I wanted to see it because I wanted to see if it had my face. Then the game warden gripped my shoulder and I cried out in surprise. *Not too close,* he said, *you get too close and he'll reach up and hook your eye.* I said, *I thought he was drugged,* and he said, *Yeah, but what if I'm wrong?*

"The drought?" I asked.

"No," Rolly said. "I bet some damn fool left some food out there."

He'd want to go and have a look, and of course he'd find the fish I'd heaved into the woods. Coop had calmed down some with Rolly's finger hooked in his collar, but he was showing his teeth and making that rumbling sound deep in his throat, and you could tell the bear was still close.

"You want me to go look?" I asked.

"Are you out of your mind?"

We stood there looking out at the night, though neither of us had any idea what we'd do if we actually saw something.

"I start Monday," I said. "That job at the club."

He looked at me sideways.

"How'd that play out?" he asked.

"Sally took it hard."

"What happened?"

"She called me a bastard."

"And then?"

"And then—" I said, and lay my forehead against the glass, "—then she asked me to stay the night."

"That's Sally for you. Why didn't you stay?"

I was looking out at the yard but I sensed that Rolly was still watching me, cataloguing the wounds, tallying the pain I'd been banking for a week.

"Urgent business," I said.

"I may need to borrow some money," he said, "come Christmas."

"You can have as much as you want. You can have it all."

"I'd just need a little to help with the cruise. I was going to use my bonus to pay for it."

"How did you know it would lead to this?"

"What," he said, "the bear?"

"The job. Getting me the lifeguard thing, it leading to this."

"I didn't."

"Rolly," I said, "don't lie to me, pop."

He turned toward me, leaned against the glass and crossed his arms. Looking very old and wasted, like he didn't want to be here doing this.

"De Soto," he said. "The Magician, they call him."

"Right," I said.

"He came to visit me at the dealership. I thought it was bad enough just being seen with him, so I had Ellen invite him in, told her to hold my calls and closed the door, then asked him to say his peace and get out. And he said he had just one thing for me. From my brother. A gift of a job for you. He told me he'd heard about the bills, how you weren't going back, and by way of thanking me for watching over you all these years de Soto would see to it that if you took the lifeguard job, Werner would hire you into the office."

"How the hell does he do that?"

Rolly rubbed his neck.

"Jake," he said, "I don't think your dad was the only one who was cooking the books. And now I guess he's got a lot of rich people on the line who got away with it. Only they didn't get away with it, because he owns them."

"And that was it?"

Rolly's fingers brushed the latch, diddled with it, fucked around with it like he didn't know what to do with himself, an old man there in his boxers looking foolish.

"He laid ten hundred dollar bills on the desk," Rolly said. *Take Werner to lunch with that*, he said. *At Semaphore. And everything is solved.* And then he walked out. Left the money sitting there. God help me, Jake, I took it. So now *I'm* on the hook to de Soto. Like a common *criminal*. You know what I was thinking, looking down at that little gift?"

I wanted to say, *But it wasn't a gift, Rolly. It was de Soto buying a fifty-thousand-dollar profit on a thousand-dollar investment. Buying fifty-thousand with a single fucking lunch.*

"That my dad owed you," I said.

"I've hated myself for it, ever since," he said. "But, yeah, that's what I was thinking. Maybe it's for the best. You'll make a lot of money, get your life back on track, and that somehow makes up for it. Not so bad of me to compromise, am I right? After a whole life of doing the right thing. I mean, it's just one job, right?"

Coop gulped and sat down.

"Anyway," I said, "I don't think I'm going to have it long."

"You're going to throw it. Take a dive."

"Yes," I said. "And see that Sally gets it."

He reached up and latched the door.

"Good boy," he said.

TWENTY-ONE

A TERRIBLE THING HAPPENED WHEN I walked into the executive washroom for the first time, at twelve minutes past ten o'clock Monday morning. As I pushed through the door and addressed the chrome and black granite Xanadu, the door *whisking* efficiently closed behind me, I beheld the impression that I had ceased to exist, the mirror before me revealing a room with my presence neatly removed. After an instant of exquisite horror, I realized what had caused the illusion: The room's symmetry had tricked the eye. There was no mirror before me, just a line of basins here, a bonsai in the center, a line of basins there, a bonsai in the center. A newspaper on this counter, a newspaper on that counter, both equally undisturbed. I had read every inch of that newspaper at the breakfast table two hours ago, scouring furlongs of fresh ink until I found it: a disinterested postage-stamp-sized brief about a fire alarm being pulled at the Zion Tavern last night, patrons evacuated without incident. No injuries. No suspects. No explanation.

No leads as to why.

This is looking like routine vandalism, a police official was quoted as saying, and suddenly I'm flooded with sweet syrupy relief. Okay, so they rooked me on thirty thousand. But that means I'm off the hook, the debt paid. I'm actually feeling like I can glimpse the end-point of this, the closing bell at which the game is declared over, tied at zero.

A cavitation of chromed plumbing to my right, the swirl and eddy of draining water.

A stall door opened and Werner's second in command, Blessington, emerged wiping his hands on a terry-cloth towel. This he threw in the hamper with a no-look pass as he addressed the handsome combed cad in the mirror, washing his hands beneath the no-touch faucet. It was all preselect and automation, this room, everything engineered for mechanized efficiency and contact-free comfort, and in that moment I realized that this was what happened as you moved up the ladder of wealth: You stepped into a science-fiction film.

"Jacob," Blessington said, with what sounded like genuine pleasure, looking at me in the mirror. "How are things going on your primary action items?"

I didn't know what my primary action items were. This was unsurprising in light of the fact that I didn't know what an action item was.

"Very well," I said, "things are going very, very well."

Thinking that surely that second *very* had been a mistake.

"Listen," he said, looking at himself now, "I was thinking you should re-prioritize the Shamokin thing. That other thing—the thing with what's-his-name. I think that can wait."

"All right," I said.

"Ping Fischer and see what he thinks about it."

"About the other thing?"

"No, about Shamokin."

"I will. I'll do that."

"But don't trust him."

"I won't."

"Listen to him. *Learn* from him. But don't trust him."

"I will. I mean I won't."

"Werner trusts him. But we can see where *that* got him on Shamokin. Anyway," he said, "we all know we're here to protect Werner from himself."

Here he looked at me, clearly expecting an informed, witty, and circumspect response. And all at once I was verbally immobilized, trapped as surely as a mosquito in amber, entirely unable to continue the line of conversation—and it was, sweetly and surprisingly, my father's words that helped me recover, one of his sayings, a phrase engineered to carry you through situations where you had no idea what anyone was talking about but needed to find some purchase.

"Well," I said, "you can't tell which way the train went by looking at the tracks."

He paused for a moment, drying his hands on another towel, and looked at me with a puzzled expression. I thought, *This one could go either way.* His expression resolved itself and he grinned into a little bark of a laugh.

"I guess that's true," he said. "See you at lunch? We'll talk about Fischer."

"See if we can learn anything."

"That lying little fuck."

He knocked on the granite countertop three times, as if for luck, then whisked by out of the room in a bright backdraft of tasteful aftershave. I dipped a palm under the cold tap and wet my face, lashed two cups of coffee into the glossiest urinal I'd ever seen, washed my hands, and tried the same terry-cloth no-look toss.

And missed.

I can drink water but that's all, Sally had said when I called her during the drive to work, dared to lead with a joke, and when I heard the smoked laughter in her response I had to pull to the side of the road, so great was my relief. *I poisoned myself. For lunch I'll make some congee, lots of ginger. It works every time. But then it's right back under the covers.*

Is there room for me?

Always.

I'm invited?

Jake, she said, *I told you: It's my house.*

Back at my desk, I hunted around in the ridiculous eighties-era Rolodex that had been left for me, and found only one person with the last name Fischer. I had spent the last of my courage the night before so it was something else I harnessed to make that frightening call—the sense, maybe, that good acts heal even the most sickened spirit, and present the opportunity for some sort of regeneration. As I dialed Fischer's number, I noticed that someone had placed a red asterisk beside his name, which I gathered was an indication that the man was some sort of exception to a rule.

"Allan," I said, "it's Jake Asprey at Chime Creek. Thom Blessington said I ought to speak to you."

"*That* asshole . . . What does he want?"

"Tell me true, Allan," I said, "what do you know about this Shamokin thing?"

I listened and wrote down everything he said, and by the time the conversation was finished I felt I understood the problem with Shamokin, a camp built and operated the next town over by Fischer, and Fischer's apparently hot to sell it to Chime Creek. This being Werner's new plan to bump membership and member rates: He operates a summer camp that's free for new members, thinks he can boost numbers by fifteen to twenty percent if he can add the camp enticement—bus leaves right from the Chime Creek parking lot, and mothers new to thinking they can spend the whole day by the pool. Only there's a problem: Last summer a parent sitting on a Shamokin bench having a nice conversation with a friend tells her daughter, *Sure, when you're done with the sprinkler you can go on the swings.* A moment later she hears her kid screaming, looks over and sees her daughter dancing with pain beneath the swing sets. Twenty minutes later she's in the ER and the doctor is telling her the kid has second degree burns on the soles of her feet. Fischer, it seemed, had unwisely installed black rubber mats beneath the swings, and now he's telling me the uproar is just parents trying to cash in on a manufactured case, the cases won't hold up in court when he tells the judge he installed a sign saying NO BARE FEET.

"Anyway the numbers aren't as bad as they look," Fischer said. "Skip over Blessington and go to Werner, and I'll make it worth your while. Werner will understand if you talk to him the way you're talking to me. Tell him it's a good move, they can run a good camp here April through October with pure profit the first year and he's going to get plenty of new bodies up in Chime Creek for it. The numbers aren't as bad as they look."

I hung up.

Four minutes of hunting revealing that an independent arbiter on a similar case had personally measured the surface temperature of equivalent mats at one hundred sixty-one degrees on a July afternoon. Another eight minutes revealing that selling the camp indemnifies Fischer against liability, now it's Werner's problem, and NO BARE FEET a worthless protection. Another twelve minutes of research plus basic math revealing that it would be at least fourteen years before camp profits paid off the cost of replacing the mats.

I called up Blessington.

"He's lying," I said.

"Put an asterisk beside his name," Blessington said.

"Someone already did," I said.

I hung up feeling somehow pleased with myself. Like I ought to call up Rolly and let him know what had just happened. He'd listen and then drop one of his lines, tell me to wait a minute and call out, *Zooey, it's JP Morgan on the line. He wants meat loaf tonight.* Letting me know he was pleased. I sat there for a few minutes in a trance of astonishment, feeling as if I'd negotiated a tricky obstacle course without hesitation or flinch or error. Werner's insistence on absolute mutual trust in business dealings had nearly cost him fourteen years of losses.

Half an hour later, an unpleasant thought caused me to pick up the Rolodex again.

Artem.

Asgar, Ashby. Asner.

There it was, on the next card: *Asprey, Rolly.*

An asterisk beside his name.

I'm thinking that's the stain of a single visit from the Magician, the stain sticking with Rolly from here on in.

Knock-knock on my door, Wendy standing there with her spectacles low on her nose, earpieces clipped to a long rhinestone chain.

"Visitor," she said.

"What," I said, "like a meeting?"

She sighed with the patient disappointment of a mother who just *knows* her kid is someday going to get it right.

"Your calendar shows no meetings until half past two," she said.

I looked at my calendar and the numbers swam before my eyes.

"She has a badge," Wendy said, eyebrow raised. "Shall I tell her you're busy?"

I tried to *look* busy—but I couldn't think of a single legitimate thing to do before Lisa knocked on the door, her credentials showing from the breast pocket of her suit. An aggressive move, showing up at a workplace like that, badging your way into the deep offices. They'd tried that with my father, came to see him at the condo office. He stood at the front door looking out through the glass with his hands in his suit pockets, his lips white and thin. Just as bad as pulling up in front of a house with your cruiser lights going. Which they had also done. A move not so much about telling the person inside of your intent as it was about telling everyone *around* that this person is under suspicion, and are you sure you want to be doing business with him?

"Wow," Lisa said, taking a seat opposite me, running her hands over the leather, turning to get a load of Wendy, then facing me again and actually spinning the seat all the way around in a circle, the way a little girl would visiting her mother's office for the first time. "Like, a tie and everything. I came looking for you down at the pool. Expecting to see you up in the chair. One of those tasty mummies says to me—in a whisper—*He's up at the office now*. The way they always whisper when they're talking about, you know—" her voice dropped to a mocking, embellished whisper "—*affairs*."

Twinkly again.

"So now you're one of them?" she asked. "Using the *good* entrance?"

"Same piece of shit car, though."

"In a hurry to get away from the hot pool deck, Jake?"

"My uncle's out of work months. He loses all that commission plus future business plus salary, money's going to be tight. I had no choice."

"Tough break. A nice guy. He be okay?"

She sounded sincere but I couldn't be sure.

"Sure," I said, "if he can lay off the ice cream."

"Some problems with impulse control in your family, am I wrong, Jake?"

I sat there sweating into my starched shirt, waiting for her to tell me they'd got a make on the Zion fire alarm last night, *We took a little walk, and guess what we found a quarter mile off in the woods? Oh, that shed'll be habitable in five or six lifetimes, once the anhydrous moves through the groundwater. So: You want to come with me now, or do I send a cruiser, the lights going?* Instead she sat there with an expectant expression on her face, as if she anticipated some sort of edifying response to the plain sense laid before me, and for the second time that morning I found myself summoning forth words I'd first heard spoken by my father.

"If the band keeps playing," I said, "sometimes you have to get up and dance."

"Your father was full of shit, too," she said.

"Excuse me?"

"Oh, sure, he's charming enough, from what Tibbens tells me. How did your uncle get off so easy? Just having the eating thing?"

"He's always been that way."

"And what about you?" she asked. "Where are you weak? Does it have to do with your friend, the chef?"

The phone rang. I didn't think I'd ever been so grateful for a phone call.

"Asprey," I said.

"What the fuck are you doing talking to *her*?" Colonel Tom said.

I coughed into my first and said, "What?"

"The hot *chispita* sitting right the fuck in front of you, bright boy."

I licked my lips and said, "How do you make that?"

"Because I'm looking at you right now."

I rotated my chair and peered through the glass at the Arcadian expanse of the golf course, the handsome ninth hole verdant in the bright midday light, the water trap beyond, a little copse of woods, then another green, more trees, and then the ultramodern million-dollar houses beyond, with their scalenes and rectangles, their pulleys and counterweights.

"See, now you're searching," Colonel Tom said, "seeing if you can spot me. But you won't. Meanwhile she's there studying you, trying to figure out what the fuck you're doing. Say something about the course so she thinks this is business."

"They mow it twice a week."

"That's the best you can do?"

"And it takes half a week to mow."

"So?"

"So," I said, "they're always mowing."

"Good. Keep going."

"Park-style course, a tricky seventh—"

"Enough."

"Should I come back later?" Lisa asked.

I turned to her and held up my index finger—*one second*—then turned back to the course.

"So," I said, "you see how it is."

"I do," Tom said.

"I'm just wondering how well you see."

"It's this sweet Kowa fluorite scope, Jake. Oh, everyone says they're going to use it for hunting long range, but no one does. They use it to watch tail undress across town. That's what everyone does, except for me—I'm the one guy who *does* use it for hunting. And right now I'm hunting you."

"Okay," I said, "what would you like to talk about?"

"I'm three-quarters of a mile away right now, but I can see that you nicked yourself shaving over by your left ear, can see the nice lady there, her name on her badge. Wait a second." The sound of a few quick clicks. "Soto or Sobo or something? I can almost make it out. And I'm sitting here wondering what the fuck you're doing talking to a cop. Because, Jake, unless you have her there for a hot lay on that nice couch, things are looking a little unclear to me."

"I can't really have this conversation now," I said. "I have a surprise visitor, just showed up without an appointment. I don't even know why she's here. But I'm interested to hear more from you."

"I'm calling because things have got fuckin' complicated, Jake," he said. "Two things have happened. One bad and one very bad."

"Elaborate for me," I said.

"Really, I can come back," Lisa said.

"Someone went and fucked us, Jake," Tom said. "Fucked us good and hard out of fifty grand of product. Can you appreciate just how upset that makes me?"

"Yes I can."

"I'm thinking, Jake, that it had to be you, it had to be Quinn, or it had to be our friend Mr. Magician. One of you motherfuckers went and siphoned off my pretty little treasure last night, pulled the fire alarm on the pool hall as a nice *fuck you* to seal the deal. See, having the cops *and* the fire marshall out at my place in the same night gets me—well, it gets me *jumpy*, Jake, and I got that ticklish feeling over my coffee this morning, and went out back to check—no word from Quinn, a fire alarm, a visit from Tibbens, something beginning to add up here—and that tank was *empty*. I just about coughed my guts out from the smell of it before I even got inside—which tells me, Jake, that the person who went and did that siphoning off wasn't Quinn. He knows how to handle anhydrous. Whereas the person who did this job just pulled as much of it as he could sloppy and *ran*. And I need to know if that someone was some strung-out meth head got a lucky find, if it was Quinn in a hurry, or if it was *you*. Now tell me true, Jake—did you go and fuck me? Because if you did, you're going to get exactly one chance to make it right, and you're going to do that by giving me a *name*."

My shirt damp against my back now.

"I'm in the dark on this one," I said. "A one-time thing, someone pulling out at the last minute—that's going to happen sometimes."

"This wasn't a one-time thing. This was just going to be the *first* one."

And that shut me up for good.

"You keep your ear to the ground," he said. "Because Quinn is *gone*. You understand? He's not out baggin' thousand-an-hour hookers, or snorting a barrel of coke in some Philly five-star. I pulled fifty jobs with that boy, and I'm here to tell you that he is *gone*. What I don't know is if he's gone because he decided that money was too good to share, find that shit hard to believe with someone coolheaded as Quinn, he's smart enough to know you stick around for a score's going to keep coming our way. No, what I'm thinking—what's got me fucking anxious, Jake, is wondering if he's gone because someone else *wanted* him out of the way. Which might just mean that same someone else wants *us* out of the way."

"I'm worried about that, too."

"You better be. Because we're tied together in this. I go down, you go down. I do time? You're going to do it alongside me, someplace your daddy won't be able to protect you. I end up toes up in a hole back in the woods? You're going to be there beside me. So you best keep your fuckin' ear to the ground and remember that right now I'm your best friend and your worst enemy. All in one. And I'll be watching. You ever think you're sitting there all alone? You're not. I'm right there with you. I'm right there *beside* you."

And he's gone.

"That was quite a conversation," Lisa said.

I pressed five trembling fingertips to my brow.

This was just going to be the first one.

The first job of many.

"It's this Shamokin thing," I said. "A lot of money tied up in it, a lot of lawsuits. You hear about the kids burning their feet?"

"I read about it. How do you see that playing out?"

"In pain," I said.

I folded my hands and waited.

"Sorry to surprise you this way," she said. "I just wanted to let you know I'm being called away."

"Back to the big city."

"If you call Harrisburg big. Not enough to go on, keep me here. I talk to Werner," she said, "he tells me nothing's missing. But I know the problem is just that he hasn't found out what it is, yet."

"Maybe it was just a couple of kids."

"Sure," she said, "pulling an IRA-style smash and grab. Oh sure."

"Kids are scarier than you think these days."

Her cell phone rang and she silenced it.

"Werner tells me your girlfriend quit today," she said. "I can't help thinking, Jake, that her quitting was exactly what he was hoping for."

"He likes things neat and tidy."

"I don't see this being neat and tidy, though. Earlier this summer, boy drowns. Then this, plus it's coming out he's got a former chef and a new business-class employee with one degree of separation from an unsavory element. If you were to ask me," she said, "he's probably going to be out of a job soon, too, don't you think?"

"I guess it's possible."

She said, "Does that mean you move up? You know: a little promotion while everyone in line shuffles up to Werner's spot?"

I blinked twice.

"I guess it does," I said.

"To the manner born."

"You could say that. Or just lucky."

"Huh," she said. "Funny how people benefit from the worst things. A kid drowns and you get a job. Someone loses his job, you get a promotion."

"You think it's over, then?"

"No, just beginning. This is going to become what we call *deep*, a lot of layers to get down through. Daylight armed theft in a town like this? That element doesn't just whisk away. There'll be more. And then I'll be back."

"I'm happy to help, if I can."

She folded her hand.

"See?" she said. "Just like your dad. Every bit as charming."

"A talent we share?"

"Along with a few others. A habit of consorting with dirty money because it helps yours seem that much cleaner. Only it's not."

"You're putting me on."

"I'm not. Oh, I can't prove you were in on it, Jake. But I know you were. You could probably sue my ass even for suggesting it, but you won't. Because you've figured out the same thing I have. It made no sense for them to get her key to the supply closet and yours to the kitchen. They would have got both from her. Easier, cleaner than that mess with you and Rolly. Except that's how it went down. That was quite an event, you taking a shotgun butt to the face. Something no one would ever question. Right?"

That terrible mad itch came to me, then, the itch that lived where the match used to strike. It came surging up and out of me in a high bark of frightened laughter.

"Lisa," I said, "you're joking, right?"

"No," she said, shaking her head and standing up, "see, Jake, you made a mistake. But I can't show you that, because you got in the game too late. This game, you have to be born into it. I'm not even going to lean on you. The reason: You're going to come to me. That's my favorite part of the job, when the bad guys realize—*surprise*—they're dealing with other bad guys, which means all the rules out the window, anything allowed, and suddenly they get *scared*. You're going to be begging me to take you in, Jake. Because if you don't, you're going to end up missing one day. No sign of you ever again. Will you let me help you?"

I licked my lips and said, "I suppose you think you're being clever, acting like I had anything to do with this."

"The sooner you give me a name, the sooner I can protect you. Because I can't help you until you give me a name, something to go on. You're going to figure that out, that you need me. I just hope you don't figure it out too late. Hey," she said, "maybe you'll even convince me that you were like Sally, involved in a way you didn't even know. Not your fault at all. Maybe you plead out, watch the other guys go down. You may even get to keep this cushy job."

She reached out and rapped on the wall.

"For luck," she said. "You'll need it."

For the next hour I tried to work, throw myself into parsing the spreadsheet of recently canceled memberships, trying to find a common pain-point there and ways to get them back. Doing it the way I used to heave myself in the pool, get in there and then you've got no choice but to swim. It was impossible, though, beyond me: I kept feeling a terrible itch between my shoulder blades, and imagining Colonel Tom still deciding how many reasons he had for keeping me around. He wanted a name, Lisa wanted a name. Everyone wanted to identify who was to blame. Even me.

In the end I did the thing I least wanted to, and dialed a *call out* message to the switchboard at Slippery Rock. And then waited.

Waited more.

Waited a lot more, the shadows clawing their way across the greens, even Werner having looked in to say he was leaving. I was just about to give up when the phone rang with the number I'd been waiting for, the pay phone from his cellblock.

"Sorry, kid," he said, "I was in this hot game, twenty cigarettes at stake."

"I need to speak to the Magician," I said.

He sighed.

"It's going to cost me all twenty," he said.

TWENTY-TWO

HE LIKED GOOD SUITS, AND he liked to eat, de Soto, a man in command of his appetites, and as I watched him address the elegant plate of lamb chops before him, delicately working with the knife, the fork, I recalled that for all the meals I had shared with him at restaurants years ago, I had never in my life seen him pay a bill. He had the unhurried reflexes of a man accustomed to getting what he wants. *Semaphore*, he'd said, *we go as a celebration*, only I didn't know what we were to be celebrating, with the product gone and an armed Colonel Tom on the hunt for a fall guy. Before me on the table, a plate of braised pork belly with lentils and parsley salad cooled into the night air, as beautiful in its composition as modern art. We were nearly alone on the outside terrace, the sweet-smelling stream rushing alongside us, at its edge the watercress the staff picked daily for salads, on the far side the night buses gliding quietly by with their interior lights on, now and then the silence cleaved by the sound of knives being sharpened as they braked to the little bus stand up the road. Four tables away, Tico's bodyguard, a tall slim import in a black suit, sat reading the racing papers, beyond him a couple celebrating what looked like a few anniversaries too many.

"Colonel Tom is leaning on me," I said.

"Of course he is," Tico said. "He is unhappy that the deal is going bad. Knowing that I am unhappy too."

"Maybe he thinks you're going to take him night fishing."

"If he is wondering that, feeling nervous, then he is a smart man. Because there is nothing I hate more than being double-crossed, I put in the effort and the time, I front the money and take the risk, and then where is my payday?"

"What money did you front? Aside from the grand you gave to Rolly."

"So Rolly is telling you," he said. "An honest man. Though not so honest that he returned the money. No, he kept it. As he should have."

"He told me."

"Then you know that you owe me for the job you have."

"As I understand it."

He reached out and gripped my hand in his, and in the moment before he spoke I had a terrible sense of being in free fall, and I'm thinking, *Why here, Tico? Why here, in this fucking backwater, where nothing matters? Why not in the big city, advising the cocksuckers from the big banks, a gleaming Rolls waiting by the curb and a blonde broad in the backseat, living the good life in a penthouse?*

Answer: Because here he could be the big fish. And eat what he pleased.

"Good," he said, "then you understand how things are between us."

"And how are things?"

"Things are," he said, "that you are in my debt."

"I understand that I was," I said.

The bodyguard looked up from his racing papers. Even the couple stopped eating and fixed their gazes on us, entertainment suddenly on offer, too far away to hear what we're talking about but close enough to read the tone of my voice. Tico still gripping my hand firmly, maybe a little too aggressively, and I'm feeling like I want to take it back.

"Nice meal," Tico said, looking out over the water. "It would be a shame to ruin it with a disagreement."

"No disagreement here, Tico. Because there's nothing to discuss. We're clear. I was never paid. I settled the debt and now I'm done."

"Jacob, Jacob," he said, pushing his plate aside, shaking his head, all sincerity now, "this is not about money or favors, this is about *succession.*"

He leaned forward on his elbows, close to me, his voice lowered so that even the bodyguard couldn't hear.

"Forget Colonel Tom," he said, "his silly fears. I can protect you, make sure he touches not one hair on your head. And here is why: We lose one job, sure, but what is one job when you are in such a position? You see how you move in this short time? As easily as falling down, except you are falling upward." He let go of my hand, held his own hand out, palm up. "And you are moving easily because there is a hand behind you, guiding you, lifting you up."

"It was your choice, doing that."

"Of course. But the assistance has been there, nevertheless. Now—how is the saying?—you are like one of those people born on third base who believes he hit a triple. And that is not the case. You are in your place because you have been helped by your good friend. This is why we must remain close. The hand of God, it always brings you low, in humility. But the hand of a friend—" He sat back in his chair and opened his hands. "Isn't it funny, Jake, that magic tricks are all about defying gravity. Laws set by God. You make a candle light in the dark with no match. You cause a coin to levitate. Or," he said, "you cause a man to go away. And in doing so, you become Godlike yourself."

"You cause men to go away?"

He smiled at me, the reflexes still slow, and to give my hands something to do I popped a match alight with my thumbnail and placed the flame to the tip of another Winston.

"I do, occasionally," he said. "Yes."

"Where is Quinn?"

"Quinn? You never see him again."

"Where did he go?"

"He went where everyone who makes a terrible mistake must go. He went *away*."

"What was his mistake?"

"His mistake," Tico said, "was to try and renegotiate the contract after it was signed."

"He wanted to change the rules."

Tico tapped his ashes.

"He came to see me the day after the job," he said. "Can you imagine—he is telling me that he has proof he cannot be trusting you. I borrow the Colonel's Kowa scope, he is saying, and the morning after the job I'm spotting Jake checking out where we go through the gate, talking on his phone, talking to Hippolyte, talking in the dining room to the lady detective. *Magician*, he says, *I am thinking that he is putting it all together, and losing heart. I am thinking that he is a talker. So I think*, Quinn says, *I make Jake fall with an accident*."

"What did you say to that?" I asked.

"I tell him I disagree. And he tells me he disagrees with *me*."

He shook his head.

"A terrible mistake," he said, "this Quinn, telling me to go fuck myself after all I am doing to support him, get all the people in the right position, make sure I get my share but they get plenty of the cut. Because now I know he could be making trouble for me in this job. Fear is useful sometimes, it makes someone do what you want him to do. But sometimes fear makes people act on their own behalf. He makes you fall with an accident to save himself, he only brings attention, messes up something I have carefully set in place. I'm wondering how much we can trust *him*, so I tell the Colonel to check our investment. And he gives me the news: *Magician*, he says, *it is gone*. Now I know Quinn and this kind of business—it's a bad mix. So I send him away."

"Why trust him?" I asked. "If he stole from you."

"Because now I know exactly what his price is. He fears prison. So I put him where prison will never be a risk—now he is managing a job of mine in Mexico City. A bodyguard. He will be happy, have all the girls he wants, good coke, be rich. A house with a pool and all he must do is carry a weapon and drive one of my associates all day. A good life, don't you think?"

"You better tell this to Colonel Tom. He's the one who's scared, now."

"He called me this evening, I let him know. Things are smoothed out with him, now. But you don't have to worry about Tom. As long as you are with me, you are with me, and those against you—they are no concern of yours. I make them go away to Mexico City, too."

"Except I'm not with you. I'm not with anyone."

"A problem," he said. "You don't work for me, how can I protect you?"

Tico turned to wave to the waiter in the doorway. The waiter disappeared inside for a moment, then carried an espresso out to the terrace and slid it gently beside Tico's elbow.

"You see?" Tico said, having a sip. "Business is so simple. Ask, receive, money changes hands. Everyone gets what he wants. It is what comes after that is complicated, the mess that must be tended to when people want to renegotiate. So why aren't we just doing business and everyone is happy? You've seen how neat and clean I keep things. There is no trouble with doing business with me."

He patted my hand.

"You know what I am seeing in you?" he asked. "I'm seeing in you a boy-king, a young boy-king who is sitting on wealth he does not understand. This is happening to all boy-kings, they cannot imagine the reach of their power, of their wealth, so they are making things more complicated than they are needing to be. Why make things complicated when the wealth is there for us? A bottomless well of money we tap now and then—just a bit—no one is any wiser, and we are all rich from doing good business over many years."

"You threw away the keys."

"Until they have more keys go missing, they don't bother to worry. In this way we are telling them it is over. But it is not over. In a few months we do it again. And again, the year after. And so on."

"How do you expect to get in next time?"

"With you holding the door for us," he said. "So I am upset our first shipment goes missing. So I am feeling betrayed by Quinn. The problem is resolved. I know who was responsible, and I send him away to Mexico City. Who cares if we get nothing this time? There will be many more, one time here, one time there. A beautiful bottomless gold mine."

"I don't understand," I said. "I don't get it. Why don't you—how come you don't wait until I'm inside, then? Then none of this is necessary. That mess by the airport, giving me a shotgun butt to the face. All of it."

"I needed to know if you were my *one*," he said, "*before* I let you move ahead. I can't trust you to do business with me, someone else is getting that job inside the club. Now we know—and if we do it this time and they understand nothing, how are they to catch us when you are the hand on the latch? A harmless way in, a harmless way out. No one is getting hurt."

"But people suffer. People die, using what you're asking me to steal."

"They will die anyway. You truly believe that if I don't make it, they won't find it somewhere else? But all powerful men must have this doubt. You build a factory here, the man over there loses his job. You unseat an enemy, but another always takes his place. Even on his wedding night—what do you suppose the king feels when he considers the marital bed, the beautiful fool he does not love but must produce an heir with nevertheless? Perhaps not as interesting as her sister," he said, and sat back in his chair, "but infinitely more willing to play the game."

"You mean Kimber."

He nodded.

"A beauty," he said. "Even if you don't love her, it will be some comfort, I think, to have a woman like that in your bed. Rest assured she doesn't love you, either—not really, though she believes she does. No, she is in love with the *idea* of you, of the boy-king Colonel Tom has been telling her about. She thinks she wants to go to Hollywood, but she won't make it. She won't make it a hundred miles before her nerve gives out, and she comes back to us. This is why she can be trusted. Because she knows the wealth she has always wanted is here for her."

"A life with me."

"With you. Like all boy-kings, you have a good life ahead of you. But to live it you must be playing the *role*, Jacob. Not just in work, but in the bed. You must be committed to it with your blood. And with"— he gestured below the table— "other things."

"I just realized," I said, "what a beautiful fool *you* are, Magician. To think that I have this in me."

"Oh, but you do. I know your blood, the way money talks to it. I can hear it right now. Do you know what it is saying?"

"It's telling you *no*."

"Then you make me lean on you with what I have at hand. Maybe I let Colonel Tom feel anxious about you, let him know I am anxious, too, and what are we going to do about it? Or maybe I tell him the older sister is another problem. A liability is a liability. And bad things are happening to liabilities, when time in the hole is at stake. Maybe you are showing wisdom," he said, "and like the smart ones out there, realizing nobody tells the Magician to go fuck himself."

I sat watching the bacon grease harden on my plate. The cigarette, untouched, had burned down nearly to my fingertips, the ash intact.

"So we're in agreement," he said. "You see how things are. It is too late to be saying you don't want to go in the pool, because you are already in, all the way in the deep end. Now you commit yourself to it and see how life turns out for you."

I stood up to leave, and when my chair tipped over backward I realized I was drunk, three glasses of wine on an empty stomach, and perhaps it *was* that final drink that gave my voice what it needed—the sound of a suit with money behind it, something I was trying on as if for the first time. It must have worked, because the bodyguard looked up from his paper again, and the couple paused with their forks halfway to their mouths.

"Here is my answer, beautiful fool," I said, and then leaned forward and mashed out my cigarette in his lamb chops. "My answer is *no*. No to you, no to the Colonel, no to your life, and no to the fucking monkey over there. You have to lean on me, go ahead. The day's coming when my father will be back on the streets. He's not a violent man. But he hears it's his own son being threatened that may just change the math. And then another debt gets paid. My blood may very well be his blood. But rest assured his blood is *mine*. Nobody tells you to go fuck yourself? *I* tell you to go fuck yourself."

The Magician silent with astonishment as I walked away, up the side terrace stairs and around the hedge, the tinkling music of the bodyguard's laughter following me to my car. When I was in the driver's seat I was possessed by such a terrible case of the shakes I had to steady my hand just to get the key in the ignition.

TWENTY-THREE

I WALKED IN THE DOOR at sunup and found Zooey at the table gripping her tea and looking worried, Rolly for once sleeping in because he didn't know what he was going to do with himself all day. Figures if he gets up too early he's just going to crab at Zooey.

"Coop didn't come back," she said.

"If this is where the food is," I said, "he'll be back. When did he go?"

My mind still stuck in the moment, forty-five minutes ago, when I'd awakened to find Sally smiling at me from the facing pillow.

"First thing, still dark out," she said. "Maybe an hour ago? I brought him out and he bolted straight off into the woods. Like he had somewhere to go."

I poured myself a cup of coffee and stood at the window looking out at the back woods.

Thinking, *The bear. He's all turned around by it.*

"Maybe he thought there was something more out there for him," I said.

Zooey's thinking, *First the scare with Rolly. Now Coop with the bear.*

"It's my fault," I said. "That bear."

"It would have come around anyway. Sooner or later."

"I'll go shake him out."

"You don't want to be late," she said.

"It's okay," I said, "I'm not going in."

The grass was sparkling with a light dew. I stepped into my flip-flops and crossed the lawn into the woods calling for Coop. Rolly had been trying for years to clear what was growing back there so he could install a slate walk, but the brush always grew in faster than he could cut it back, Rolly falling behind like a tired rower losing to a fast current. The clearing dried up just ten steps in, the pile of unused slate still stacked there under a tarp, and then the trees closed in overhead as I began calling Coop's name, scaring the crows every time I gave the piercing two-fingered whistle that always brought him galloping back to the front yard. Not this time—no response but the crows cawing back at me from the high branches. Feeling a little prickle at the back of my neck now—that same feeling of being watched, the air sluggish with humidity—I kept calling his name and dropping those piercing whistles, the crows protesting, and stopped when I entered a small clearing carpeted with ferns and saw Coop.

He was sick, leaning his sagging weight against a birch trunk and panting, his tongue draped out of the side of his mouth like he'd just run a couple of miles full tilt. The ferns around him were torn up, like he'd been eating and eating at them, his belly spasming as he retched and coughed, and when he saw me he tried to take a step, though it was the step of a drunken man and his hind legs collapsed.

"Coop?"

He looked at me with his eyes full of the big hows, the whys, struggled back to his feet and stumbled toward me through the ferns in a weaving, panting gait, coughing foam and pink spray, his body quivering. The crows applauding somewhere up overhead. Little whining gasps were leaping out of Coop with every breath, the sort I often heard at night when he was in the midst of a very bad or a very lovely dream—rabbits, nirvana, the terrible first owner and what he had done, famished nights with nothing but a beating to look forward to tomorrow. Sometimes I'd stand over him, watching him sleep and dream, and wonder if I should wake him or leave him alone, not knowing which it was. I dropped down to my knees in front of him as he drew close to me, but he was still five steps away when blood burst coughing from his eyes and nose and mouth, and with one final step and a high piercing gasp he collapsed in the ferns.

"Oh, Jesus, Coop," I said, and bent over him, my hands on him.

His blood was all over me, my shirt, my arms.

A lock of black hair, long and lustrous, coiled like a snake, was tied to his collar.

Only one person I know with hair like that.

"Oh, Coop," I said, but he was dead.

Rolly and Zooey were in the kitchen waiting for the police to arrive. Coop's blood had dried on my hands and shirt in dark garnet slashes, Zooey crying softly behind me as I walked into the woods again. I didn't allow myself to look at Coop's body, knowing it would bring a rush of understanding, my mind's eye showing me the night of pain and fear he'd suffered alone in the dark of morning, unable to get back home, that lock of hair knotted to his collar.

Placed there on Coop's collar as a warning. As if the Magician himself had spoken in my ear: *This is what I do with people who tell me to go fuck myself.*

"I'm sorry, Coop," I said to the empty glade, my vision going mazy. "I'm sorry, I'm sorry."

At the far side of the clearing I found what I was looking for: a half-empty bag of supermarket bread, and beside the bread a bag of the glass shards they'd secreted inside the bread before feeding it to him.

"Oh, Jesus, Coop," I said, and looked back at him, his body barely visible among the tall ferns.

Driving to the mountain I passed a police car going the opposite direction, the cruiser's lights spinning, no siren, and wondered what a cop would make of me now if he stopped me: striped with black blood, no wallet, nothing to identify me, no money, hardly any idea of what I was doing but sure of myself nevertheless.

The pool hall was empty this early, just one vehicle out back, that truck I knew so well. I parked beside it and used the back entrance, passed the fire alarm I'd pulled just two days earlier, forever ago, and apprehended Colonel Tom in his office, in the moment of applying a match to his first cigarette of the day. Tom sitting at his desk with his long graying hair unbound and hanging in his face, looking lost and frightened, every surface in the room screaming with the reflected light of the hard overhead lamp.

He said nothing when he saw me standing in the doorway, the war paint striping my hands and shirt canceling out his thoughts.

"Quinn's not in Mexico City," I said.

The match burned down to Tom's fingertips and he dropped it, cursing, in the ashtray, sat back in his chair with his thumb in his mouth, his jacket gapping open to reveal the holstered piece.

I held up the lock of black hair.

"He's dead somewhere," I said. "Your friend. And no one's ever going to find him."

The first thing I did back at home was call Werner, my knees so weak I had to grip the counter to stay upright.

"You're late," he said.

"I'm not coming in. Not today, not ever."

He let that sink in.

"How do you expect to find a job after this?" he asked. "Even as a lifeguard?"

"Swim," I said.

"You think I'll give the job to Sally," he said, "you're wrong."

"But you will. Because I'm telling you to."

And I felt it happen. I imagined I could even *see* it happen—Werner subside back against his chair, beaten. This respectable, proper, correct man somehow taking orders from his wealthiest members to *give the kid the job, Werner,* to make opportunities for the son of a con artist, *get the kid inside the office.* The Magician behind all of it, *the hand of a friend*, invisibly placing me where he wants me to be, and Werner helpless to resist.

When he spoke again his voice was pleading.

"Who is it?" he asked. "Behind you. When your father's just a common thief, up in prison. Who is it behind you?"

"Refuse me and you'll find out," I said.

In the wake of that bluff thinking, *But maybe it* was *you all along, Jake, not the Magician but somehow you, born into this life and meant for it.* In a way I hoped he *would* refuse me, and then I would find out who and what I really was. I hung up on him before he could respond, then walked out to the garage and lifted the shovel off the wall. Tibbens met me on the slate walk coming the other way, the sound of a walkie-talkie broadcasting from back in the clearing, something like this the worst violent crime in a nice neighborhood like Rolly and Zooey's in ten years—and I realized that tomorrow was Wednesday and that I wasn't going to visit my father, not tomorrow or ever again. I'd paid my debt to him in full—he'd tried to run to Canada for me, so I owed him that much. But no more. I imagined him sitting in that room in his jumpsuit, waiting and waiting for a visitor who was never going to come again.

"Where you been?" Tibbens asked. "Jake, where?"

He gripped my shoulders, tried to stop me. His hat fell off and we stamped around for a moment in the damp ferns, almost fighting. "Jake, wait," he said. "Sit down. There, sit. Here, drink this. Get some water down you. Just breathe. Breathe, kid. You don't want to see what's back there."

"I already did. It's his blood's on me."

"Just breathe. You're looking crazy."

"Maybe I am."

"Where are you going with that shovel?"

"To dig the hole," I said. "Bury my dog."

PART FOUR

✚

SWIM

TWENTY-FOUR

THE FIRST SNOW OF THE year arrived on the last day of November. Tow trucks brought in three cars, two had blundered into high curbs and snapped their axles, the third in need of a new radiator and a good bit of bodywork. I had just got the first one up on the lift and was checking the cracked sway bar when Rolly walked in through the bay door, dusting snow off his shoulders. He was looking younger every day in the new suits and shirts he'd bought after he lost all that weight, Zooey keeping after him about his eating, maybe he can cheat a little on the cruise, he's doing so well.

"You going to fix that thing or just scratch its belly?" he asked.

And he realized a beat too late that this had been a poor choice of words. I wiped my hands on a rag and decided to leave it alone.

"You want to get some lunch?" I asked.

"I've got a mark lined up," he said. "Maybe have a Sazerac at the Skeller later?"

"If you can."

"One of these wrecks needs a loaner," he said. "Can you run it over? The industrial park past the airport. He'll give you a ride back."

"If Vic will let me."

But Rolly would have already thought of that. He tossed me the keys and stood squinting up at the snapped axle for a moment.

"Don't you end up like that," he said.

I was about to put the loaner in gear, blowing into my fists to warm them, when Sally called.

"I don't know what I'm doing," she said.

"The spreadsheet giving you trouble again."

"The numbers won't add up."

"Ask Wendy. She'll show you how."

"Was that how it was with you? Always asking her?"

"For one day."

"From what I understand," she said, "you saved them a mess on the Shamokin thing. In just one day."

"I doubt Werner will write me a thank-you."

"Things okay there?" she asked.

"Yeah, terrific. Plenty of business in this weather," I said, and after a pause added, "though I guess that sounds a little callous, doesn't it?"

"So long as no one got hurt," she said, "I think I'll give you a pass." She hesitated for a moment.

"Did anyone get hurt, Jake?" she asked.

I said, "No one knows."

"It's nice not knowing, sometimes," she said. "Isn't it?"

"Not at night."

"We won't watch the news, then," she said. "We'll just watch each other. Okay?"

I hung up and sat waiting for the air flowing through the vents to go blood-warm, shivering and hollow inside and somehow feeling wrong and right at the same time. Wondering if maybe this was something I was going to have to get used to, if maybe I could call up Kimber—not Bethenny but Kimber—and ask if it was enough, running away, if I'd been wrong and she'd discovered the true remedy for our particular disease. But then I thought: *no, so long as one doesn't know for* certain, *one is still allowed to believe it's possible, the Escape Cure, and that it can be taken if the pangs become unbearable.*

She'd vanished just two days after I buried Coop, taking the handsome oil-black Camaro and two suitcases and, for good measure, the family silver, probably pawned along the way, the last anyone had heard from her. But we'd seen her, Rolly and me. Just once. There we were, almost bedtime, and before us the appurtenances of our late-night ritual: the little television, a dish of ice cream for me, Rolly eating strawberries. We're picking apart that dance show, the shirtless joke on the beach talking into his mike like a brother, and watching the camera pan over the dancing crowd, drinking in the rapture of tanned flesh and youth and awful blue sky, vibrations of heat and sand and sex rising up as fragrantly as coconut lotion. Just before they cut to commercial, the camera zoomed in on a lone dancer, and Rolly and I instantly fell silent.

"It's her," he said.

And it was. She was dancing with her eyes closed, her head tilted off to the side, listening to the rhythm of she knew what, unaware that the camera had engaged her and liked her and would be back. And what camera wouldn't love that? To return to this lovely woman dancing alone, eyes closed, dressed in a green bikini that somehow seemed to promise immortality.

Traffic was crawling all the way to the airport road, nothing going in or out, the plows raking the runway with their orange lights revolving, rooster tails of snow kicking up in their wake, and as I passed the control tower, sipping a carton of milk, I spied the familiar truck coming the other way.

I guess you could say that I felt a certain tightening in my chest.

He did what he always did as he passed: raised two fingers straight up from the top of the wheel, a grim little salute. I returned the same, not even a nod exchanged between us.

And then I did what I had been sentenced to do for the rest of my life: I looked in my rearview, a little frost of perspiration chilling the back of my neck, and made sure that Colonel Tom wasn't showing his red brake lights through the curtain of mazy snow, made sure that he hadn't experienced that itch of doubt, changed his mind, and decided that the right thing to do was stop, turn around, and pursue me. As if I were someone worth pursuing.

If he did that—if he came after me?—

—If he turned that truck around, chased me down, and, standing at my car window on the empty, snowbound airport road, his gapped jacket revealing the holstered piece with its two fresh notches on the handle, said to me, *What I did with the Magician, his driver—you're the only one alive who knows. So I need you tell me true, Jake: Should I be worried?*

If he asked me that?

Well, I suppose I'd have to give him the only answer I know to be true: *I can do silence.*

ABOUT THE AUTHOR

Keith Dixon is the author of two novels, *The Art of Losing* and *Ghost-fires*, and a memoir, *Cooking for Gracie*. He is an editor for the *New York Times* and lives in Westchester with his wife, Jessica, and his daughters, Grace and Margot.